TARNISHED
Gold

TARNISHED
Gold

Barbara Townsend

Fine Nib Publishing

Copyright © 2017 by Barbara Townsend

Cover by Dan Van Oss at CoverMint Design

Wyoming, USA

ISBN-10: 0-9972340-7-5
ISBN-13: 978-0-9972340-7-7

To the gold miners who rushed to the South Pass region

hoping for riches

and ended up enriching a community

With Gratitude ...

To Lois Gross, Christine Thorp, and Robert K. Townsend for their stellar reviewing skills and enormous moral support.

To South Pass icons:
Steve Gyorvary for his infinite patience, sharing geology and mining knowledge, and his reviewing skills of the manuscript,

John Mionczynski for his generous giving of plant and historical knowledge, and for his inspirational musical skills.

CHAPTER 1

Lander Gazette Local News
"Placer Claims" reported by Em Olson
May 15 – May 25, 1933
- *The Assayer's Saloon and owner Jamison Smith hosted a reception for newlyweds Esther Jennings and brother Steve Smith last week. Jamison regrets the celebration's "excitement" and promises to fix the bullet holes in neighbors' roofs.*
- *Spring melt caused Quartz Creek to rise, and a logjam blew out Bert Smith's bridge to his cabin. Bert says he'll use his hip waders until he rebuilds the bridge.*

Pounding on the entrance door jolted Em from her sleep. Her heart thumped in her chest as she threw back her bed covers, grabbed her cotton robe, and tugged its sleeves over her flannel pajama gown.

Nothing good comes from this, she thought. She squinted at her windup clock on the nightstand, but the room was too dark to see.

The log hotel creaked, shoved by the wind's force. The night was a nasty one, a dangerous night to be roaming in these mountains. The snow, driven by what Em hoped was spring's final blast from the north, hissed against the single-paned window. When yesterday's last light faded the hard-packed drifts were over two feet tall.

She scuffed in her slippers along the dark hall toward the front door as she cinched the robe's tie around her slim waist.

A thought flitted about slipping her father's Colt Dragoon in the pocket but that massive steel would be a bit noticeable.

"Coming," she called out to the repeated pounding on the door. The pounding stopped.

Her hands, slick from the udder ointment she'd rubbed on her dry, cracked skin, slipped on the round knob. She hurried knowing the person wanted to get out of the storm.

She grabbed the edge of her robe and wrapped it around the rusted knob to gain purchase. With a groan, the latch released. The night, like the house, was dark and she squinted to barely make out a hairy beast at the bottom of the step.

"Come in, come in." Em pushed open the screen door. She pulled her robe tighter as the frigid wind sucked her breath away. Pinpricks of snowflakes stabbed her face. She blinked and grimaced against the pain.

Snow swirled in with the hairy mass. The beast stamped snow off its boots and breathed heavily.

Pulling her robe tight, she stepped aside to a wall-mounted oil lamp. She lifted the hurricane glass and slipped a match from a box nailed to the wall. As she struck the match, its glow immediately made the room feel warmer.

With a practiced twist of her wrist, she turned the thumbwheel to raise the wick, touched the match's flame to the woven fabric then turned the wick lower. She replaced the glass and faced the panting beast. The fur hat was wrapped tightly around his head and covered his face.

"I'm sorry for the intrusion," a voice gasped from the hat. "I'm Finch Stone. You received my letter that I was coming?" A face emerged as he pushed back the hat.

"I did, with your deposit." Em took in the cleft on his square chin. "You were to arrive two days ago—at a reasonable hour." Em tried to put on her angry face, but his rugged face swept away her irritation.

"My pickup broke down in Idaho Falls. I tried to send word to you, but Placer City doesn't have telephone service. I got lost on my way here and twice I got stuck in drifts and had to dig out. I apologize for any inconvenience, and I'll pay for the lost nights' rate." He hesitated as he tried to catch his breath. "Do you have a room available?" He held out his hand to indicate the night's storm. "Please say you have a room available."

Em fought against giggling at the boyish face silently pleading with her. Any irritation at him vanished. "Your room's still available. Welcome to the Olson Hotel. I'm Em Olson—Miss Olson." She felt foolish emphasizing "Miss." Em blushed as she extended her hand. "Even if I didn't have a room available, I wouldn't send you back out into this storm."

He shook her hand and bowed slightly. "Thank you. Doctor Finch Stone at your service. Call me Finch." His eyes turned dark in the flame's light as he took in Em's still-young face. A jolt of pleasure raced through Em's body, a feeling she'd never experienced before. Her face turned hot; her body's warmth grew to match the heat on her face.

"Well, Doctor—Finch, let's get you settled." She held out her arms for him to turn and for her to remove his overcoat, buffalo from the fur. She pulled back her hands. "Would you like to get anything from your automobile first?"

Finch pulled off the rabbit-fur hat and handed it to Em. "I'll wait until morning. I don't want to go out in that again, even for a short distance."

She turned to a row of hooks on the wall and placed the hat gently on the hook. "This is your hook during your stay. This way you can always find what belongs to you."

"Makes sense," he grunted. While he unlatched his coat, he glanced at Em's figure.

Em shrank under his gaze. She tucked a foot behind the other as if that action would hide the clumped fur on her elk-hide slippers under her threadbare robe.

Finch turned so Em could help him remove the heavy coat. She grunted slightly under the weight, but managed to push the coat onto the hook's bottom half.

She held out her hand to pull his attention to the register. The thick, heavy-leafed book stood open on a battered wood pedestal. She unscrewed the inkwell cap, picked up the fountain pen and dipped the tip into the bottle. She held out the pen for him. "Please write your name and address. I fill in the dates of your stay."

Finch's fingers brushed Em's as he grasped the pen. Her breath caught.

He stooped over the book and with great flourishes wrote the required information. He handed the pen back.

She stepped to the book. "You'll be in Room Two. You'll stay two months as stated in your letter?"

"That's my schedule so far. Two months. Although my boss said he'll send me to Salt Lake City a few times on company business. I'll let you know as soon as possible when I'm leaving and when I'm expected back."

Em filled in the information that Finch was to stay intermittently for two months and in Room Two. "Let me show you around, unless you'd like to rest first."

"I'd like to look around. That would be fine."

"Obviously, you found the front door, even in this storm. Your room is upstairs."

"Am I the only guest tonight?"

"Yes." Em suddenly felt unsettled. A strange man was the lone guest, but she'd never had a guest act untoward to her. "For right now. Usually a big storm brings more guests because they're stranded in the local area—well, assuming their vehicle can make it through the snow."

Em lifted the lit oil lamp off the wall bracket. As they ascended the steps, Em felt ashamed at the steps' steepness whenever she preceded a guest. Her father had built the steps to the sharp angle because he had insisted they needed the landing space more.

At Room 2's door, Em removed the skeleton key from the lock and extended it to Finch. "Here's your key. It'll work with the hotel's front door should you find it locked."

She pushed open the door and stepped in, knowing if she stayed outside the room to let guests enter first they'd remain in the hallway and peer inside. Human nature sometimes baffled her.

4

She set the oil lamp on the dresser and struck a match from the box affixed to the wall. She lifted the glass from another oil lamp on the dresser and lit the wick. The room glowed with the light of the two lamps. With a gentle puff, she blew out the match and placed the burnt stub on a tiny metal shelf above the matchbox. "Please place your used matches on this shelf. Never place it in the trash. My housekeeper will collect them."

Finch grunted his understanding. "No electricity?"

"No." Em bit her tongue at the oft-repeated question. "Each room has several oil lamps and candles to carry with you as you move around. Since the sunlight is lasting longer each day they'll be less necessary."

She tugged open the top drawer and pulled out a blanket. "More blankets are in the closet should you need them." She whipped open the wool blanket, the best one she had with no holes, and draped it on the bed's quilt.

Kneeling near the floor's heater vent, she flipped the lever. The massive coal furnace her father had installed in the basement proved to be a godsend. As long as she could afford the coal, its constant warmth made living through the winter bearable and she didn't have to hire someone to chop wood and stack the 35 cords necessary to warm the place. She held her hand against the grill until warm air began to flow. "It'll warm up soon."

Suppressing a groan, she pressed her hands against her knees to straighten and opened an adjoining door. "Your bathroom. This room is the only one with a private bath. The other four rooms share one bathroom."

"My last hotel only had shared facilities for ten rooms. It was terrible."

"How awful for you." Em squirmed at the image in her mind's eye. "Let's go downstairs, and I'll show you the dining and living rooms."

On the room's oil lamp, she turned the thumbwheel to dim the flame. She picked up her lamp and led Finch down the stairs. On the main floor, she paused to ensure Finch followed her then opened the door off to the side.

"Watch your step there. Watch your head here — there's a low overhang."

At the bottom of the few steps that led into the dark kitchen, they paused. "I keep a pot of coffee going all day. You're welcome to stop in for a cup any time."

They stepped through the kitchen into the dining room. "Family-style meals are served here. Breakfast is at seven o'clock sharp."

"It's quite large." Finch peered into the dimness.

"We can host parties or large meetings here. We've even hosted weddings. In a few days we'll host a wedding reception in this room, so I'd appreciate it if you could avoid this room while the event's going on."

"No problem." Finch rubbed his arms to raise some heat as he stared at the old wood stove standing cold in the frigid room's center.

Em noticed his movements and focus. "It'll be warm in the morning, I promise."

He studied Em. "You run the entire hotel too, in addition to rescuing stranded travelers?"

"I have some help but, yes, I do quite a bit of the work."

"So how does a young lady run this hotel, do much of the work, and stay so lovely?"

"Thank you, Finch." Flushing furiously, she changed the subject. "You're a medical doctor? Do you have a specialty?"

Finch laughed a warm guffaw. "Everyone assumes that. I'm a geologist. And please, don't make jokes about my name. Stone ... geologist ... I've heard them all."

Em shook her head. "I don't make fun of people's names." She held his gaze. The warmth in his eyes held off the cold. In the dimness, they studied each other.

She broke the scrutiny to lead him through another door. "In here is the guests' common area. Some folks call it the living room or a parlor. So, feel free to spend your evenings relaxing here."

Dark oak furniture loomed in the oil lamp's soft glow. She held out a hand to indicate a desk. "If you need to work, there's a large desk and chair. The oil lamp on the desk has been in my family for more than a hundred years, and it works beautifully. Beside every oil lamp, either on a desk or mounted to the wall, is a matchbox and a metal tray for the burnt ones. Over there, I have a small library if you need a diversion from your work."

"Miss Olson, if you're here, you'll be quite the pleasant diversion." The flame reflected Finch's white teeth.

Em squirmed against the chill. "You're most kind. Well, I suggest retiring. Seven o'clock will come soon enough."

~ * ~

"Where is that girl?" Em mumbled, shivering in the kitchen. She gathered kindling and newspaper to restart the wood stove's fire that died during the night.

Already out of sorts, her missing cousin and worker didn't help her irritation. After receiving the unexpected guest last night, she had forgotten to set the alarm even though she lay awake thinking about the handsome man in her second-story room. Only because of her early rising habit did she wake with enough time to prepare breakfast.

She stuffed the newspaper wad in the Monarch's firebox then balanced kindling on top. Stiff fingers struggled to strike the match and hold the tiny flame to the paper. Holding her breath, the paper caught. The flame spread to the kindling. As the kindling crackled, she added thicker branches then closed the firebox's cover. She lifted the large coffee pot from the stove and stepped to the water pump at the wooden sink.

The spring storm had passed during the night, leaving this morning's sky a brilliant blue. She squinted against the harshness. Through the west-facing window, the sun reflected tiny rainbow dots in the pristine whiteness. High winds had scoured the hilltops of snow and deposited tall drifts pointing southwest, revealing the wind's northeast origin. An abandoned prospector's log cabin up the hillside stood distinctly with rows of snow striping the near-black logs. Bare aspen branches outside the window didn't move.

Em checked the thermometer fixed to the outside wall. "Nineteen degrees," she muttered. The thought of such cold so late in the spring made her shiver even harder.

Like her muscles, the water pump handle was stiff in the morning. She pressed with all her weight to get it to move. The icy metal sucked any remaining warmth from her body. Within seconds, pain radiated through her hands and up her forearm. As she started to pant from exertion, water gushed from the spout and splashed into the wooden sink.

She held the pot steady to collect the near-freezing well water into the coffee pot as the door to the two-story squeaked open. Perfume preceded the teenager as she hurried down the few steps into the kitchen.

Em threw a glance over her shoulder. "I need you to start biscuits right away. The guest who was supposed to arrive two days ago arrived during the night, so there'll be him and me for breakfast."

"Good morning to you, Auntie Em." The brassy tone permeated Sylvia Wartzen's high-pitched voice, which only increased Em's sour mood.

"Good morning, Sylvia. You've got to get down here in the morning. You can't just waltz in here when you decide to get up."

"You were late yourself." Sylvia's voice was accusatory.

"And how would you know that?" Em's anger rose because Sylvia had to have been awake, yet didn't get up. With a grunt, she hefted the full coffee pot from the wood sink and hurried to set it on the warming cookstove.

Sylvia froze. She'd been caught. She snatched an apron and headed for the flour bin. Within moments, a thin cloud of flour floated and dusted the surfaces.

In silence, Em sliced ham steaks and scrambled eggs while Sylvia brooded over her biscuits and set the table.

As seven o'clock neared, Em's heart lightened at the thought of eating breakfast with the ruggedly handsome new guest for the next few months. "I'll be right back," her euphemism for going to the toilet. She slipped out the two-story door and stepped down the hall. Above, the floor creaked as Finch walked around his room as he settled in.

In her private bathroom, her fingers smoothed the light hair piled on her head. Her sleepless night had darkened the circles under her eyes. Smiling into the mirror, her fingers stroked the ever-deepening creases around her eyes while she recalled Finch's compliments.

Moments later, Em hurried toward the kitchen, wanting to be the first to greet him when he came downstairs. As she pulled open the kitchen door, Sylvia's high-pitched voice echoed from the dining room. Finch's open-mouthed laugh rang out. *He's downstairs? How did I miss him coming down?*

She peeked through the dining room door in time to see Sylvia stroke an errant lock of hair on his head. Finch smiled as she stood over him.

Appalled at Sylvia's forward behavior and disappointed in Finch's apparent ease of female distraction, Em swallowed hard. *He's just a guest.*

"Sylvia," Em called out to her own surprise. She quickly looked around to find something for Sylvia to do. Em called again. With a glance at the coffee pot's percolator glass top, a dark liquid bubbled. After a pause, she decided to pretend ignorance of Finch being in the dining room. She lifted the pot, grabbed a hot pad, and stepped into the dining room.

"Good morning, Finch! How did you sleep last night?" Placing the pad and the coffee pot on the table beside the biscuit platter, she wondered if he had given permission for Sylvia to call him Finch.

"Finch slept well last night." Sylvia's eyes reflected she'd been granted the privilege.

He stood from his chair in greeting. "Well, good morning, Miss Olson. I'm sorry for my sudden and late arrival and for disturbing your night." He smiled at Em with a warmth that made her cold sadness vanish. His brown eyes twinkled, and in the full light she could see how handsome he was.

"Why not at all. Call me Em. Please sit. Sylvia will serve the rest of our breakfast."

Finch held out a hand to indicate the two place settings on the table. He pulled out a chair for Em. "Does this mean you'll join me for breakfast?"

Em smiled. "I eat with my guests when I can." She sat in his offered chair and he pushed it forward. "Thank you."

"Sylvia, you won't be joining us?" Finch asked.

"No. I'm the resident menial. This morning I'm to serve breakfast, not eat it, because I have urgent chores to do. Don't I, Miss Olson?"

Em flashed Sylvia an angry look. Sylvia's face flushed as she slunk toward the kitchen.

Glancing from Sylvia to Em, he cleared his throat. As he sat, he reached for a biscuit from the platter and then for the butter. The silence grew more tense.

"Em. Is that short for a formal name?"

"No, just Em. A proper name."

Finch lifted the coffee pot and poured some into Em's cup then filled his own. Drips of coffee dotted her white linen tablecloth. She hid a grimace. "Thank you," Em said.

"You're welcome."

"So, Finch is a unique name. Is that short for something?"

Nodding, he pursed his lips to blow on the steaming coffee. His soft breath sent the rising steam into a contortion. "Fincelius, after a frontiersman."

The tiniest bell tinkled in Em's memory. "I seem to recall such a name in our region's history from the last century. Closer to Atlantic City though."

He nodded as he chewed a piece of ham. He swallowed. "Sylvia said she's your cousin. Do you have other family members here?"

Em shook her head as she plucked a biscuit then reached for the butter tray. "No. I have only a sister living. Rose is in California. Her husband owns an orchard. My two brothers, Edward died as an infant, and my eldest brother Michael died a few years ago."

She smeared the butter pat on the biscuit. "My parents, Bea and James, are also gone."

10

Well, Mother is passed away, she thought. Her father abandoned the family two years before. The shame of it she kept to herself. To erase the memory, she focused on the table to ensure Sylvia set the table correctly and check the food presentation. She frowned slightly at the too-brown bottom of the biscuit on her plate. Again, the girl neglected to remove the biscuits at the right time. The ham steaks Em cooked on the griddle were perfect, as were her scrambled eggs.

"The breakfast is sumptuous. You and your cousin must slave away every morning." Finch said.

Em acknowledged his compliment with a nod. "Thank you. We do try to cook good food for our guests."

They ate in silence. Em began to squirm as any question she wanted to ask him seemed too nosy, too inappropriate to ask this guest. *Does your wife ever travel with you? How many girlfriends do you have and do they travel with you?* As she chewed, she avoided looking at him.

"Oh, before I left Montana, my boss gave me a request. Do you have a room starting next week for him and his new wife? Sometimes he travels behind me to see for his own eyes about the opportunities."

Em thought about her largely blank reservation book. She received many inquiries into mining opportunities but only a few requested a reservation. Even if the country weren't gripped in an economic depression, sightseers rarely wandered through Placer City. Most people needing a room simply showed up at her door.

"I do. They can choose a room or a cabin. If they prefer a room, they'll have to share a bathroom. If they prefer a cabin, they'll share an outhouse and bathe in the creek, but they'll have a chamber pot."

Finch threw back his head and roared a ringing laugh. "That won't make either one happy. They're particular, especially his new wife. Not to say anything untoward but they can afford the best. Tell you what, if you don't mind I'll move down the hall and share a bath. They can use my room and have the private bath."

"How generous of you. The problem's solved." Em felt relief, yet irritated anyone was so particular they couldn't share a bath. No matter how rich they were, it would be good for them to share once in a while. Being sheltered only made one weak, she thought.

A question she could ask him entered her mind. "Do you have a specialty in geology, Finch?"

He nodded his head as he chewed. He didn't rush to swallow, but rather held Em's gaze with an enjoyable light in his eyes. Finally, he swallowed and took a sip from her grandmother's fine china cup. "Sorry, I didn't want to hurry that bite of ham. That is the best I've ever eaten."

Em smiled a huge smile and slouched in embarrassment over his enthusiastic praise.

"My specialty is precious metals. I travel quite a bit to find opportunities in areas where my boss is interested. I'm working the Mountain West region right now."

"Our little region interests your boss?" Em's eyes gaped at the nosy question that popped from her mouth.

"Oh, yes. I assume you get many prospectors."

Em nodded. "This is a gold region. But you already know all about it, don't you?" Em smiled at him to show she wasn't being nosy or cheeky.

Finch leaned closer. "I'm here to find all things precious." His eyes became darker.

CHAPTER 2

Several days later, Em straightened from lugging her third table from the basement and placing it just so in the large dining room. Leaning back, she rubbed the small of her back to ease the ache that never seemed to go away.

She stabbed her fists on her hips and stepped back to survey the tables' placement. The room had to be perfect for the wedding reception for two childhood friends that afternoon. Em's life-long friends and long-time Placer City residents Nancy Burns and Pat Moreno loved the old hotel and its land. She was pleased they wanted their reception nowhere else.

One table appeared off-kilter. When she pressed the top, the table lurched. Em sighed. "Magnus!" Em waited. "Mag—"

"Here, Em."

Em jumped at the little man who appeared at her elbow. She sighed. "I never know how you can move around without making a sound."

The edges of Magnus' thick drooping mustache rose a bit as a smile lifted his cheeks, but he offered no explanation.

"Could you please fix this table? It wobbles. We can't have that."

"We can't have that." Magnus repeated. He picked up the table in his powerful hands and shifted the table to the corner to work on it.

He's not much taller than the table, Em thought. Magnus reached almost five feet tall. Born several miles up the road in a hardscrabble prospector's cabin sometime in the latter half of

13

the 1800s, of seven children he alone survived into adulthood. He could still lift more rock than most prospectors around.

The appearance in her mind's eye of Magnus' little cabin on the corner of the Olson Hotel property caused her to shiver. Magnus Ollsen wasn't a member of her family, but he became one as he settled into the caretaker's cabin before Em was born and stood as uncle to all the Olson children. She'd been in Magnus' cabin once. The grime he lived in turned her stomach. She privately refused to step in there again — although to spare his feelings she never told him why.

He drank whiskey often, but only in his cabin and he never showed up to work hung over. She'd heard rumors he distilled his own with Placer's assayer, Bill Newbury, who was said to bootleg the spirit to Utah.

The Olson Hotel needed workers for maintenance, cleaning, and cooking. Em could count on Magnus to take great care of the hotel and grounds, but finding — and keeping — reliable workers for housekeeping and cooking were a constant headache.

Em stepped into the living room to ensure the room was perfect and tidy. She swept her finger over the old rosewood piano and inspected the dust patch on her finger. She sighed again. The hotel was hard to keep clean, what with dirt roads, stiff winds, and windows constantly requiring glazing.

"Sylvia!" Em hated to order Sylvia to do her chores, but that was usually the way it was. She opened her mouth to holler again when Sylvia dragged her feet into the room. The slouch told Em she was in for a battle.

"Sylvia, please dust this room. I thought I told you to do this yesterday."

"You told me to prepare that room Finch is moving into. Then you said I had to get ready for the dinner meal," Sylvia shrieked.

Em tamped her anger. "Sylvia, you were to dust in addition to all those things. You can't just do one or two things and then stop for the day. Here, you have to work. When I tell you to do multiple tasks, I expect you to do them all. Don't make me follow you around."

"I am not a slave!" Sylvia screamed. She snatched the towel draped over her shoulder and slapped it against an overstuffed chair beside her. The sunlight streaming through the large window reflected the swirling dirt cloud that hung in the still air.

Em's lips grew tight. Cousin or no, she did her family a favor by taking in this lazy woman. "Sylvia, you were sent here to work. When you arrived, you agreed you'd work hard. I don't see you working hard; I see you hardly working. If you can't or won't do the work, let me know. You can return to your parents. I'll find someone to replace you."

The teenager's face turned red. She swayed in fury that Em would send her back. Em knew she'd touched a nerve. Sylvia's parents could afford to give her every luxury. Through letters, Sylvia confided to Em how much she hated her parents and how alone she felt. Her parents didn't care about her and the servants weren't friendly. In her seventeen years, Sylvia hadn't worked or shown any interest in any profession. Her threatening to run away at the very discussion of wifely homemaking caused Sylvia's mother to think she could benefit from working for once and in western mountain air. Sylvia agreed she would work for Em at the hotel in any capacity.

Since her arrival, Sylvia's enthusiasm for cleaning and cooking dwindled rapidly. The first few days she seemed interested in the work. Soon the drudgery sank in. After her first cleaning of the cabins' chamber pots, milking the cow, and feeding the chickens, Em was forced to push, prod, and cajole Sylvia into doing the work.

"Fine." Sylvia's voice was piercing. She slapped the towel against the chairs and ignored the flying dust.

"Stop! Do not slap at the chairs, Sylvia. You know how you're supposed to do it." Em stabbed her fists on her hips and let the sharpness spit out with her voice. "I don't have time to watch you. You know very well this reception is important to me. I expect you do it right. If you can't—or won't—let me know right now." Em's chest heaved.

Sylvia stared at the chair she had swatted.

Em fought the urge to tap a foot to hurry Sylvia's decision.

"Fine." Sylvia said, her voice flat, emotionless. She moved the lamp and swept the rag over the table.

Em watched Sylvia for a moment then walked back to the dining room. The wobbly table Magnus moved aside was back in its place. She pushed on the table and its stableness surprised her. She smiled.

Magnus always did what she needed him to. With him there was no ordering, no cajoling, no pleading. Trusted Magnus did his job. Her heart warmed as she thought about her family's most faithful friend.

~ * ~

The hotel's front door squeaked open and a nose appeared. "Mail call!" The nose retreated and the door closed.

Em smiled as she reached for the doorknob and pulled open the door. "Afternoon, Lewis. I didn't hear your truck. How was your trip up the mountain?"

Lewis Roberts had been the Sweetwater region's mailman for decades. Gray eyes twinkled through a leathery face atop stooping shoulders. Only ten years earlier he'd switched from horses and buckboard to a Ford pickup. After receiving an inheritance from an elderly aunt he splurged on an older Model T pickup with front skis and double-axle rear tracks for winter conditions.

Even with a truck so equipped, at times he'd still strap on his snowshoes, hoist a 30-pound backpack and trudge through the rugged terrain.

Once, he confided to Em that although he was honored to have the series of nearby gulches named Roberts Gulches after he was caught in a sudden blizzard west of Placer City for a harrowing two days and a night several years ago, he was more honored to have survived.

"Mighty fine, Em. Here's that Sears catalog you've been expecting. Got a letter from Rose too." Lewis held out a short stack of mail as he stood on the small porch. The old wood step sagged under his slight figure. "And quiet. I borrowed my brother's automobile. At least his tail pipe is still on."

He turned to indicate a dusty Dodge coupe. "The ruts through Red Canyon finally tore off the last of the baling wire holding on my muffler. I couldn't take the noise anymore. It's in the shop."

Em breathed a silent sigh of relief. The rumble of his truck announced his arrival for miles. She held out an arm toward the kitchen. "Time for coffee?"

Lewis hesitated. His eyes darted to the north edge of the hotel. "Do you know Samuel Quint is staring at your barn from the chicken coop enclosure?"

"Sam's on my property?"

Lewis gave a quick nod of his head. "Want me to stick around for a while, Em?"

She turned to stare at the building's corner, around which Sam Quint snooped. "No, thank you, Lewis. I can take care of him myself."

With a forefinger, he touched the bill of his cap, nodded, and turned away.

Em spun on her heels, tossed the mail on the counter as she dashed through the kitchen, trotted through the dining room then the living room. Through the door's window that faced the chicken coop, she watched.

Samuel Quint stepped outside the enclosure and studied the coop's walls. His head towered above the coop's five-foot-high peaked roof. His dirty blue jeans sagged and his once-white shirt appeared to have been slept in. He raised a hand to touch one of the boards.

"What the …?" Em seized the doorknob and threw open the door. She hurried down the porch steps.

As her heels struck the steps, Quint turned and watched Em approach. He held up his hands, palms out. "Now, Em, don't get your pants in a wad." The local freighter and alleged-whiskey runner who lived to the northwest of the Olson Hotel always seemed to enjoy belittling her and her family. He slowly stepped toward the gate.

"What the … are you doing?" Em cried. She stopped feet from him and tipped her head back to look into the huge man's face. She crossed her arms.

Quint's chin nearly touched his barrel chest as he stared down at her. "I'm just checking out the place to see how much I would pay you for it."

Rather than be intimidated, Em forced herself to take a small step forward. "Last month when I chased you out of my barn, I told you this place is not for sale." She raised her arm toward the gate. "Now leave. I wouldn't traipse around your property without your permission and I don't appreciate you snooping around my place without my mine."

He raised his hands to his chest. "I'm a charitable man."

Em snorted.

"I heard you're having a rough go since your dad left for the California gold fields. Then there's your mother — God rest her soul." Quint snatched his soiled cowboy hat off his head, slapped it to his chest, and then clapped the hat back on his damp head. "She left you all alone. I thought you might be about desperate to sell and I'm seeing what this place and the mine is worth."

"You already know the hotel is not for sale. Not now, not ever. And the mine's not worth what Father paid for it, even if he did get it cheap."

Quint stared at a distant hill. His lips and cheeks bulged as his tongue moved around his teeth. With a loud "sip" sound, he looked down at Em.

"Oh, yeah, the restitution Walt Denton bestowed on your father for shooting him when they were both drunk." Quint watched the two chickens pecking at the ground. He spun back. "Tell your father to sell me the mine or this hotel." He stomped toward the gate.

Her chest heaved from the building anguish until the sensation changed to fury, finally erupting out her eyes. With her sleeve she wiped off the stream of tears. "You know darned well and good I don't know where he is!"

CHAPTER 3

Em rose with the other celebrants crowding into the pews as Nancy Burns glided along the center aisle of the Old Church. The bride's white silk shift shimmered then exploded into vibrant colors as she stepped into a stream of sunlight shining through the small stained glass window.

In front of the altar, her groom Pat Moreno wore a white suit and shifted nervously from foot to foot with a huge smile on his handsome face. His face seemed to melt as he caught sight of his bride.

The pastor, a short chunky friend of the Burns family, stood motionless, stone-faced, apparently taking his position in the ceremony seriously.

As Nancy reached Pat, they giggled like children. Her face transformed from glowing pale to a deep blush. Pat stared at his bride while he blinked back tears.

The congregation sank and squeezed into the pews. Taller heads blocked Em's view of the ceremony so she stared out the few open windows. Sunlight highlighted the green shoots poking through last year's matted, dead grass. A yellow flash reflected the sun as a warbler flitted amongst the willows and sang a song. A mountain chickadee dropped from its perch on an aspen branch. It snatched a seed then zipped up to trap the seed between its feet and rap its beak to break open the shell and expose the meat.

Attendees snickered as the couple's giddiness disrupted the somber readings of Bible passages. Em turned back, craning her neck to glimpse the couple's happy faces. Tears pooled in her eyes, in part for her friends' joy and partly for the aging spinster in herself. Loneliness washed over her. Would she ever find a love, a life-mate for herself? Her sister Rose's voice echoed in her mind: "Come to California. There are loads of beautiful men out here who would love to meet a mountain woman."

Em turned to stare out at the darkening logs of the Olson Hotel across the road and at the hills beyond. The old hotel's humbleness belied a deep soul. The mountains' wilderness and rugged terrain sang to her heart.

She studied the simple log church's interior. The beams were stained dark, stark against the whitewashed beadboard wainscoting. The pews were little more than sanded split logs. The pastor's podium was a beautifully carved, hand-hewn stump; its lone candle not needed on the brightness. Behind the podium stood an antique pipe organ, unused since it had developed a high-pitched wheeze. To her, the church's modesty was holy and she perceived Jesus would approve.

At the shouting and clapping for the new husband and wife, Pat swept his new wife in his arms. Em averted her eyes at their passionate first kiss.

After the newlyweds ran laughing down the aisle, Em scurried to the side aisle and out the side door. She trotted over the creek's footbridge toward the hotel to be the first there to ensure the decorations and cake were ready and to receive the wedding party into her hotel.

In the quiet dining room, she wandered the decorated tables, straightening slightly askew utensils. She studied the cake, a white buttercream smoothed over a yellow cake. Yellow flowers mounded the top.

"What a beautiful room."

Em spun to see Finch eyeing the room. "Yes, the room dresses up wonderfully." She nudged a spoon straight.

"You're particular, aren't you?" Finch sauntered toward her, skirting the round tables. "You're proud of this place. It shows."

Em smiled, pleased he had noticed her attention to detail. "Thank you." She hesitated. "You've had a good day?"

Finch nodded as he studied the cake. He didn't take his eyes off it as he leaned his head toward Em. "Think they'd noticed if I slipped a finger into the frosting?"

Em giggled. Her eyes suddenly popped at herself and stifled a gasp. *Did I just giggle?* She quickly asked, "Have you had a good chance to study the area?"

Again, Finch nodded. "Had a guy show me around some gulches. He even pointed out an old wrecked truck in one … over some miners' feud apparently."

He didn't give any specifics and Em wouldn't ask. His activities weren't her business. Her brow furrowed as she searched her memory about a wrecked truck in a gulch. After a quick shrug, she poked another spoon for something to do. Through the door's window, she could see the wedding party lingering outside the church steps. Finch watched them through the window.

"Does this event make you think of your own wedding?" Em blurted. She froze, horrified to have asked such a prying question. She wanted to kick herself for being impertinent.

She felt him watching her. From the corner of her eyes, he shook his head. He seemed unsure how to answer, which made Em even more uncomfortable.

"I'm sorry. That was none of my business." Hurriedly she added, "The dining room is reserved for the reception. The living room will be crowded, but you're welcome to use it since you're a guest of the hotel." Em spun on her heels to head to the living room. Embarrassment weighed heavily and she needed to hide her shame.

Finch shifted in his stance, blocking Em's way. She couldn't meet his eyes. He stepped close. Her heart rate quickened. Her chest heaved at his nearness. She forced her eyes to meet his.

"I'm not married," he said softly. He looked deep into her eyes. "Or engaged."

A chorus of voices entering the living room made Em start and step back from Finch. The bride and groom swept into the dining room to a cacophony of chatter and laughter. Nancy rushed to Em and held out her arms. They embraced while

Nancy swung Em side to side. "What a beautiful ceremony!" Em cried.

Pat grabbed Em's arm and kissed her on the cheek. Em stood aside to show them the room and the cake.

Nancy squealed her pleasure at the cake as Pat swept his finger across the frosting and swept the gob into his mouth. She faked a gasp, giggled, and tapped his hand.

Beyond Nancy, Finch slipped into the living room. Relieved he left yet sad he did, Em turned back to Nancy and Pat to ensure the room was to their liking.

"Well, Miss Prude ..."

Em froze. *Oh, no. Samuel Quint. Again.* She spun on her heels and faced the big man. At least he'd washed his face, she thought. The buttons on his fresh white shirt strained. His trousers were so snug the pocket openings bulged. She reminded herself to "turn the other cheek." *Gosh, how infuriating he is.*

"Don't be so formal, Mister Quint. Call me Miss Olson." She turned to stalk away. Sylvia stood in Em's way, unsure what to do. The pause in Em's escape from Quint allowed him to catch both women.

"Well, Miss Warts ..."

Sylvia's head snapped up to Quint's insult. She met him the last time Quint came to inspect the hotel. The experience was not a pleasant one. Hatred boiled from her eyes.

Em jabbed a finger at Quint, almost poking his chest. "You will address her as Miss Wartzen. Show her proper respect or I'll order you to leave the premises."

Quint's mouth fell open at the shock of Em's words then contorted into a grimace. "I'm a guest of the reception. You can't throw me out."

"I will if you don't behave. This is my place. I expect decorum." Her eyes held his in anger.

"Sam, what did I tell you about behaving today?" Margaret Quint snuck up behind Sam.

The big man hung his head at his wife's sudden appearance. "To be nice."

"Yes. This is a happy occasion, isn't it?" Margaret stepped close to her husband, transfixing him. Em couldn't help but stare at the sheepishness in Quint around his wife.

He nodded his head. "Yeah, I just don't like getting gaudied up. That's all."

"I know," Margaret purred. "It's just a few hours. Be nice." She watched him for a moment before shooting a quick smile at Em before moving away.

Em turned aside. His hand pressed on her shoulder, stopping her. The pressure forced her to face him.

He leaned in close, so close she could smell the cheap whiskey she'd heard he guzzled by the gallon. "I could buy you, you know," he whispered.

Her eyes grew big. Before she could raise her hand to slap his face he quickly added, "Your hotel. You are the hotel. I could buy you out. With cash. Lots of it. Think about it."

With a casual swipe so others wouldn't see her anger, she pushed off his hand. "Think about it," he hissed.

She turned away, but he didn't touch her again.

More celebrants streamed into the dining room. Most Em knew, and she greeted and was greeted by the revelers.

"Em, the room looks divine. Doesn't it look beautiful, Bill?" Margaret cooed, this time herding her younger brother. She nudged him. Bill Newbury was the town's assayer. She was taller than Bill by half a head and almost as burly.

Bill nodded his assent. "It's beautiful, Em."

"Thank you, Margaret, Bill. Hosting Nancy and Pat is my pleasure. I love the thought that this hotel is a part of the memories for dear friends."

Margaret leaned close to Em and placed her hand on Em's arm. "You look like the weight of the world is on your shoulders. Are you all right?"

Startled by Margaret's announcement, Em blinked, feeling shame at not hiding her stress. "I'm managing. I just want the best for their reception." Self-conscious, she lightly touched her face. "I hope it's not real noticeable."

Waving away Em's concern, Margaret grinned. "You'll always be annoyingly pretty, Em. Don't forget if you ever need a hand around here for a few days, you let me know. I'm still working at the Assayer's Saloon in the afternoon, but I can help in the morning. Sam's good with me working. Okay?"

Em reached for her old friend's hand and squeezed it lightly. "Will do. Thank you."

Margaret gripped Em's hand tightly, leaned close, and whispered, "Em, you may want to be vigilant. Walt Denton's on a tear. He was already liquored up at the wedding." She patted Em's arm before heading for her table. Staring at Margaret's back, foreboding caused the butterflies in her stomach to flutter.

"Em!" A voice Em knew well called out to her.

"Pauline! I'm so glad you could make it."

Pauline Highsmith, a tiny elderly woman who lived alone between Atlantic City and Placer City, looked 1800s in her vest and skirt that appeared to be adorned with chaps. Her face was deeply wrinkled, yet still beautiful. Her large eyes took in the room's decorations and the people crowding in. She laughed. "My old 'T' begged for mercy, but she made it up the hill just in time. I didn't want to miss Nancy's wedding. That tick bite made her so sick last year, but I'm thrilled to see how wonderful she looks."

Em turned to watch the radiant bride. Nancy chatted happily with the many well-wishers, her arm wrapped around her new husband's waist. Em smiled and turned back to Pauline. "Your tinctures worked wonders for her." She held out an arm. "Your table is over here." She leaned in to whisper, "I sat you with some nice people. I think you'll like them." She led Pauline to the table to make the introductions, but the little woman knew them already.

Em stepped back and bumped into a soft tower. She spun, crying out, "Oh, I beg your pard—"

Walter Denton stood inches from Em. He swayed as he stared at her. Blue veins crisscrossing his bloated face stood in stark relief to his pale glistening skin. His thinning hair stuck flat against his sweat-beaded scalp.

Much of Denton's substantial wealth came from loaning grubstake to miners and landowners. As the country spiraled into economic depression, Wyoming had been spared the worst—so far. Several people who could escape the unemployment and poverty made their way to Placer City. Playing the benefactor, Denton was quick to offer his loans to those in need—the Olson family had been one. Between Denton's high interest rates, strict conditions, and enforcement of payments many greenhorn prospectors were forced to abandon their properties and mining claims, which meant Denton became the owner of yet another property or gold claim.

Denton dropped his eyes. He swayed slightly. His eyes rose and appeared to study Em's face—but avoided her eyes. He never met anyone's eyes when he was drunk. After a small belch he slurred, "Bea."

His heavy eyelids sank then rose. "You look like your mother." He seemed to recall a sudden thought. With a gruff voice he blurted, "Watch where you're going." He nudged her as he moved to his seat.

Stunned, Em felt her face grow hot as her brow furrowed at his comments. She wondered what the crowd's reaction would be if she were to slug the mealy mouthed beast. Likely, she'd hear applause. She moved on and almost didn't hear a small "Hello, Em."

The voice's gentleness stopped her. She turned to see Walter's petite wife, Betty Denton. Her soft, aging face turned up to Em's.

"Hello, Betty. It's good to see you. Oh, I love your white dress. It reminds me of Nancy's dress." Em shook Betty's offered hand and tried not to recoil at the limp, cold claw. "So glad you could be here." She stepped away.

A wave of pity swept over Em for the abuse Betty suffered when Denton was drunk. Yet, she felt anger for any woman who would tolerate it. Denton's great wealth from questionable business dealings meant Betty could help herself to his bank account and leave. Yet, she chose to remain.

Em slipped to the far side of the huge room and stood to watch the festivities and help out where necessary.

~ * ~

After the food serving line, the cutting of the cake, a stuttering toast by the too-drunk best man, Em and a few partiers moved aside a few of the tables for a small dancing area to the accompaniment of a local quartet, the Cow Chips.

Suddenly the crowd dwindled. *These guests know you don't leave before the bride and groom.* Nancy and Pat didn't seem to notice as couples pressed in to dance.

As the dance floor became more crowded, a furrow crossed Em's brow. Walter Denton danced with an unknown blonde woman, though Nancy and Pat seemed to know her. The tight dress highlighted her shapely figure. His squinting eyes peering from his bloated mug never left her face. They danced closely — too closely — with suggestive motions.

Em, unable to witness the sight, wandered into the living room. Several guests who she thought had left were lounging in the living room on her overstuffed chairs. She sauntered around making small talk.

Sylvia flitted around the room, picking up soiled plates and glasses. When the girl caught her eye Em nodded her pleasure, to which Sylvia's face tightened. Oh well, Em thought.

"Wonderful party," a soft voice whispered in her ear.

Em smiled into Finch's face. "They're wonderful folks."

He stared into her eyes. "Wonderful."

Em blushed, then grinned her farewell.

Screaming and cursing burst from the dining room, followed by hollers and the crashing of wood.

Em dashed into the room. A table had been upended. Two chairs had been knocked over. The tablecloth from the cake table lay tangled on the floor. The maid of honor pressed against the wall holding the remnants of the pastry. Despite the pandemonium, the Cow Chips didn't miss a beat.

27

In the middle of the screaming and flurried action, Betty Denton gripped the strange blonde's hair and kicked at her shapely legs. Walter Denton grabbed his wife's hair and yanked her head back to pull her away. Betty screamed in pain. The blonde swung her fist in a roundhouse, connecting at Betty's cheek with a loud *whack*. "You bitch!" The blonde screamed. "Walt, get this cow away from me!"

Em stood flat-footed, unable to move.

"Betty Jean, you dunce. Leave a real woman alone!" Denton yelled as he pushed a weeping Betty to the floor. He swung back his arm, his fist clenched, to strike her.

"Don't!" Em screamed. She lunged to shove Denton, anything to stop what was to happen. Before she could reach him, Finch slipped in front of her and grabbed Denton's raised fist. Seemingly in slow motion, he twisted the fist until Denton howled in pain. Finch gently led his captive to the door. Em trotted after Finch and the bellowing Denton through the parlor, out the exterior door, and down the porch steps.

Once on the ground, Finch released Denton's fist and stepped back. He held out an arm in front of Em to shield her from an attack.

Denton stooped low and lunged for Finch. With an agility lightning fast yet molasses slow, Finch evaded a right cross from a charging Denton. With his momentum Denton plunged to the ground.

A snicker behind Em caused her to look back. The entire wedding party stood behind her. All grinned, some clapped their hands in glee. A man from South Pass City yelled to Finch, "Give 'im his comeuppance, boy!" A round of laughter spread through the crowd.

Denton pushed himself off the ground, eyeing Finch as if deciding to throw another punch., his fists pulsed with anger. Finch stood still, legs spread wide.

"Think you're something special," Denton growled. "You're a pissant. A pissant. And I'm the man to stomp you."

"You'll find me a tougher punching bag than your wife." Finch said loudly. He ignored the whispers behind him. "You

28

think you're a big man because you can beat a woman? Only a small man is that cruel."

Not taking his eyes off Denton, Finch leaned his head toward Em. "Miss Olson, would you prefer this man to leave the premises?"

His sudden reference to her caught her off guard. She glanced at the crowd behind her. All eyes were on her. She leaped at the chance.

"Yes, Doctor Stone." She emphasized *Doctor*. "I'd like him to leave immediately. And he's to never return to this property."

"Not even when he's black and blue?" Someone shouted out behind her. Laughter exploded from the group. They'd probably all been cheated or intimidated by Denton at some point. He was invited to the wedding only because he was related to the groom.

"Go to hell!" Denton screamed at the shouter.

"Enough." Em ordered. She had reached her limit. If Denton swung at her, she'd meet him again sometime and he'll look down her gun barrel.

She stepped up to Denton, her hands on her hips. "Walt, you're to leave."

Denton swayed as he tried to gain his balance and his composure. He studied the faces of the crowd. He belched. He glared at Em then Finch as hatred seeped from his squinty eyes. "You'll regret what you did, boy."

"I won't." Finch said, simply. He didn't move.

Denton swayed a bit more as he appeared to weigh his options. He bent to pick up his hat then swung a fist at Finch's face. Em gasped.

Finch evaded the clumsy uppercut then followed with one of his own into Denton's chin with a loud *smack*.

"Uhh," wheezed from Denton's mouth as he fell. He hit the ground with a thud.

Finch stepped back, barely avoiding the flying dirt. "You heard the lady. If you don't leave for the lady, then do it for yourself, Denton. You're looking mighty foolish."

The silence hung so thick Em could hear magpies squawking a mile down Quartz Creek. Denton grunted as he rolled out of the dirt. "I'm gettin' my woman first."

Em stood in his way. "You must not have heard me. You're leaving. Betty can leave when she's ready. And that ... lady you were dancing with can leave now too. Now, get off this property." Her fists stabbed onto her hips, her legs spread wide in her calf-length skirt.

"You'll regret this too."

I regret anything to do with you. "Perhaps if you apologize to us all, most especially your wife, we can put this behind us." Em stated. Defiance rang in her voice.

Denton stared at Em's face before turning away.

She didn't move as the fat man slapped dirt off his suit as he staggered the driveway. His Chevrolet Deluxe Coupe sat in the Old Church's dirt parking lot across the road. Denton always parked across the spaces, taking up spots for three automobiles, an arrogance that irritated everyone in town.

As Denton reached the end of the driveway and stepped off her property, laughter rang out. Em turned and held her arms wide. "It's over everyone. Let's get back to celebrating at the reception."

The chattering crowd turned and reentered the hotel. Em watched Denton gun the coupe to a roar and launch the big automobile from the parking lot. Rocks spewed behind in a large arc. The vehicle raced up the hill toward Hamilton City.

Em approached the door but held back to shepherd everyone in. Finch hung back to allow her to enter first but she placed her hand on his arm. The hardness and warmth of his arm muscles jolted her abdomen. Her breath quickened and she blurted, "Thank you, Finch. You were wonderful! And such a terrible situation. I can't thank you enough." Em blushed at her babbling.

Finch placed his hand on hers, pressing her hand tightly into his arm. Em's eyes almost closed, taking in the sensuousness of his warm hand. Her lips parted as she looked up at him.

"I'm glad to help … you." His voice was soft as his eyes caressed her face. The screen door screeched open. Em jumped away from Finch and pulled her hand from his arm. He dropped his hand.

"Auntie Em, aren't you coming?" Sylvia's high-pitched voice scratched the air, causing Em to want to strike her for breaking the moment. Sylvia stepped out the door and grabbed Finch's arm. "You were great! Where did you learn to do that? Are you a boxer? I hope you'll dance with me. Say you'll dance with me!"

Finch faced Em and smiled a sad smile. "Well, Miss Olson, your presence has been requested inside. May I escort you in?"

Em took Finch's offered arm and returned the smile. She let the screen door slam in Sylvia's face.

CHAPTER 4

Now where is that girl? Em felt particularly irritated this morning. Exhaustion from hosting and cleaning up after the wedding reception and Denton's incident had set in. Her legs hurt. She couldn't sleep all night what with replaying the events in her mind.

The ugliness of Walter Denton jerking Betty's head and trying to hit her haunted her. Remembering Finch's touch and warm eyes failed to rid her mind of the ugliness, though the sudden thought of his handling of Denton made her snicker.

She hurried to the flour bin to start the biscuits. She pulled open the flour bin. The grit on the handle caused her to look at her floury palm. With a glance, she noted white dust coated the kitchen. *Sylvia needs to wipe down the kitchen.*

At the giggles through the opening door, Em prepared to chastise Sylvia for arriving late—again. Her mouth hung open in shock as Sylvia and Finch came through the door together. Each laughed at the other.

Sylvia adjusted her skirt as if she'd just put it on and patted her hair as if she'd just put it up. Finch buttoned his shirt. She teased him how his misaligned work shirt looked ridiculous.

Em turned back to her dough in shock. *Did they sleep together? Of course not. Don't be ridiculous.* She concentrated on mixing the dough with her fingers.

"Good morning, Em."

Finch's voice was disgustingly happy this morning, she thought. *There was no caution, no embarrassment at having been caught sleeping with a seventeen-year-old girl—and in her hotel!*

And the girl — how could she throw herself at a mature man? Had she no decency!? She gets the boot, Em decided.

"Good morning." Her voice sounded far away as she sprinkled more flour on the sticky mixture. As she kneaded the dough, her fists grew more agitated, harder and harder she pounded. Tears stung her eyes as she felt a betrayal she had no reason to feel.

"Last night Finch taught me the moves he used on Denton. Almost for the whole night." The suggestiveness in Sylvia's voice stabbed at Em's heart.

"How nice." Em pretended she could see their faces in the flour so she could beat them both as she kneaded.

"Don't exaggerate." His voice had a chastising note.

"That's right. We did other things too," Sylvia laughed.

"So, is that how you get your biscuits so light and tender, Em? Beat them into submission?" Behind her, Finch's voice rang with a smile.

Not daring to look at him, she patted the dough flat before slicing the dough into biscuits she said, "Sylvia, please set the table for two this morning."

"Two! You said yesterday I could eat with you both. You said I could." The sharp petulance made Em want to throw the dough at her.

Em swallowed hard. "I won't be eating with you two this morning. I have some things that must be done." Like crying into my pillow, Em thought.

"Oh, good." Sylvia retreated into the dining room. Soon, the clatter of dishware echoed. She cringed. *Will I have any china left when Sylvia leaves?*

"Are you alright this morning, Em?" Finch's voice was directly behind her. She jumped at his nearness.

"I'm fine," she said in a small voice. Oh, how she wanted to turn and let him hold her. She took a slow breath to calm the desire to weep.

Em stepped to the wood sink and gripped the pump's handle. Tight this morning, she pushed up hard on the handle then leaned her weight to force it down.

"Let me help you." Finch slipped beside Em and gently nudged her away. He gripped the handle and pumped until water gushed. "This pump is nearly frozen. Why don't you change to those new-fangled faucets? They're not expensive and it'd save you a lot of energy."

"I like it the way it is," Em snapped. Bracing for the frigid blast, she plunged her hands into the icy water. She picked off bits of dough to flush down the drain.

His breath brushed the tendrils of her hair at the nape of her neck. "I can't believe you like it this way. Please, tell me what's wrong — if it's something you can share."

From the corner of her eye, she saw Finch lean against the counter beside her to study her face. She blushed.

"I don't know if you have the strength this morning to hear my problems after being up all night with Sylvia." She draped a towel over the biscuits on a baking sheet.

Finch crossed his arms as he stared into the kitchen. Finally, he nodded. "Ah, I see." He leaned toward Em. "Let me guess: judging from how Sylvia and I looked as we came in the door, she adjusting herself in a great show, me rebuttoning my shirt, you think we slept together."

Embarrassed at his forwardness, she swallowed. "Yes." Her trembling voice betrayed her hurt feelings. Finch pushed himself off the counter and headed to the dining room door. His departing presence dragged away her soul like a vacuum.

"Sylvia!" Finch leaned through the door. "Set the table for three. Em will join us."

Em, shocked, looked over her shoulder at him. Finch turned from the door and winked. He returned to lean on the counter and crossed his arms. "Em, I thought you knew my feelings better than that. But I understand how you came to believe what you believe."

He shifted close, his arm almost touching hers. His body heat washed over her, intensifying his closeness. His brown eyes twinkled. "I'm not that kind of boy."

Sylvia leaned through the doorway, a look of irritation in her face. "Auntie Em, now you're eating with us?"

A satisfied look flitted across Em's face. She glanced at Finch while she answered, "Yes, I'll be eating with you."

Sylvia groaned and shoved off from the doorjamb. Soon, more clatter of dishware echoed.

A knock on the kitchen's exterior door interrupted Finch and Em's gaze. "I'm sorry. Excuse me," Em muttered as she dried her hands on a clean rag. She stepped into the pantry and opened the door to find a bruised Betty Denton. "Betty! Oh, please come in." She led Betty into the kitchen. "I only have a minute. I'm sorry, but I must get breakfast going."

Finch pushed himself off the counter and stepped toward the dining room door. "Good morning, Missus Denton. It's good to see you."

As he turned to leave, Em thought, "What a gentleman he is to leave during this moment."

"Oh, thank you for taking Walter outside yesterday." She reached out a hand to stop him. "He can be … a bit abrasive." Betty raised a hand to hide the bruise on her cheek where the blonde woman struck her.

A bit abrasive – he's more abrasive than a drilling bit.

Finch tipped his head. "Anything I can do to help, madam. Excuse me." He nodded his head toward Em then stepped into the dining room.

In the awkward silence Em brushed the biscuits with softened butter and placed them in the oven. The fire wasn't quite hot enough so she stuffed wood sticks in the firebox to stoke the fire.

"Would you like a cup of coffee?" Em asked.

Betty shook her head. "I stopped by to apologize for yesterday. I can't believe he would bring his tramp to the wedding. And to dance with her, in front of me!" She lightly touched the bruise under her eye. "And the way he danced with her, like he was … having sex with her. I lost myself. I'll apologize to Nancy and Pat when they return from their honeymoon. I'm sorry. I don't know what else to say."

"I understand, Betty. I've never seen him so drunk. I don't know what I would have done under the circumstances." I wouldn't be in that circumstance, Em thought. *Any man who'd cheat on me in front of the whole town would have been cut loose a long time ago.* "I hope you two had a talk and settled it."

Betty shook her head. "I started to walk home. He didn't wait for me anywhere."

Em's brow furrowed. They lived five miles out on a two-track road that wound its way through a forest. "You walked?" Appalled at Denton's inconsideration, she exclaimed, "You might have run into a cougar or a wolf! Did you get home before dark?"

Betty nodded. "Dusky. I hoped he would've waited at the road. I was scared to death since last week Bill Newbury told me the bears are about and Lewis Roberts swears he saw a wolf by South Pass. But Bill saw me before the turn-off to the house and gave me a lift most of the way. Walter didn't come back last night. I haven't seen him since. I can't help but think that he abandoned me—like your father did you!"

CHAPTER 5

"Sylvia, I've given Finch the key to Room One. He's moved out of Room Two so it needs cleaning and linen. His boss and his wife will have that room for the private bath. There's no telling when they'll arrive today so you need to get started."

Sylvia's lip curled in a sneer and waggled her head. Though she faced away from Em, the reflector on the wall-mounted oil lamp mirrored her movements.

"Don't you make a face at me like a child. I don't know why you think that's acceptable, but knock it off." Em's voice raised to a shout.

Sylvia stalked out the kitchen and slammed the door behind her. In frustration, Em whipped the kitchen towel against the wood stove. "Oh!" By habit, her eyes scanned the now-clean kitchen after the breakfast seating, then she decided she needed fresh air.

Stepping out through the exterior pantry door, she let the screen door slam. At her favorite spot, her spirits lifted. The swinging wood bench hung from ropes under the one-hundred-year-old fir tree and swayed gently in the breeze. She plopped on the bench and pushed off, and let the zephyr blow away the anger.

I don't know how to get through to her, Em thought. Why is she so difficult? Granted, Sylvia wasn't used to working. Being spoiled, she resented the requirement as if labor were beneath her station. Work was not for her. No, there was no reason to keep her.

She could send Sylvia home. But who would replace her? Margaret's offer to help was thoughtful, though she could offer only limited services, what with her job at the Assayer's Saloon. Help—decent help—long-term help—was hard to find. The rest of the country was in the midst of an economic depression with thousands desperate for work, but those willing to work for room and board and a low wage couldn't reach this county. Em sighed in resignation.

She looked around the Olson Hotel property. God, how she loved this rugged country. She felt the mountains' strength to her soul and brought peace.

The Olson family had owned this ground for more than sixty years since gold was first discovered and Placer City founded. The pull to protect that legacy was strong.

But, did that mean she had to remain here? She could sell it on her father's behalf. He was the owner, but he had left. Lord knows, she'd been offered goodly sums for the property. Samuel Quint offered again to buy it, but the thought of that scoundrel owning her hotel and what she envisioned he'd to it didn't appeal to her.

Rose often sent letters encouraging her to sell and move. Perhaps in California she could find a man to love.

An image of Finch materialized in her mind: handsome, warm, teasing. Em liked him. She was attracted to him. She had to admit it. He seemed attracted to her. Finch wasn't the first man attracted to her, but he was the first man she'd been attracted to. At the Olson Hotel, single men—and married men—showed up to stay a while, flirted, expressed their devotion to her, then left.

The sequence was always the same. Finch would leave like all the others.

She needed to put up an emotional wall to prevent this man from breaking her heart. If that weren't hard enough, she'd send her only family member back to her parents. She'd be alone again with a crushing workload. As a wave of loneliness swept over Em, tears welled.

One tear dribbled down her cheek. She swept away the tear though no one was around to see it.

"May I intrude?"

The softly spoken question made Em jump.

Finch leaned against the tree. He'd materialized without her seeing him. She must have been lost in her misery.

With a sad smile she said, "You're not intruding." Her voice was soft, sad, she knew. She didn't care whether he knew. He'd not be around much longer.

Finch pushed himself off the tree and sauntered to the swing. He sat on the swing as far from Em as he could. He turned his head to watch her.

Together, they pushed the swing in silence.

"May I ask if you're alright?"

"I'm fine." Em let her voice sound noncommittal.

Finch nodded his head in time to the rocking.

"Are you angry with me?"

Finch's question surprised Em. She shook her head. Realizing he needed some explanation although he didn't deserve one she said, "Just a rough morning."

"I'm sorry."

"How has your morning been?" Em changed the subject.

"Guess I'm on pins and needles waiting for my boss to arrive. He's a good guy, but his wife can be … a bit demanding." He turned his head to watch Em's reaction. She made sure he saw none.

"I look forward to meeting him and his wife," Em said, her voice crisp, businesslike. "That's one thing I love is meeting new people."

"What do you hate about this place?"

How personal and impertinent. "Nothing."

"Nothing," he echoed. His lips tightened as he nodded in time with the swing.

They watched the sunlight flicker through the waving fir trees. A doe mule deer with her last year's fawn stepped tentatively through the western section of the property. They sat silent until the doe and the baby disappeared in the willows behind them.

"Are you sure you're not angry with me?" The plaintiveness in his voice softened Em's heart and cracked her wall of protection.

"I'm not angry with you, Finch. I have decisions to make that aren't easy." She clenched her hands tightly and watched as her knuckles turned white.

"Can I help you in any way? You seem so pitiful and sad. I'm a good sounding board and I don't gossip."

Em smiled at that. Everyone knew everyone else's business in this town. And if they didn't know, they'd make it up. *Perhaps someone who'll be gone soon can give me a fresh perspective.* She turned to stare at the old hotel—her hotel. "I've had an offer to buy the hotel and I'm thinking of accepting it," she blurted. The ease of how the words escaped surprised her.

Finch started and breathed deeply. He glanced at her before facing away.

"It's not just a huge decision, it's the loss of what's left of my family's memories." Em pointed at the hotel. "See the difference in the aging of the log buildings?"

Finch shifted in the bench to study the hotel. The whitewashed lean-to kitchen was sandwiched between the two-story's light brown logs and the one-story's logs hewn in the last century had aged to near-black.

Swallowing hard Em said, "At the start of the gold boom in eighteen sixty-eight, my grandmother built the one-story hotel and the lean-to kitchen. Two years later she added the two-story." She crossed her arms and pressed her hands against her ribs.

"Six years ago my brother Michael was passed out in his room in the two-story. There was a fire. The sheriff thought Michael had thrown a match into the waste bin and it was still burning." Em clenched her hands tightly. "We lost that building and most of our belongings ... and Michael."

"Oh, Em." Finch whispered so softly the breeze almost carried away his words.

"That's why I insist on matches being discarded on the little metal shelf. We managed to rebuild the two-story." A smile flitted across Em's lips. "That's why I have indoor plumbing now."

After a deep breath Em continued, "Michael's loss and the loss of the two-story started my parents to fighting and Father to drink heavily." She paused as the doe deer and her fawn stepped into the clearing from the willows. The doe watched them for a moment before leading the fawn back into the willows and vanished.

"Soon after, Rose left for California. My father followed for its gold fields. Mother died last year." Em stated, almost lightly so as to not invite questions. "Help is hard to get. Another family could buy the place. They could do well."

He reached for her hand and held it. "I'm so sorry, Em. You deserve good things to happen to you."

Slowly she removed her hand and placed it in her lap. Her message was clear: leave me alone. "Thank you. I appreciate your thoughtfulness for listening."

Finch nodded, still watching her. "I shall leave you to your decision-making. Good day, Em." Finch stood from the swing then briskly walked toward the hotel.

In the lingering emptiness, guilt engulfed Em. "Good day, Finch," she whispered though he had disappeared into the hotel. Tears welled and rolled down Em's cheeks. In a gasp, she gulped for air as she wept.

Sobs wracked her slender shoulders. She leaned forward and covered her face with her hands. "Oh, God," she murmured between sobs. With only loneliness for company, Em cried until she couldn't cry any more.

~ * ~

Later that afternoon, Em lifted a foot to climb the stairs to the second floor. The hotel's front door pushed open and a nose appeared. "Mail call!" The nose retreated and the door closed.

Em turned for the front door and opened it.

"Afternoon, Lewis. How was your trip up the mountain?"

41

"Mighty fine, Em. Here's your property tax bill for the hotel." Lewis held out an envelope.

With a sigh Em said, "I'm so relieved to get that."

Lewis smiled at her sarcasm and nodded. "I'm hearing the taxes are going down. Properties aren't selling for much now."

Em nodded. "Got your pickup back I see." The battered Ford was already covered in mud.

Lewis studied his vehicle. "Yup. Glad to have the ol' boy back." He lifted a finger to the bill of his cap. "Gotta dash, Em. Got a special delivery for Denton."

"Perhaps next time you'll have time for coffee and cookies, Lewis." Em waved.

Lewis tottered toward his truck and raised an arm in understanding. "Hope so, Em!" He suddenly spun back. "Oh, Doris Beers and her three kids are here for the summer. Thought you'd want to know for the 'Placer Claims'."

Lifting the envelope in salute Em shouted, "Good to know. It'll go with Nancy and Pat's nuptials."

She closed the door and stepped into her private office. After contemplating how to pay the taxes, she tossed the envelope on her desk. Grabbing scrap paper, she quickly jotted a reminder about Doris Beers and the Moreno nuptials. Right now she needed to inspect Room Two before Finch's boss and wife showed up.

The stairs felt particularly steep. Her legs suddenly refused to propel her up the stairs, forcing her to drag herself up by the railing.

Panting to catch her breath, she stood in Room Two's doorway. The curtain had been swept aside; sunlight streamed across the bed. The quilt looked straight. Em lifted a corner at the bed's head. The wool blanket was askew. Em pulled down the quilt. After she straightened the blanket, she hesitated then lifted the blanket to ensure Sylvia had changed the sheets.

She swept her finger on the nightstand. Her fingertips were clean. The bathroom was set. Mirror was clean. Tub was clean. The towels were slightly uneven and Em straightened them. The floor looked clean. The key was in the door's lock.

Em closed the door to Room Two and trudged for the stairs. A shriek of giggling stopped her. Em sidled down the hall. The sound came from Finch's room.

Sylvia and Finch were laughing over something. Regret beat the wave of jealousy and self-pity. She pushed him away. He couldn't be expected to moon over her. Finch was a good catch, but one who would leave her like all the others. Em headed for the stairs.

In the kitchen, she closed the door against their laughter. She sat at the counter and stared out the window.

A few moments later, she thought about asking for instructions from her aunt on how to send Sylvia back. Before she could push back from the counter to stand, a soft vibration of a large machine outside massaged Em's muscles.

A vehicle pulled into the front yard. Her guests had arrived. She hurried to the door and watched a red Packard roadster the size of a ship pull into Em's boat dock of a driveway. The machine idled in the suspended dust cloud.

When the driver turned off the machine an unsettling stillness enveloped her. A large man wearing work clothes and a beautiful young woman in silk emerged from the land yacht that appeared to be brand-new. The woman brushed off the dirt from her skirt. I just hope they're nice people, Em thought.

Em pushed open the door to meet them on the porch and held out her hand. "Welcome. I'm Em Olson. I own the hotel. You must be Doctor Stone's employer and wife."

Barclay gripped Em's hand warmly. "This is Doctor Clarence Barclay." The woman emphasized *Doctor*. "I am Missus Doctor Virginia Barclay."

Missus Doctor's eyes inspected the darkened logs and the windows' chipped white paint. Em turned to Virginia and held out her hand. "Oh, you're a doctor too? I apologize for not knowing your achievement."

Missus Doctor squinted at Em with cold eyes. Em dropped her hand.

Her eyes lowered to take in Em's faded cotton dress and cracked-leather shoes. Her lips tightened slightly.

"In Europe, a wife takes her husband's title."

Em fought the urge to become angry at Missus Doctor's attempt to belittle her. She might be poor, but she was her own boss, a queen in her own castle.

A snort escaped from Barclay. "My wife's educational specialty is shopping and spending my money." His voice was genial if it weren't slightly annoyed at having to explain.

"Please, come in. Let's get you settled in so you can relax." Em turned away.

"One can relax here?" Missus Doctor asked.

Em openly eyed Missus Doctor with contempt. She led the way into the hotel then held out her hand to indicate the register on the stand. "Please sign in. I've already written in that you're staying in Room Two."

"Do you expect us to just accept the room you give us?" Missus Doctor's sharp voice plucked at Em's stretched nerves.

Should she be cordial? *No.* "Yes." Em faced Missus Doctor. "Unless you prefer a room that shares a bathroom or a cabin that only has an outhouse." She felt satisfied when Missus Doctor's eyes widened.

After Barclay signed the register with tiny strokes with the pen, Em said to Barclay, "Please feel free to call on me if you need something or if you have a question about the local area. I can also arrange for a guide."

"We already know this area," Missus Doctor snapped. "We arrived a few days ago, but stayed in Lander."

Em clenched her jaws. "Up the stairs."

In silence they climbed the steep stairs. At the door to Room Two, Em pushed open the door and stepped inside. "This is your room. Your key to this room and the hotel's front door is in the door lock. There are extra blankets in the dresser." She ignored Missus Doctor as her eyes swept around the simple room. Em stepped into the bathroom. "Your bath."

"What time do you provide room service?" Missus Doctor's hands curled to her chest as if she were afraid to touch anything.

"I don't provide room service. Breakfast is at seven. Lunch is a cold pail lunch by prior request, and dinner is at six."

Missus Doctor spun to face Em. "I want a proper lunch at two and dinner at eight. Those times are far too early." Her voice challenged Em.

"If you wish to have those meals at other times, you'll have to go to the Assayer's Saloon or the Sage Restaurant." Em turned her back to Missus Doctor and held up a hand to indicate the oil lamp mounted on the wall and the tiny oil lamp on the dresser. "For lights, we have oil lamps around the room. Some are mounted and others are set on the dressers to carry from room to room. There are matches near each lamp. Place the burnt matches on the metal plate, never in the trash."

"No electricity?" Missus Doctor's eyes widened. Her upper lip raised slightly.

"No." Em spun to step out the door. "If you'll follow me, I'll show you to the dining room and the living room."

"We need to rest. We'll find your dining room and living room later," Missus Doctor spit out.

Em turned to see Barclay lie on her bed and drop his shoed feet on her quilt. "Please do not place your shoes on the quilt, Doctor. My mother made that quilt." Her tolerance for indulgent guests fell lower.

Barclay said nothing but moved his feet to hang over the edge of the bed. From down the hall, Sylvia's voice echoed loudly from Finch's room. A thought to let him know his boss had arrived flashed in Em's mind, but if he were concerned he would have waited out front to greet him instead of gallivanting in his room with her unmarried cousin. If his boss knocked on Finch's door she wondered what he'd find.

She shook her head to rid her mind of the image and thumped down the stairs. No doubt, later she'd find the Barclays wandering around. Then they'd be angry because they didn't know where to go for the dining room or the living room and act like their being lost was her fault.

Maybe I should talk to Samuel about accepting his offer.

CHAPTER 6

Lander Gazette Local News
"Placer Claims" reported by Em Olson
May 26 – June 1, 1933
- *Nancy Burns and Patrick Moreno wed in the Old Church and held their reception at the Olson Hotel. The newlyweds are off on their honeymoon in Yellowstone Park.*
- *Doris Beers and her three children arrived for the summer from California as they decide whether to move here. This will be their tenth summer in Placer City.*

A few days later on Sunday morning, Em tossed back the covers on her bed. To push off the heavy quilt and step out of the warm, soft bed was painful enough, but facing guests was an agony she didn't want. The world awaited to irritate, annoy, or ruin any good mood she possessed. She slouched on the edge of bed, staring at her worn shoes tossed in the corner. They look old and tired—like me, she thought. *Who could make me feel shiny and new?*

She had only the Olson Hotel, a rundown old lady like herself. She could stay slouched on the edge of the bed until the hotel deteriorated to dust. Her sister Rose's words echoed in her mind: "Sell the place for whatever you can and run to California. Here the zephyrs will blow away your cares."

The ticking clock on the nightstand tolled its seconds like a gong in a sideshow. When she had guests, she preferred to rise early, giving her plenty of time for a relaxing workload and enjoy the morning's beauty.

This morning, however, she would have much less work. Last night the Barclays invited Finch and, surprisingly, herself and Sylvia to the Sage Restaurant for Sunday brunch. Though a generous offer, she declined. She wanted to attend church then come back to wash her clothes and bedding. With few clothes, laundering had to be accomplished weekly.

Perhaps today wasn't so bad. She hopped out of bed.

~ * ~

After church, in the basement, Em stopped cranking the handle for the washtub's rollers. With a grunt, she hefted her damp bed sheet and whipped it to loosen the wrinkles. She grabbed some clothespins then draped the sheet over the clothesline strung from the joists.

Sylvia had been washing clothes for Finch and for a few prospectors who stayed in the past month. Behind the washing machine, Em unscrewed the glass bottle attached to the drainpipe. She swirled the water-filled jar in the light streaming through the lone window and watched gold flecks sink to the bottom. Carefully she poured out the water then dumped the speckles into a small pail. Flecks dotted the bottom—not enough to pay the hotel's bills. She reached in and pinched between two fingers a tiny nugget. *At this rate it'll take until Doomsday to save enough to pay my debts.* She let the nub fall into the pail.

"So, what do you think, Mother?" Em called out to the low floor joists above her head. She looked around the dim basement as if hoping her mother would materialize. She listened to the creaking building. The wind had kicked up. Great, another incoming storm, she thought.

Em stuffed another load of laundry into the round tub. *Sylvia needed to take care of this yesterday. Where is that girl?*

Trudging up the steps, Em felt a growing pain in her legs. The achiness crept up her calves to her thighs. *Why does this pain return every time I'm down?*

The light of reality brightened her mind. Are they connected, she asked herself. "Mother, what do you think?" A

47

popping noise sounded from one of the logs. *Did Mother answer her question?* "Are you here, Mother?" Another popping noise from the log. *So what's the answer?*

"Fresh towels."

The sharp voice jabbed a needle into Em's balloon of thought, bursting it. She jumped, wincing at the pain in her legs. The Barclays, Finch, and Sylvia returned earlier and Missus Doctor declared herself too dusty from the walk and a bath was required.

"Is that a problem?"

The voice and its intent spiked Em's anger. She craned her neck to look up the stairs' opening and into the face of Missus Doctor, who leaned over the banister upstairs. The loosely tied silk cord barely held her robe together.

Em bit her anger into her tongue. "No. You startled me."

"Well, have your mother get them."

"I'm not sure why you think she can. She's dead."

Self-satisfaction washed over Em when Missus Doctor's lips tightened. "Oh!" She pushed away from the banister and stomped back into her room.

Em rolled her eyes as she headed to the upstairs linen closet. She had to pull herself up the stairs since her legs' pain increased. At the top landing, she huffed slightly at the exertion. A giggle down the hall reminded her Sylvia was again with Finch in his room. Her shoulders drooped as she pulled out the key to the linen closet from her apron pocket and pushed the skeleton key into the hole.

"Em …"

She stopped. Finch had spoken her name, but she couldn't hear the remainder of his sentence. Laughter burst from Sylvia and Finch. Tears stung her dry eyes as Em pulled open the closet's wood door. She reached for the towels, but the towel bin was empty. Sylvia hadn't filled it, and Em hadn't seen the towels in the basement. *Oh no.* Now, she'd have to knock on Finch's door to ask Sylvia about the towels. Em hesitated. She had to get Missus Doctor her towels, but to do so she'd have to interrupt Finch and Sylvia … in whatever they were doing.

Both acts were unpalatable. Sylvia's giggles echoed through the hallway.

Em studied the door to Missus Doctor's room. She recalled her decision not to allow Finch into her heart. If that decision was final, why hesitate?

With a toss of her head, the Olson Hotel proprietor would do what she must. She strode down the hall and rapped on Finch's door. Come what may, she thought to herself.

The soft murmuring behind the door stopped. In the sudden silence, she heard a soft draping of fabric. Em felt a hot flush cross her face.

The lock switched. The door slowly opened a few inches. Finch's brown eyes widened.

"I'm sorry, Doctor Stone," Em switched to a formal address. "I need to find Sylvia. I believe she's here." She allowed the coldness to come through her voice. Finch's flinch informed her he received the blast of frigid air.

"Um, just a moment." He closed the door softly.

Em stared at the doorknob and felt anger rise. In her hotel, she shouldn't have to tolerate shenanigans between unmarried people. That's not the way she was raised. And married guests resided down the hall!

The door opened a few inches. Em didn't move, but stood steadfast. That twit Sylvia was not going to get away with anything now. Now more than ever, Sylvia was going back home to her spoiling parents.

"What do you want?" The bluntness of Sylvia's voice set off Em's fury. With a bravado she didn't know she possessed, she pushed open the door and didn't stop until the door shoved Sylvia and knocked her to the floor. She yelped and pushed herself up.

"You," Em ordered to Sylvia, "Downstairs. Right now. I'll speak to you in the kitchen." A red curtain of rage draped across Em's eyes.

"How dare you talk to me that way!" Sylvia screamed.

"I do and I will." Em stepped aside for Sylvia to leave.

Down the hall, Missus Doctor's door cracked open.

"You'd better go." Finch said, his voice contrite, soft.

Sylvia staggered, tripping over her feet and muttering curses under her breath.

"And you, Doctor Stone," Em turned to face him. "Pack your bags. Leave right now." She tightened her lips to show anger. Better for him to know she was livid than for him to know her heart was breaking.

"I protest this low-class screaming."

Em started at the harsh words spoken behind her. She spun to see Missus Doctor standing in the doorway, hands stabbed to her hips. "I want towels and all I get is screaming. What kind of a backwoods place is this?"

Em opened her mouth and turned to square off at this spoiled woman who dared to insult the Olson Hotel and her.

"I am so sorry, Virginia," Finch purred as he slipped to the door. He lifted his arms wide to lean against the doorjamb, blocking Virginia's view. "We had a incident here." Finch turned to indicate Em. "Miss Olson here diffused it. Quite deftly I might add. Without her, a most unsavory occurrence might have exploded into the hallway." He cocked his head as a large smile crossed his mouth.

Em watched in wonder as Missus Doctor's posture relaxed and her hands flew to her face. She blushed, either at his words or his face. "I am so sorry, please forgive me, Finch." Missus Doctor's hands fluttered. One reached to touch his chest, but pulled up short. "I will excuse myself." Her face looked remarkably like a child experiencing her first communion. She caught sight of Em and her face turned to cold steel. Missus Doctor spun on her heels. The door's slam echoed down the barren hall.

Em stood, stock-still. She barely breathed. Finch straightened and stepped beside her. His body exuded heat that warmed her. She felt his breath on her neck. She wavered on her vow to make him leave her life.

Then she saw the half-empty whiskey bottle on the dresser.

She spun to face him. His face was close enough to kiss. She faced him dead on. "You bring liquor into my hotel? You know very well I don't allow spirits." Her shoulders trembled. "Doctor Stone, you will pack your bags and leave my hotel. I will not tolerate shenanigans between unmarried people in my hotel and spirits being brought in despite my prohibition."

She paused at the door. "I'll have your bill made out. I can refund your pre-payment." Even as she turned, she worried how she would refund his money; she'd already spent the money paying Magnus' wages for the past two months. Perhaps she could borrow the money back.

"Miss Olson," Finch also jumped to the formal address. "I think you misunderstood what's been happening here." He reached for her, but she lifted her arms and stepped back to evade his grasp.

"Your seduction techniques will not work with me. Pack your bags. I'll meet you downstairs." She headed out the door and tried not to mirror Missus Doctor's stomping.

"She's practicing her tailoring."

Em stopped at the soft voice behind her. She turned, deciding to allow him to defend himself and Sylvia before Em booted them both out.

Finch walked with his hands stuffed in his pockets. His head hung low, but he tilted his head so he could peer at her. He stopped in front of Em, who stood her ground, defiant.

"She told me you wanted her to learn a trade. She considered tailoring—since apparently she has many tailor-made garments and knows what she's talking about. I thought a tailor would make a fine trade. She practiced on my clothes."

I wonder what else she practiced on him, Em thought.

He seemed to read her thoughts. "Nothing else happened. I promise on my sainted mother's soul." Finch pulled out his hands from his pockets and raised his right hand, his left on his heart. "I would not tarnish Sylvia's reputation—and mine—by doing anything untoward with that girl." He leaned toward her. "I'd prefer to kiss a more mature woman." A small smile flitted across his mouth.

Em leaned away from him, feeling her face burn. She swallowed hard.

"As far as the whiskey, I know you don't allow it. But I opened the bottle at my last hotel. I couldn't leave it in my truck; it would get broken. Since I've been here I resolved not to drink any out of deference for your restriction."

He stepped close enough she could smell his warmth. "Even if you don't want me," he said in a barely audible voice. "I wouldn't do anything to hurt you or damage the reputation of your hotel."

In the silence of the hallway, Em watched his eyes as they searched her face. He tightened his lips before spinning on his heels. As he walked away he called out over his shoulder, "I will pack now. As you wish."

Her shoulders slumped at his words. She watched Finch's broad shoulders as he turned into his room. Her eyes wandered to his slim waist, then his tight backside encased with chino. Ashamed for her overreaction, jealousy and self-importance got the better of her.

Drifting back to Finch's closed door, she stared at the battered wood. She lightly tapped on the doorjamb. After a moment, Em reached up her fist to rap louder when it opened.

Finch leaned against the half-open door, expressionless.

Em took a deep breath. "I apologize," she stuttered. No coherent words came out. She hung her head, blinking back tears stinging her dry eyes. *Come on, girl.* "First, thank you for being so thoughtful as to not drink while you're here. Second, I had no idea what Sylvia was doing."

"What do you think she was doing?"

Em's face burned so hot she thought it might ignite. Her heart pounded in her chest at her embarrassment. Unable to actually say the words she decided, "You know."

She continued to stare at the door's edge unable to meet his eyes. Finch didn't answer for quite some time.

"No. I don't. What do you think we were doing in here?"

Sweat trickled down Em's chest, the tickle edged its way between her breasts. Pinpricks raced along her back as pores opened, ready to ooze sweat.

Em decided to face the question. She fixed her gaze into Finch's eyes. "I thought you two were being … intimate."

She held his gaze for several seconds. Finch's lips tightened. "We were not."

Em dropped her eyes. Neither moved for several seconds until Em decided to end the confrontation. She looked up. "I'm sorry. With what I was hearing …" *Would he think I eavesdropped?* "When I was down the hall … I heard a lot of giggling … from down the hall. And you two … seemed … very close. Yes." She looked back into his eyes. "I assumed." Em took a deep breath. "If you can forgive me and accept my apology, please stay."

Finch still hadn't moved since he opened the door. He appeared to consider her offer. Suddenly he stared at the wall behind Em and seemed to be thinking out loud. "Well, what are my choices? I can stay here, a single man with two beautiful single women for company. Or, I can move into that decrepit cabin by the Assayer's Saloon so I can stay by my work. Or, I can pitch a tent in the springtime Rocky Mountains and take my chances with the snows. Or, I can go to a hotel in Lander and travel sixty miles round-trip every day to my work. Hmm. What to do … what to do …"

Em wasn't sure if he teased or vented his anger. She apologized and meant it. If he wanted to tease her, she felt too much physical and emotional pain to tolerate it. She decided to cut him loose. He could make his own decision.

"I must go," Em said. "You're welcome to make your decision for what works best for you. Now if you will excuse me, I have another guest to tend to." She turned on her heels. *And a spoiled rotten girl to tend to.*

As Em passed Missus Doctor's room, the door opened. An obviously naked Missus Doctor peered out. While she made an attempt to stay behind the door, she didn't seem to care how much skin she displayed. "My towels?"

Em focused on Missus Doctor's eyes. "I'll get my assistant to fetch your towels. I will be back as soon as I can."

Missus Doctor slammed the door.

"Uhh!" Em groaned under her breath. That stinking Sylvia better have a good excuse for this aggravating situation.

At the top of the stairs, pain stabbed through her legs and they collapsed. She seized the banister to keep from falling. She bit her lips to keep from crying out, a sound that would reverberate down the sterile hall. She gasped as strong hands grabbed her arms and held her steady.

"Easy there. Are you all right?" A soft, yet strong voice purred in her ears.

She froze, panting in pain. A slight groan escaped from her lips. Her head shook.

"Here, let me help." The hands shifted to ease her to the landing. As she crumpled, the hands removed themselves, a loss Em strongly felt. Tears again welled in her eyes.

Finch sat beside her. He twisted his body to lean against the wall and watch her. Em focused on the wallpaper, trying not to look back. She didn't trust herself to stop her body from flinging into his and settled on a simple, "Thank you. I appreciate your help." For some odd reason, she didn't feel so lonely with him sitting beside her nor embarrassed for her physical condition.

"Can I help you in some way?" Finch asked softly. From the corner of her eye, she could see his gaze never left her face.

She shook her head though she wanted to nod. "My doctor says I have a stress-induced condition. It flares up occasionally." She forced herself to concentrate on her breathing, trying to calm herself. "It'll pass in a bit."

Em and Finch sat beside each other, not saying anything for moments. He seemed content to remain, and she didn't want to move away.

The pain subsided and Em's breathing slowed. The sweat dried on her body. Neither Finch nor Em moved.

Finally Finch asked, "Are you feeling better?"

She took his question that their time together was ending. She nodded. "It's passing. Thank you for sitting with me." She grasped the banister to pull herself up.

"This is nice, Miss Olson. I rather enjoy sitting here with you. Please don't have to leave on my account." A small smile crossed his face.

Self-righteousness in her heart softened. Her hand lowered and rested in her lap. Her smile mirrored his. "It is nice, I admit. Thank you."

Finch leaned lightly toward her, not touching, but close enough she could feel the heat from his arm. "It is okay to sit with a man, isn't it?"

She turned in a flash of anger at his teasing. At his gentle smile, the anger softened.

"I won't do anything you don't want me to," he said.

"I have to protect myself," blurted from Em's mouth. *Where did that come from?*

They sat in silence for another moment.

"From what? Or from whom?"

Em's face turned to stare into Finch's. She blinked at the logic and reality.

What was she afraid of? Her heart breaking. "The hotel has a lot of single men stay here. Many flirt with me. I generally don't mind it because it's harmless and they always leave. But I didn't know it was so painful … when it's someone I like."

Finch nodded in understanding. "Does my flirting cause you pain?"

Tears welled and she hated herself for not stopping them. They trickled down her cheeks. Finch's fingertip brushed her cheek. At his touch, she gasped in a huge sob. Hysteria overwhelmed her. "I must go," she cried. She grabbed the banister and heaved herself up. As she trundled down the steps, she gripped the banister for support.

Finch did not follow her.

CHAPTER 7

Icy water splashed on her face shocked Em from her self-pity. Staring at the pretty face in her bathroom's cracked and cloudy mirror, the stress and work of the hotel was aging it fast. Lines seemed to deepen every day. At this pace, when would the flirting stop? When would she become known as the old lady who owned the hotel?

Em splashed more water on her face before reaching for the thin towel draping the nail hook. She studied the woman's face in the mirror for puffiness around the eyes. Finally, the puffiness faded.

An image of Sylvia jumped into her mind. *Oh no. Missus Doctor's towels.* With a groan she draped her towel on its hook. She smoothed her cotton dress with her hands and straightened up.

"Alright, Miss Proprietor, be strong," she muttered. She opened the door with a purposeful yank and strode toward the kitchen.

"Where are my damn towels!" Missus Doctor screeched through the open kitchen door. The harsh tone and foul language jolted an already unsteady Em.

Missus Doctor towered over a cowering Sylvia, bent across the wood stove, hot from burning all day. She fought to keep her balance. Her hand touched the hot steel. She yelped.

"Watch your language!" The strong voice that shot from Em surprised even her. Em raced the few steps toward Missus Doctor, who stepped back in surprise at the shouted order.

Quickly, Missus Doctor regained her composure. "What kind of a hotel is this that a guest can not get a simple request fulfilled. Never in my life—"

"This is a fine hotel. One that does not tolerate any guest, no matter how fine or low they are, berating another guest or worker. Step back from Sylvia. If you have a problem come to me. But you will not approach her in an angry manner again." Em panted for breath and forced herself to speak in a calm manner. "Normally, we fulfill our guests' needs immediately. We've had a bad day today. I am sorry." Em turned to Sylvia. "Where are the clean towels so we can get Missus Barclay's need met?"

"You will refer to me as Missus Doctor Barclay." She emphasized *Doctor*.

Em ignored the command and turned back to Sylvia.

Sylvia hung her head.

"Sylvia?"

"I haven't washed them yet," she said in a small voice. "I hid them in the basement."

Em's face grew cold. Those towels would not be ready for several hours.

"Well, I have never in my life been so poorly treated." Missus Doctor pushed past Em to head back to her room. "What kind of a slum is this," she muttered as she shoved open the kitchen door. The stomping of her feet up the stairs shook the kitchen.

Em fought to keep her temper. Lord, help me, she thought. She opened her eyes to glare at Sylvia.

Sylvia sank to her knees, her shoulders shaking. Gasps of sobs erupted. Em's brow furrowed. Never had she seen any emotion except hostility or indifference from Sylvia since her arrival. So, she met a justifiably angry guest. She's either thin-skinned or something else is going on.

Em knelt beside the weeping girl and patted her on the shoulder. Sylvia shrugged off Em's touch.

Okay then. "What's wrong. Did she insult or strike you?"

Sylvia shook her head. She wiped her eyes and face with a vicious swipe of her arm. "What do you care as long as the slave keeps functioning."

"I don't treat you like a slave. You get plenty of time off. You take plenty of time off. Perhaps, young lady, I should point out we wouldn't be kneeling on the floor if you had done your job, namely washing and drying towels." Em almost shouted. "I expect you to act like an adult, not some spoiled rich child." Her voice continued to raise as her anger took on a life of its own. "You were so relieved to get away from your parents. Do you remember? Now you accuse me of slavery? Be ashamed of yourself!"

"You old women don't remember being young! You're so hooked on this rundown hotel you can't stand to have a young lady take the attention of a handsome man!" Sylvia screamed back. "You're just jealous you can't attract any man to take you away from this dump!" Sylvia's eyes blazed with fury.

With a rounding swing, Em slapped Sylvia so hard her head snapped to the side and her body flung to the floor. She wailed like an infant. Slowly, she pushed herself to her knees. Her body moved faster and so did her fist as she punched Em in the face.

Em gasped and pressed her hands to the floor, not knowing which hurt more, the punch or the insults. In a flash, her hand swung up. "You ungrateful witch!"

Before her hand could contact Sylvia's face, a gripping hand snapped her arm to a standstill. Shocked at this sudden brace, Em looked up. Finch gripped her arm. He stood over her as she knelt.

In one smooth movement, he lifted Em off the floor and led her away. "Peace, Em. Her poor decision is not worth family violence." He led her toward the dining room door.

"Try flirting your way out of this, you aging bitch!" Sylvia screamed behind their backs. Both turned, stunned, at her terrible words.

"Be silent, you ... you ..." Em spun away to return to Sylvia but Finch held her back.

"You're jealous I may be with child and you will never be!" Sylvia screamed as she pushed herself off the floor.

Silence fell as Em and Finch froze in shock.

"What? How? … When?" Em's mouth barely worked. *Scandal!* Breathing hard, Em realized a stranger, a guest, was witnessing a family tragedy. She became conscious of Finch's hand on her arm and took comfort in his warmth and his hands' soft pressure.

"Who would do such a thing to you? He will pay mightily for putting you, an underage child, in such a wicked condition!" Em's voice was tight. Anger grew by the second.

Sylvia's eyes softened and turned to focus on Finch. "Why, the good Doctor Stone."

CHAPTER 8

At Sylvia's shocking accusation of Finch being the father of her baby, a pall hung over the kitchen like the smoke cloud when the woodstove backflowed. Sylvia's face appeared proud, almost defiant for Finch to deny his paternity.

Em moved first. She stepped away from Finch to stare at him. Her ego deflated. Numbness crowded out any emotion, logic, or compassion. Finch's face paled and his mouth fell open. Although she had pulled from his grasp, his hand blindly reached for Em's arm.

"What are you saying, Sylvia?" Finch demanded. He still hadn't moved. His eyes widened until Em thought they would fall out.

Em closed her eyes. Her heart hurt. Although she fought against it, she allowed too much of this man to enter her heart. Now, she found out this abominable act had taken place in her hotel and to her unmarried cousin for whom she was responsible. That Finch had bald-faced lied to her about his feelings hurt most.

She pushed herself away from the counter as she made her way toward the door. She needed to get away, to think, to hurt in silence and in private.

"Em." Finch said, his voice nearly inaudible.

She shook her head as she groped her way to the door. With her back to them, she allowed the welling tears to fall. They would not see them; they were too taken with each other to notice her. As she reached for the door, a more urgent "Em!" sounded behind her.

"Leave me alone," she tossed over her shoulder as she pushed open the door.

"Please stay. You need to hear what I have to say." The pain in his voice hurt.

"I do not." She closed the kitchen door then staggered toward her private space.

Behind her, the door to the kitchen slammed open then shut. She started and turned, expecting to see Finch and Sylvia head to his room.

Instead, Finch's red face highlighted his white lips from being pressed so hard. He skirted her in the hallway and stood between her and her bedroom door, blocking her way to safety and privacy.

"I don't know what is up with the women in this hotel, but I have had enough." He bent until his face was inches away. His eyes, squinty with anger, held hers. She couldn't look away even if she wanted to.

He lifted a hand to point at the kitchen door. "I don't know what that girl is up to, but I told you the truth she only practiced her tailoring. She's a child and a self-centered child at that."

He lifted his finger to point at his heart. "I am not a man who has to find … indulgences … with spoiled children." He panted, trying to catch his breath from the exertion of anger and shock.

He clasped her thin shoulders in his hands. He gently squeezed, feeling the bones through her thin skin. "I swear to you, on everything I hold dear, I have not done anything familiar to that girl."

After a pause, he dropped his hands. "I don't know what more I can tell you. She's lying. Why? I don't know. You need to ask her." Finch stared into Em's eyes. "Either you believe me or you don't." He spun to stare at the closed kitchen door. His body trembled. "But I'll tell you one thing: I'm sorting this out right now."

He skirted Em and stomped for the kitchen. He threw back the door and descended the steps into the kitchen.

61

Yelling rang through the door and ricocheted off the wall before it slammed closed.

Perhaps they might come to blows. Em didn't know what she'd do if they did. Perhaps letting them duke it out was best. Maybe they'd kill each other. That would solve most of her heartache and problems.

Em turned to head into the kitchen.

"What's going on here?" demanded Missus Doctor as she leaned over the second floor banister. "What is wrong with this place?"

Em decided to forgo any semblance of respect. She held up her hands and shrugged her shoulders in resignation.

"Augh!" Missus Doctor spewed as she straightened before heading back to her room. The door slammed closed.

With a sigh, she turned her attention to the kitchen. Finch towered before a shrinking Sylvia. She slouched and wept.

Em slipped down the stairs and watched quietly.

Sylvia screamed to Em, "Get out! This has nothing to do with you."

Em lowered her voice, hoping to calm the situation. "This concerns me in many ways." Sylvia was her responsibility and Finch was a paying guest in her hotel.

"Sylvia," Finch said, sternness thick in his voice. "Tell Em you're lying, and I deserve to know why."

"No," Sylvia said. Smugness laced her voice. She moved her hand to indicate Em. "Even she knows how much time we have spent in your room."

Finch's mouth worked but nothing came out. Finally he said, "You know nothing happened. Who're you lying for? Who're you protecting?" His face turned beet red.

Sylvia twisted at the waist at a singsong pace and said in a singsong voice, "Myself." She stopped her twisting and smoothed her flat stomach. "And your baby."

Finch staggered back, his face ashen. "You filth. You have a mental problem." He raised his hands in resignation. He looked to Em. "I need some air." This time he staggered from the room. Em's eyes squinted in concentration as she carefully watched Sylvia.

Sylvia had an oddly proud look on her face. Em thought of all the lies she'd caught Sylvia telling. *Why would she lie now?*

The realization of "why" blinded Em by its brightness. Sylvia knew she was to be sent home to her parents. A pregnancy would keep her here, hidden from the world in this broken-down town while her scandal, her unmarried pregnancy, was hidden from her parents. She would blame a man who had no defense. Sylvia had a tailor-made excuse to ensure Finch had no alibi.

Sylvia made sure Em knew of her giggling in Finch's room. Who would believe a single man did not have intercourse with a young woman in his hotel room? Sylvia flirted with him constantly and there were times he returned the flirtations. He'd been here long enough for a romance to turn serious.

Em fixed Sylvia with steely eyes. Sylvia's eyes darted to look around the room.

Em knew the truth. Her hand swung hard and caught Sylvia across the cheek, flinging her against the counter. Sylvia pressed her hand to her cheek. "Why would you do this to a pregnant girl?"

"You're lying!" Em advanced on Sylvia, who slinked along the counter. "Admit it! Not only are you lying, but you're tarnishing a good man's character! Have you no shame?" Em's voice rose to fever pitch, echoing off the wood walls.

A wail came from Sylvia. "No! I am pregnant!"

Em was so angry she barely noticed the kitchen door open and Finch enter. "You're lying in a horrible fashion in order to remain here. I don't know why you want to stay here all of a sudden when all you do is complain about it."

Sylvia hunched over the counter, weeping.

"Tell the truth." Em yelled.

"I am pregnant," Sylvia screamed as she pushed herself off the counter. Anguish gave way to anger. She shot her arm out to point at Finch. "And he did it."

Em looked at Finch, who stared at Sylvia. His eyes reflected anger, anguish, and fear.

She turned back to Sylvia. An odd sense of calm washed over her. Seeing everything clearly she said in a soft voice, "When you choose to tell the truth, let us know."

She turned to Finch. Hope stirred in his eyes.

"Doctor Stone, let us step out for some air until Sylvia decides to admit what we already know." She held out her arm to guide Finch to the door. She turned, not waiting for him to follow yet knowing he would.

They left a screaming and wailing Sylvia in the kitchen.

~ * ~

She walked Finch over to the swing on the acreage she called the "West Forty." For moments, they sat in silence as Finch's longer legs pushed the swing in a slow rhythm.

Finch let out a huge sigh. "Em, I can't thank you enough for believing me." He shook his head. "I don't understand why she would do such a thing. To me." He looked over at Em. "To you."

At his "to you," Em studied his brown eyes then turned back to focus on the new grass shoots under their feet. She breathed in the fresh spring air to help clear her mind. "Sylvia has been most difficult. Partly because she's had a difficult life." She snorted in disbelief. "No. She has not had a difficult life, but a charmed life. An easy life. It's hard to imagine one with a charmed life would find reality so difficult."

"That's no excuse for making such a horrid accusation. It's embarrassing. It's hurtful." He looked Em full in the face. "It's wrong. I could lose my job."

Em nodded. "What she's doing is horrible, and not just to us but to herself." She picked at her fingers, roughened from all the labor. "I wonder if this humiliation will make her grow more resentful."

"I wonder if this humiliation will make her grow bolder."

Em lifted her head to watch the big fir tree's branches sway in the light breeze. She considered his words. "Interesting point." She nodded in understanding. "So, you think because she failed to prove her superiority over us, she'll want to do something else to prove it."

Finch rocked as he considered Em's words. He nodded. "I think so." He looked over at Em. "Perhaps this is a warning to you to be prepared for more mischief. Perhaps this means you cannot trust anything she says or anything she does. You must be careful, especially if she deals with guests." His voice went flat in complaint at the last part.

She lightly nudged his elbow with hers. "You're right. We—I—must be on my guard. I must watch her more carefully." At this she turned to face Finch and hold his gaze. "I can't impress upon you how sorry I am this happened to anyone, but especially you. I apologize for … so many things." Em hung her head and gripped her hands. "It seems like apologizing is all I ever do anymore," she murmured.

They swung in silence. They watched juncos flit from the fir tree to the ground. A robin tugged on a worm. A hawk soared overhead while a cottontail rabbit froze then darted under a willow.

"I'll feel better when she retracts her accusation," Finch said. "Until then, my reputation is slandered. My boss might hear of it. He might think less of me and this hotel." He turned his head to Em. "Less of you."

She forced herself to focus on the robin running on the ground. "I know. But I can't control her. She's not my daughter. She doesn't have my background and raising. She's been raised to do what she wishes with any consequences smoothed out by her doting parents." Em allowed the sneer to drip from her voice about Sylvia's parents, her Aunt Dee and Uncle Stephan, of the Boston Wartzens.

She shook her head. "I told her yesterday she's to return home. I'm waiting on instructions on how she's to go back." She rubbed her eyes in frustration. The disgust came through her fingers as she pressed into her eyes. She wanted to cry, but the sobs and the tears wouldn't come. She was all dried out.

Finch lifted her hand from her face. He patted her hand and she curled her fingers so he couldn't see her rough fingertips and the chewed nails. He kept patting her hand as if to keep it in place. His touch felt warm and the roughness of his fingertips matched her own.

"Exactly how long have you been alone here?" Finch's voice was soft, curious.

Now the tears worked and the welling water stung her eyes. She looked away and thought of yanking her hand from his but she didn't want to. She wanted to sit on this swing, watch nature, and hold his hand until the mountains eroded.

Em swallowed hard, trying to release the tightness in her throat. Her sorrows tumbled out before she could stop them. "I told you about my brother Michael burning down the two-story. The thing is he was drunk—passed out—at nineteen. That's why he couldn't escape. My sister Rose and Michael were especially close and she suffered horribly. We all did. Father blamed himself.

"While we rebuilt the two-story, he started drinking constantly. His drunkenness led to bad decisions like being suckered into taking out a second mortgage on the hotel and buying a gold mine. He didn't ask Mother. He hid that from her. That's when the fights got out of control."

Swallowing hard at the memories rising from a hidden place in her soul, Em continued. "Mother, Father, and Rose often battled. I tried to stay out of the way. During a bad financial spell, he sold some of Rose's prized stamps to pay on the loans. She was furious over it. She screamed at him Michael's death was his fault for encouraging him to drink."

Finch grunted.

"He hit her." Em blinked hard. "He berated her so badly she grabbed the first miner and ran away to California. One morning, Mother and I were loading a friend's car who was taking us into Lander to sell Mother's wild strawberry jams to a market, which would pay for that new-fangled sink and faucet for the kitchen. He yelled at her that everyone would be better off if he left for other gold fields."

Em paused to tamp the rising emotion. She'd never talked to anyone of that day. "I remember clear as today him climbing into his Model T—a flatbed. He tossed his rucksack Mother made for him on the floor of the passenger side. As he slammed the truck door closed, he plopped his left arm on the door. His elbow poked through the split fabric of the red checked shirt." The edges of Em's lips lifted slightly at the fond memory.

"He straightened his gold fountain pen in his shirt pocket and loosened his bolo tie I made for him. He hollered he wouldn't be here when we got back—California would be right for him. Mother didn't believe him. He stared at Mother for the longest time." Em groaned and rubbed her eyes to press out the memory.

"Late that evening when we returned we learned Magnus had been hurt—real bad. He was more dead than alive. We moved him into the hotel to care for him. We learned quick enough Father kept his word. He must have left right after Mother and I did. He was so mad he left without his clothes."

Em stared into the willows for a moment then smiled a sad smile at Finch. "Maybe that's why I don't want to change the water pump; maybe I'm just desperate to have things the way they used to be, before we lost Michael and the original hotel, when we were all together and happy."

Finch patted her hand. "Perhaps that's all the more reason to move on to a new, happier life and make your life easier."

"Perhaps." A bigger smile crossed her lips then faded. "Less than a year later, Mother died. I blame Father for deserting us. Mother had so much shock and worry and stress. He killed her, Finch, all for booze and gold. I've been all alone for almost a year until Sylvia arrived a month ago." She almost snorted in derision. "She's my only family here and I have to kick her out."

Em's chin trembled and she hated herself for being so weak in front of Finch. Her nose ran and she discretely swiped at her face so he wouldn't see her bodily functions. Her sinuses swelled, forcing her to breathe through her mouth. Mortified, her nose dripped more but she forced herself to breathe through her nose. She did not want this handsome man to see her runny nose and her breathing through her mouth.

"Miss Olson, I don't want to hurt you. If I have given you pain with this question, I'm so sorry for asking." His hand gently rubbed hers.

"Oddly, it feels good to talk about it."

He lifted her hand and planted a soft kiss, then lowered it to resume his rubbing.

He seemed to care and comfort her so much she couldn't help the sob that wracked her shoulders. She yanked her hand from his clasp and leaped to her feet. She started to run back to the hotel, back to where that hated cousin lay in wait, back to that spoiled Missus Doctor who would only screech about a lack of clean towels and the noise.

Finch grabbed her by the shoulders and spun her to face him. In the same motion, he pulled her to him in a soft embrace. "I am sorry you're in such pain."

She had no strength to push him away. She let herself melt into his chest. In a slow movement, he rocked her. His face settled beside hers. Their cheeks touched. The heat of his cheek warmed the cold traces of her tears.

"Now I know why you're so keen on proving Finch didn't seduce me."

Em jumped, startled at the words, and backed from Finch.

An angry Sylvia stood beside the fir tree, hands on her hips. A grimace slowly crossed her face. "You don't care about me at all! You're only looking out for yourself, that you want him. You don't want him to want me!" She stepped closer and leaned forward in her exertion. "Wait until I tell everyone what you have done here, you called me a liar—me—a pregnant girl, seduced by him!" She pointed at Finch as she said "him" for emphasis. "In your hotel!" Sylvia's voice reached higher until she was screaming. Turning to run, she screamed over her shoulder. "I'm telling! Especially Finch's boss what manner of beast he is!" She trotted toward the hotel.

Finch shoved past Em to dash toward Sylvia. He sprinted to close the distance. Em thawed enough to race after them. Fear washed over her that she accused Sylvia of lying when she was in a most difficult situation.

Within seconds, Finch closed the distance between himself and Sylvia. As he neared her, he seized her arm and whipped her around to face him. He grabbed both shoulders and shook her in his fury. "What is wrong with you, you demented—"

"Finch!" Em screamed, afraid he would strike Sylvia. "Stop it!" Em panted in exertion. "Let's go into the hotel. We can close the living room door and talk." She grabbed Finch's arm and Sylvia's shoulder. "Let us settle this calmly."

Sylvia fixed Em with squinty eyes. "So you can call me a liar in private?" She tilted her face skyward and screamed, "Rather than the entire world to know how selfish you are!"

Finch shook Sylvia to silence her. "Stop this right now."

"This is hard enough to deal with without both of you acting like this. Let's go." Em's voice grew more stern.

"You can't order me around anymore," Sylvia snapped. "I'm pregnant. I'm emancipated," goading both Em and Finch.

"Baloney," shot from Em's mouth. "You'll go back to your parents before the week is out." Em shouted. "You will leave this place, pregnant or not. Enjoy the drama while it lasts."

Leaving was the only way to defuse the situation. If Finch and Sylvia chose to remain here and fight this out at least she wouldn't be a party to it.

If they chose to follow her the better. She would lead them into the living room where, when the door closed, they would have the privacy for a screaming match.

She strode across the fresh grass, concentrating on the earth's squishiness saturated from last week's melt to calm her jangled nerves. As she entered her hotel, she fought the urge to slam the door open then, when the door rebounded back, to slam the door closed. Locking the door sounded good too.

Continuing her way through the hall, into her kitchen, through the dining room, then into the living room, she wondered if they would actually follow. Huffing, she plopped into her favorite overstuffed chair. She listened to the ticking clock. She tapped her foot. She picked at her rough fingers. *Was that a sound?*

"Well, well, Miss Olson!"

A masculine voice interrupted her concentration. Doctor Barclay sat in the dim light, a book lay open on his lap.

Angry voices grew louder as Finch and Sylvia entered the dining room. "I should turn you over my knee." Finch's voice was tight. "You did already, remember?" Sylvia's voice bubbled with humor.

"Doctor Barclay," Em said, loudly to warn Sylvia and Finch they would not be alone. "Has your search been successful?" She babbled in her anxiety.

"I have been successful," he boomed. He tossed aside the book and stood to approach Em. "I have made contact with a fellow who wants to show me to a rich gold mine he purchased a few years ago." His voice was proud. His nose rose as he spoke.

Sylvia and Finch swept into the room. Daggers of hatred flowing between them vanished as they realized Barclay was present. Em caught the look of fear in Finch's eyes.

"Where have you been, Stone?" Barclay asked, his voice thick with irritation. "I grew tired of searching for you."

"I am sorry," Finch said, contrition in his voice. "I had some things come up."

"I'll say," Sylvia sneered. "Up then out."

"That's enough," Em snapped.

"It's not enough," Sylvia shouted. She looked at Barclay. "You must know something about your employee." She pointed at Finch.

"Don't," Em's voice was deep with concern.

Sylvia hesitated. "Doctor, your worker can tell you," she ordered with her hands on her hips.

Barclay turned to Finch in confusion.

Finch seemed unsure, afraid, then seemed to make a decision. "Doctor, a situation of a most unfortunate kind has erupted." He indicated Sylvia. "This young woman here is a liar and she wishes to corrupt my reputation."

Sylvia gasped, "You asshole!"

Everyone stared in shock. Sylvia fixed Barclay with a stern look then screamed, "Your man raped me!"

Everyone gasped. Sylvia indicated Em. "She let it happen in her hotel and now I am with child."

At this, a red curtain descended over Em's eyes. She grabbed Sylvia's hair and yanked the screaming girl out.

Barclay hurried to Em and grabbed her arms, forcing Em to release Sylvia's hair. "Madam, how dare you assault this woman!" He reached for the shrieking Sylvia. "My dear, tell me what happened."

Sylvia clutched Barclay, pushing her body into his. She wailed in pain and frustration.

"Doctor Barclay, I assure you Sylvia is lying about everything." Finch spoke up. "And if she's with child, I had nothing to do with it."

Barclay stared up at Finch. He looked down at the cuddling Sylvia. Em curled her lip. Sylvia played Barclay like a fiddle.

Em walked toward Sylvia, intending to pull her away. Barclay held up his hand for Em to stop. His head bent toward Sylvia, and he appeared to cuddle back. "There, there, my dear. Tell Uncle Clarence all about it. Did the big bad Finch do anything to you?"

Em's eyes widened at his childish voice. She looked to Finch who had the same expression on his face as hers, though his face paled.

"Doctor Barclay, I assure you, I did nothing to this girl. If she's pregnant, there's another man who did this." Finch said. He appeared helpless, unsure what to do.

"Sylvia, let us leave these two alone. They have real business to conduct." Em reached to yank Sylvia away.

"Leave me alone. You don't care about me!" Sylvia screamed as she grasped Barclay to keep him close to her.

71

Em gasped as Sylvia rubbed her chest against his. "You are insane," she whispered. "You are mad."

"Madam, you will leave," Barclay declared.

Em grew more agitated. "No, sir. You are out of line. I will not be ordered out of any room in my hotel. This woman is under my supervision and I will deal with her." She twisted Sylvia's wrist to wrest it from Barclay's shoulder.

"Let her loose," Barclay ordered.

"She's coming with me." She hoisted a crying Sylvia to her feet and put her wrists in a come-along hold her father taught her years before, a hold she used to practice on Rose until she squealed in pain.

Em called out over her shoulder as she dragged Sylvia through the door. "Finch, I suggest you have a chat with your boss here."

"Will do" faded as Em dragged the struggling and whimpering Sylvia behind her.

CHAPTER 9

Em hauled the shrieking Sylvia down the hallway. A door slammed upstairs and sharp clicks of high heels stamped into her pine floor. *Oh great.*

"Is there any chance I can get clean towels or is that just too hard of an achievement in this place?" sounded from upstairs.

The only answer Missus Doctor received was the slam of Em's bedroom door. She dragged Sylvia to her bed, then threw her onto it. Both women's chests heaved with exertion. Em leaned on her bed for support as she gasped for air. Sylvia dragged her feet onto Em's quilt.

Em smacked Sylvia's feet off her bed. Sylvia rolled over and displayed her backside to Em. The message infuriated Em. "Turn around and face me," a growl threaded her voice.

"Forget you," Sylvia called out over her shoulder.

Em snatched the flyswatter hanging from a nail beside her bed. With a whistling swish, the flyswatter slapped Sylvia on her backside.

"Ow!"

Em stood beside her bed, hands on her hips. "Now, it's just you and me. No innocent guests to fake. No one here who'll believe every word you say, regardless how ridiculous it is. Now, why are you lying about this? What do you get out of this? A thrill at my expense? At Doctor Stone's? Get your jollies by getting Barclay to hug you? What is it?"

"Your boyfriend seduced me," Sylvia said with a lightness that belied the serious situation. "It's that simple."

"You're lying."

"He's the father of my baby. Perhaps I should call the police. I am under eighteen after all."

The threat sent a chill down Em's back. *Could Finch be a seducer of all the women he comes across?* Sylvia couldn't be trusted. She decided to believe him. *But how to prove Sylvia was lying?* She had to think fast. In a blaze of light, an idea formed.

"Finch is a caring sort, isn't he?" Em asked, forcing her voice to soften.

"Yes. He told me that."

Em nodded slowly. "He has a good sense of fashion and style for a working man, don't you think?" Em tried to keep the tone light, almost conspiratorial between her and Sylvia.

"Yes."

"I don't feel threatened by him at all. He does seem like a girl's best friend. Easy to talk with. I feel safe around him too."

Sylvia sat up and pulled her feet back on Em's quilt. Em tamped her anger to keep Sylvia off balance and trusting.

"How odd. That makes no sense. Strange, funny." Em scratched her head, pretending confusion. "Interesting," she muttered, but loud enough for Sylvia to hear and to become curious enough to push.

The silence grew longer. Em worried Sylvia wouldn't ask. She stared out the sheer curtains that draped her west window. Birds flitted outside, looking futilely for seeds so early in the season.

"So what is strange?" Sylvia snapped, obviously irritated at Em for keeping quiet when she was so curious.

Em took a deep breath. Trembling overtook her body as she prepared for what she would say. She fixed her eyes into Sylvia's. Em hesitated.

"Well?" Sylvia prodded. "What's so curious?"

"You seem to think Finch is my beau." Em paused. "I made it known to Finch I was open to a relationship with him," she lied. "He was quite hesitant, but you know how honest he is."

"Yes," Sylvia's rolling eyes urged Em on.

"He told me a few days ago that ..." Em tried to stall. "He confessed that he ..."

"What!" Sylvia cried out, hooked.

"He does not prefer women." Em hung her head in pretend sadness. "He asked me not to tell anyone. I hope you will keep this information to yourself."

A heavy silence stretched. Em's heart pounded, not knowing what explosion would ensue. "He said he could not perform with a woman." She peeked under her eyebrows to watch Sylvia.

Sylvia was frozen, her eyes wide in horror.

Silence stretched longer.

"Did you have intercourse with a homosexual man, Sylvia? How did you manage to get him to have sex with you?" Em paused in her questioning to let Sylvia think her way out.

"Did he tell you that you cured him?"

Another pause. Sylvia's breaths came faster.

"Will your parents approve of you having intercourse with such a man?"

A gurgle emerged from deep within Sylvia's throat.

Em had another flash of inspiration. "He also admitted to me he had a disease that flares occasionally. You will have to tell Doctor Adams in Lander so you can get some medicine for it." Em kept her voice soft and helpful. "In your condition you need to go to the doctor anyway."

Sylvia started to weep. Em watched her, eyes narrowing in concentration. The girl started to rock.

Em sat on the edge of her bed, trying to act like the caring aunt she really was.

"How can I help you, Sylvia? Would you like me to take you to the doctor? You need his help as soon as possible when you have carnal knowledge with a diseased homosexual." Keep it helpful and nonthreatening, she thought.

"He's a faggot!?" Sylvia's voice sharpened.

Em flinched at the offensive word.

"So, that's why he let me tailor his clothes, because he wanted fitted clothing."

Em seized the opportunity. *Keep your voice soft.* "I'll do what I can to protect you from the locals, Sylvia. Some will heckle you for being intimate with a homosexual." Em leaned toward Sylvia. She let pity cross her face.

"Augh!" Sylvia almost screamed.

Em bit her lips so hard blood might ooze from the cuts. Sylvia needed to have the space to decide to come clean.

"Maybe Finch isn't the father of my baby." Sylvia sniveled.

Em held her breath. "Is he or isn't he?" *One issue at a time.* "If he's not the father, we can still keep it quiet that you had intercourse with him."

"I would not screw a faggot," Sylvia said harshly. "I'll shoot anyone who says so."

Em breathed a silent sigh of relief. One thing still to confirm. "So, you did not have intercourse with Finch?" She fought the urge to place her hand over her heart in relief.

"That's right," Sylvia sneered. "I would not fuck a faggot."

Em's mouth tightened at Sylvia's vulgarity. She forced herself to nod in understanding and sigh loudly in pretend— though very real—relief. "I thought you had much more intelligence in your decisions." Em nodded with auntie compassion. "So, you did not have intercourse with Finch. If that's the case, my cousin, who is the father of your baby? I will help you as best I can."

Sylvia rolled her eyes. "Oh, for crying out loud. I'm not pee-gee. I just said that to get him in trouble."

Horrified, Em let her anger come through. "You put a good man through an ordeal just to get him in trouble? Why would you do such a terrible thing?"

"Because he only talked about you. Em this. Em that. He always talked about you! He drove me nuts." Sylvia shouted. "Then you said you'd send me back home ..."

Before Sylvia could figure out she'd been duped, Sylvia had to admit her lie to Finch and to Barclay. Em would have to trick Sylvia into doing so.

"You know, Doctor Barclay must know of Finch's homosexuality. He comforted you for having intercourse with him, you know."

"I will not have him thinking such a thing," Sylvia screamed. She flung herself off Em's bed, lunged for the bedroom door, and ran toward the kitchen.

"He may be telling his wife right now!" Em called out to Sylvia as the teenager yanked open the kitchen door. "She'll tell everyone!"

Em dashed after Sylvia. She followed Sylvia through the dining room. Both women charged into the living room, panting. Both men looked at them with what appeared to be cold fury etched in their faces.

"I did not have sex with this man," Sylvia screamed. She pointed at Finch.

Shock settled over the two men, but Em was prepared.

"Doctor Stone did not have intercourse with you—is that the truth? And Doctor Stone never touched you—is that the truth?" Em asked.

"That's the truth, I swear it. He did not touch me. And I would not touch him," Sylvia screamed.

"He did not touch you? He is innocent?" Barclay seemed as if he would melt into the floor.

Em barely breathed.

"Yes," Sylvia said. "I wouldn't touch a faggot." Sneering threaded her voice as she looked Finch up and down.

"And you are not pregnant—by him or anyone else?" Em asked quickly.

"No! I am not!" Sylvia hollered at Em. She turned to Barclay. "You've told no one of this?"

Silence fell over the room. Barclay stared at Sylvia for what seemed an eternity. He placed his hand on Finch's shoulder. "I am so sorry, my boy. I hope you can forgive me and forget my angry words. Such unsavory things bring out the ugliness in me. Forgive me, please."

Finch nodded. He couldn't speak.

Barclay faced Sylvia. His brow furrowed. "Homosexual?" He indicated Finch. "Him?!"

Sylvia nodded emphatically. "Correct."

"Um," Em said quickly, sensing trouble. "Sylvia, now that you have confirmed your chastity and saved your reputation, you should leave. We'll talk later and put this matter to rest." Em placed her hands on Sylvia's shoulders, spun her around, and pushed her out the door. She quickly closed the door and leaned against it to prevent Sylvia from returning.

"Doctor Barclay, I apologize for my cousin's horrible accusation. I apologize to you, Doctor Stone. This must have been an ordeal for you. Please, now that this is resolved, I beg you to let this matter drop."

"Your cousin is unbalanced and caused a good man great harm, Miss Olson," Barclay sniffed. "I hope she receives help."

"I agree. Within a week I will return her to her parents. She has caused too much trouble for me to keep her here." Em said. Her legs wobbled from relief.

Barclay bent to retrieve the book he had dropped. He took some steps toward the door before stopping. "Homosexual?"

Em dropped her head. "Sylvia needed a reason to tell the truth, so I lied."

Barclay considered what Em had done. He burst into laughter. "That's very good, Miss Olson. You turned a terrible situation and found a way to cleanse it. Very good." He turned to Finch who still trembled. "I am sorry, my boy, that you had to go through that. Please forget everything I said." He pulled open the door and slipped out before closing it behind him.

Em closed her eyes. Her breath came faster and she was afraid to look at Finch.

"Em," Finch's voice was ragged and soft. "I owe you so much. Clarence fired me and said he'd notify the professional societies." His voice choked.

Em stepped toward Finch. "I don't know what I could have done to have prevented this." Her face felt like it sagged from all her cares.

In a smooth movement, Finch swept Em into his arms. She buried her face into his neck. She lifted her head and opened her mouth to apologize again only Finch's mouth covered hers. The warm shock of tenderness stopped her breathing.

His lips of velvet softness turned more urgent as his mouth opened and she was responsive to his lips.

Both jumped at the sound of the door opening. Em and Finch stepped apart, trying to act nonchalant.

They froze at the sight of Sylvia, who stood with her mouth gaping. "What the hell?" She glared at Em. "Are you so desperate for a man you'd go after a fag?" Her face turned beet red in anger.

Em's initial anxiety calmed. She believed Finch and freed him of this accusation. She moved to stand alongside him. She felt gratified when Finch put his arm around her. Sylvia needed to know the facts so she wouldn't go yelling another falsehood to the community.

"Sylvia, Finch is not a homosexual."

The clock on the mantel ticked seconds. They waited patiently for Sylvia to figure out she had been duped.

"What?" Sylvia asked quietly.

"Finch is not a homosexual." Em said again. "I told you that to give you a reason to admit you lied." She froze, not knowing what to expect.

"You bitch!" Sylvia screamed. She raced toward Em, murder in her eyes.

Finch pushed Em aside and stood in front of her in protection. "Who's the bitch, Sylvia? You accused me of the heinous crime of rape. You should be on your knees begging your god for forgiveness."

His shoulders trembled in rage. Em was afraid he would strike Sylvia, although she deserved it.

Finch's voice rose as he spoke until he shouted. "Perhaps I am the one who should tell everyone how you accused an innocent man. You can't be trusted. I should announce to the world—and your parents—how you thought nothing of your actions, only what you wanted. Stay away from me. You make me sick."

Sylvia stood, shaking, appearing undecided whether to rush at Em again, slap Finch, or collapse into a quivering mass on the floor and weep.

"If you know what's good for you right now, Sylvia, go away," Em said softly. "No one wants to see your face. Better yet, go to your room. Pack your bags. Tomorrow, depending upon how you act right now, I will put you on the train back to Boston." Em's shoulders straightened as she spoke.

Em turned to face Finch, determined to ignore Sylvia so she might slink away. Sylvia hesitated, then spun on her heels and slammed the living room door closed. Footfalls echoed into the dining room and faded as they entered the kitchen.

Finch turned back to Em with a huge sigh. "Now, where was I?"

He reached for Em as she encircled his neck with her hands. Her fingers brushed the fine hairs and stroked the softness at the back of his neck. She lifted her head and parted her lips to accept his, but he stopped.

His head straightened so he could see Em full in the face. "Homosexual?"

Em grinned. "It was all I could think of."

Finch grinned back. "Well done." He remained tall, studying her eyes, her face, and her hair. "Well done."

This time he bent and kissed her.

CHAPTER 10

In the tense atmosphere, Em and Finch tried to keep the dinner conversation light. At the far end of the twelve-foot-long table, Sylvia hunched in her chair and picked at her food.

Em sat at the head of the table with Finch to her left. Barclay sat across from Finch and occasionally Barclay spoke to Finch about his search. The glow on Barclay's face held a secret, Em thought.

Finch did not acknowledge Sylvia. He made it obvious he ignored her. Barclay once asked Sylvia how she enjoyed the meal, but her only response was a sullen shrug. Barclay shrugged back and ignored her after that.

As the male guests filled their plates with Em's good food, she recalled how she made supper alone. Sylvia remained sequestered in her room. Fine, Em thought, one more nail in her coffin that goes on the train tomorrow. *Good riddance.*

High heel clicks descending the kitchen stairs announced Missus Doctor would finally join them. She missed yesterday's meal because she could "not possibly be prepared to face anyone" in such short notice after finally getting her towels. Later, Missus Doctor whined to Em about being hungry, but Em simply told her she'd have to work her makeup quicker. Virginia's face grew red when Em added, "In this country, no one cares what you look like but rather how good a person you are." Em rather enjoyed the furious squinty eyes of Missus Doctor before she traipsed up the stairs, stomping the whole way. The door's slam was Em's cherry on the top.

As Missus Doctor entered the dining room, both Barclay and Finch stood. She didn't acknowledge their courtesy but oozed onto the chair Barclay pulled out for her beside him. Missus Doctor adjusted the lace collar on her low-slung bodice. She looked around the table to ensure everyone watched her, then flexed her shoulders to jut her bosom. Barclay's face turned red, seemingly with pride. Em chased the peas on her plate with a fork and tried to ignore her.

"We're glad you could join us," Finch said, obviously trying to be polite.

"Finally got some towels so I could do my necessary things," she snapped.

Oh, please, Em thought. She fought to keep her lips from curling. "So, Doctor Barclay, you mentioned some success today. You had a good day?" Em asked, anything, even something that wasn't her business, desperate to shift the topic from Missus Doctor and her bouncing bosom. She fought the urge to look down at her own small bust draped by her thin cotton dress.

"I did. As I told Finch, I signed up with a local to show me around. He said he had a lead on a promising mine, one that could be mined without having to build an expensive mill." He glanced to Em. "We'll leave early in the morning and check out the place and spend the day. First light. May we trouble you to prepare breakfast for us?"

"You don't expect me to be up early in the morning. You know I just do not get up early." Missus Doctor flipped her long, curly hair over her shoulder in defiance. "I must get my beauty sleep, Clary. You wouldn't like me otherwise."

Barclay smiled smugly. "Of course not, baby cakes. Of course." He turned to Em. "Would you be so kind as to prepare breakfast for my beautiful lady at the regular time, Miss Olson? I would be most grateful."

"If I'm the only one to eat I want breakfast later than the regular time. I can manage nine," Missus Doctor snapped.

Em clenched her jaw at the workload. Then the thought of doing something nice for Finch and for Doctor Barclay, who had been kind to her, loosened those jaw muscles. "Certainly. The later breakfast may not be as hearty as I usually serve, what with two seatings. Is that all right?" She posed the warning to Missus Doctor, who shrugged.

"My source said we'll do quite a bit of strenuous hiking, so I'm obliged to have a big breakfast." Barclay sliced his ham steak as though he would carve through the china plate.

Em considered her foodstuffs. Her pantry was full. She nodded. "I should be able to do that, just fine. What time would you like breakfast served?"

"Five a.m." Barclay stabbed the ham steak.

A three a.m. get-up. Em forced a swallow. The exhaustion she'd struggle through early in the morning coursed through her body now.

"I'll do that," she said a soft voice.

Barclay nodded as he shoved in the huge piece of meat into his wide-open mouth.

"Miss Olson, you must know this area quite well, having lived here all your life," Finch said. His slip into the formal address confused Em, but she decided that was for his boss' and Sylvia's benefits.

"Yes, I was born right here. If there's anything you have a question about, please ask. If there is a place I might be able to lead you to, I can do that as well. Well, as long as I don't have an expected guest or you don't mind a cold dinner."

A snort erupted from Missus Doctor. She tapped the ham steak congealing on her plate with the knife. "A cold dinner is most unsatisfying."

Em shrugged. She made her offer. If these men and this indulged woman couldn't handle a cold dinner they could traipse around the country by themselves—as long as they didn't get themselves lost, forcing her to search.

They sat in silence, some ate with an appetite—the men—and some pushed their food around their plates—the women.

Finch turned to Em. "Would it be alright with you if we picked your brain?" He indicated Barclay. "There must be all sorts of played-out mines or swindles you can help us avoid."

To Em that sounded interesting and would help her be aware what was happening in her area—and it would let her be close to Finch.

Barclay waved his fork as he chewed. Finch became silent as his boss demanded it. Barclay leaned forward, fixing Em with a stern, yet curious eye. "First, might I ask if you can be quiet about our questions and our findings? I demand complete confidence. If you can't assure me of confidentiality, I'll find a man who can." He stabbed the remaining bit of ham and stuffed it into his mouth.

Em wasn't sure if she was curious or angered. *A man? Who said a man would keep his mouth shut?* "I assure you, Doctor Barclay, I keep quiet. I hear more than I speak." Em made a mental note to ensure they only spoke when Sylvia was out of earshot. In no way could she guarantee the girl's silence. Perhaps they could speak openly in the living room with the dining room door open where she could watch for Sylvia's approach. The bushes in front of the windows would keep anyone from approaching too close.

Barclay watched her and she watched him back. She wanted him to know she was a match to him. He waved his spoon, now emptied of the mound of peas and mashed potatoes, to command attention. "Miss Olson, if you could assure me I have your confidence, and you will divulge all you know, I shall give you a retainer for your services."

Em's heart skipped a beat. To have a good time showing these geologists the area and be in on their secrets was a good thing—and paid for her knowledge was a great thing! She tried hard to keep from smiling in relief and excitement.

"Doctor Barclay, I can assure you of both."

Barclay nodded as he stabbed the last pea on the plate. "We will discuss the retainer after dinner, in the living room?"

"That would be fine," Em thought about jumping up and clicking her heels. Instead, she rose to stack the empty plates. "Sylvia, please help me clear the table for dessert."

Em lifted the soiled plates and hurried into the kitchen. She placed the dishes on the counter beside the wood sink. Sylvia sauntered into the kitchen carrying three bowls. "Thank you for bringing in a few bowls," Em bit back a sarcastic tone.

Sylvia said nothing as she lifted down the dessert plates and set them out individually. She trudged to the pantry and pulled open the pie cupboard's door. The cherry pie Em baked yesterday had cooled and set. She set the pie on the counter. Em slipped out her prized pie cutter her mother had used for decades. She used it several times a week and the constant use kept the silver plate gleaming. In a good mood, she decided they would finish the pie. She cut five generous pieces and deftly slipped them onto the plates. Sylvia fanned out five dessert forks. They balanced the plates on their arms and stepped into the dining room.

As cries at the huge pie pieces echoed off the walls, Em happily smiled then stacked the remaining soiled plates and removed them to the kitchen.

"How do you keep your slender figure with treats such as this, my dear?" Barclay asked.

Em smiled at him for the compliment. "I thought we should celebrate a successful partnership of exchanging knowledge," Em said. "I hope to help you with whatever you search for." She warmed to see Finch pull out her chair and wait until she sat before sitting.

Barclay nodded. "Well, if I could certify all partnerships with this treat, my job would be so much more enjoyable. Although my waistline wouldn't find things easier." He clapped a hand on his stomach as he stabbed at the slice.

"This pie is wonderful, Miss Olson," Finch picked at the flaky crust with his fork. "This is the fluffiest crust ever. It's a good thing we'll work this off tomorrow." He smiled at Em.

"Thank you both," Em said. She glanced at Missus Doctor, who stared at the pie with a baleful look. Perhaps she can't eat pie. "Is there a problem with your pie?" She refused to say "Missus Doctor." "Do you not like cherry pie?"

Missus Doctor sniffed. "Desserts are death to a lady's waistline." She pushed away the plate, then turned to look at the far corner, rebuffing Em's question.

Fine, I'll eat it later. Just don't talk and spit on it.

Except for groans of delight from Barclay and Finch, they ate their pie in silence. As soon as the dessert was finished, Em wanted to talk with them about their goals, but especially her retainer. She stood to stack the pie plates and felt gratified as Sylvia stood to help. Em's eyes narrowed as she considered why Sylvia was suddenly so helpful.

"I'll brew a pot of coffee. We can sit in the living room."

The men pushed back from the table and each patted their stomachs. Missus Doctor primly slipped from her chair and tossed her linen napkin on top of the pie slice. Em's eyes narrowed as she considered whether the napkin was clean enough to eat the pie later. Em snatched the napkin off and whisked the plate away before Missus Doctor could tarnish any more of the slice.

Sylvia and Em stacked the dishes beside the wood sink. "You want me to wash the dishes?" Sylvia asked, her voice flat, emotionless. Em blinked in surprise.

"I would appreciate it if you would." She realized she had forgotten to remove her apron after making dinner. Em reached behind her to untie her mother's apron strings, draped the apron on the nail that jabbed from the wall, and smoothed her dress and her hair. Butterflies fluttered in her stomach. Why would she be nervous? They might offer her a few dollars for something she would have done for free. The thought calmed her.

Em glanced at the coffee pot. The dark liquid percolating in the glass top indicated the coffee was ready. She stacked cups, sugar and cream, and napkins on the tray. She learned the hard way to always have napkins available. The permanent stain on the coffee table always irritated her.

"I suppose you'll want me to avoid the living room." Sylvia's voice was again flat, emotionless.

Em watched Sylvia, who avoided looking directly at Em but rather at the soap she poured into the wood sink. "To be honest, yes. Perhaps in time I can trust you again." Em said.

Her words hinted Sylvia could stay, though Em would trust Sylvia only when she was back in Boston.

She started to turn to the dining room, hesitated then turned back. "I am sorry, Sylvia."

"I understand," Sylvia said, her voice soft. Her hands rested on the wood sink's edge, her head hung low. Em decided not to give comfort. Sylvia needed to suffer for her actions. Maybe not long if she were truly sorry for her actions and learned from it, but she hadn't yet suffered enough.

Em walked through the dining room balancing the tray. The guests had moved into the living room.

"Here we are," Em said brightly as she walked through the door. Finch and Barclay stopped talking, and Em wondered if she interrupted their discussion. The men focused on Em pouring the coffee into her grandmother's fine china cups.

"Missus Barclay, a cup of coffee?" She offered the first cup to her, but Missus Doctor looked away, not bothering to answer. Em shifted her arm to offer the cup to Barclay. He took the cup, throwing a sharp glance at his wife. "Sugar, please, my dear."

Em lifted the sugar bowl and handed him a spoon. She poured another cup for Finch. "Thank you," he said brightly. "Black, please. As you know."

She stepped around the room, lighting the oil lamps. She lowered the ceiling light, lit the wicks then raised the lamp. The walls and ceiling glowed with a warm softness that made the room cozy and relaxing. Em poured herself a cup, a rare treat at this time of evening. She sat like a lady in her favorite overstuffed chair. She wanted them to get down to business, but she didn't want to seem too eager.

"My teacake, would you like to stay while we talk business?" Barclay turned to his wife, who curled her lip.

Why would she treat her husband so poorly, Em wondered. *He treats her well, provides her with nice clothes and yet she acts like he's dirt.* She caught Finch's eyes, and behind the turned faces of his boss and his wife, he rolled his eyes. Em fought not to smirk so she focused on her cup and took a sip of the hot liquid.

Missus Doctor tossed her head. "Business is not for ladies," she called out over her shoulder as she walked out.

Em's irritation spiked. *Business is for intelligent folk.* She stared at the black liquid and added a thin stream of cream into her cup. She swirled the cup until the black turned to a beautiful rich brown.

"So you were born here." Barclay prompted.

"Yes, sir. My father took us kids along to various mines. Some of them were hidden. Some were abandoned. I watched the animals and can help you avoid some the more dangerous areas, like where moose frequent. There's no elk in the close area, but you may run into them outside this area." Em said. She often told guests this information, but not with the potential for income.

"Would you be willing to present information on some workers? So we are assured of their credibility?" Finch asked. "We know few people here, and we have a lot at stake. We need to know who we can trust."

"And who we cannot." Barclay added.

"Certainly. I'm familiar with locals. If there's something I think you should know about some of these people, I would tell you—or warn you." Em sipped her coffee.

"With the understanding I have your confidence and your assurance you will help us to the utmost. I would pay you a consulting fee of five dollars a week for information. If you show us to certain areas, I will pay you an extra dollar each day you take us out. Does this sound amenable to you?" Barclay leaned forward as he studied her reaction.

Em's face grew cold. He offered her what seemed to be a fortune for what she provided free to other guests—and provided an opportunity to be with Finch. Her heart raced as she nodded. "I shall do my best for you, Doctor Barclay." She turned to Finch. "Doctor Stone."

"Splendid," Barclay said. "Let us relax and talk."

Finch winked at her. He raised his cup to her in salute. She recalled his kiss and his embrace. She started to sweat.

Barclay indicted Finch and himself. "We've been researching various mines around here, the Midas Touch, the Discovery, the Wapiti — whatever that is."

"That's Shawnee for 'elk'," Em said quickly.

He nodded. "A source will meet us and take us to a confirmed gold mine. He acquired it a couple years ago. He would sell me the mine if we could meet his demanded price or he'll allow us to prospect with a lease. He has an assayer who confirmed the high yield per ton and his belief in high grade deposits."

Em's brow furrowed. The words Barclay used rang a bell, a warning toll, in her mind. Barclay stopped speaking as he watched her reaction.

"Something on your mind?" he asked.

Em nodded, then shrugged. "Something from my past. May I ask who your source is? I'm sure he's trustworthy, but then again …" Em let her voice trail off in uncertainty.

"A fine source: Walter Denton, a gentleman. He and a man named Sam Quint own this mine." Barclay beamed with pride at his finding.

Em's lips tightened. She studied the coffee swirling in her cup. Her first tidbit of information to provide was bad. She bought time by pouring herself more coffee, then offering the pot to the men. Both held out their cups and she filled them. She had their attention and they kept silent.

Barclay prodded, "You know Denton and Quint."

She sat and swirled her cup. "Yes. I must advise you to be wary of them." She held his gaze as his eyes turned from curious to angry. The eyelids narrowed to slits and covered his blue eyes. His mouth worked. "How so?"

"I've known both of them for many years, almost as long as I can remember. I know no one who trusts them. My advice: take care." Em looked at Finch, eyes wide in shock. "If you choose to do business with him, verify everything." She looked back to Barclay. "Double-check it. Be aware of forgeries and the small print. Be wary of a swindle. I can't stress this enough." She paused. "I'm sorry to pass this on, but if Denton's your source, tread carefully." She watched Finch, who studied his coffee.

Silence hung like an old sheet, separating them all with their thoughts. "He said he had all the paperwork proving their patented claim." Barclay's voice was almost accusatory.

Em nodded. Her heart beat rapidly. "Doctor Barclay, he may indeed have the paperwork. I advise you to verify what he claims." She decided to let it go. If Barclay pursued the deal without verifying, then shame on him. She warned him.

The silence hung thick and she became aware of the ticking clock. It seemed to get louder as it ticked.

"Miss Olson," Finch said. "What would you do in our shoes, concerning this deal?"

Em's head shot up. "If I were tempted to pursue this transaction, I would go to the courthouse and review the deeds to confirm his words and the papers. I would obtain ore directly from the mine and have a trusted assayer test it." She shook her head. "I would be prepared to give up on the deal at the slightest hint—the slightest inkling—of something not right." She shook her head again. "My disclaimer, gentlemen, is I don't like them. I don't trust them."

Barclay grunted as he considered her words. "You have witnessed untrustworthy behavior or is this a local's rumor?"

"I have. My family has been victimized twice by Denton's schemes. He cost us a lot of money. Since then, I have nothing for him. We're a humble family, Doctor Barclay," she said boldly. "And to steal money from a hardworking family ..." She let her words lapse and shook her head.

She had a thought. "Denton owns many of the mines around the region. To be fair, a few produce a high yield like the Uncle Bob up by Hamilton City and the Cinderella outside Atlantic. May I ask which mine they hope to sell you?"

Barclay nodded to Finch who said, "The Ember Mine."

Em's face paled.

CHAPTER 11

"What's wrong, Em? You're as white as a ghost." Finch's anxious voice sounded far away. He quickly reached for her in support.

Em shoved herself out of the chair with an almost violent motion and stepped near the door, her back to the men. Her ragged breaths overshadowed the clock's tocks. She clasped her hands to still the shaking.

"My dear?" Barclay prodded for an answer. He stepped beside her. He clasped hers with warm, soft hands and turned her to face him. "What's wrong?" His voice was gentle, caring.

Em took a deep breath. "Doctor, I told you I would be honest with you in everything. And I will. I strongly suggest you stay away from Walter Denton. He can't be trusted in this matter."

Barclay studied Em's face. "I can see you're upset, this revelation has you in tears. But I need to know why I must step away from this deal. Denton told me the mine was called Ember because it 'exudes a glow of riches of the hottest kind'."

Finch peered over Barclay's shoulder, his eyes reflecting concern. He reached around his boss and placed a comforting hand on her back.

Em gulped. She looked up to Barclay. "I know of the Ember Mine. I have heard rumors it's rich." She paused as she recalled what she knew. "It's in a rough location with a trail to it, though it may have a road by now. It's at the end of a fissure. I haven't been there for a couple years.

"My father bought the patented claim from Walter Denton, the same man trying to sell it to you. Father worked that mine. He hired a dear family friend — my adopted uncle — to help him with the work since Magnus has what Father described as 'a nose for gold.' He named it the Ember Mine. I asked him why he named it Ember, but he would only smile and kiss me on the forehead. He said, 'Someday, you'll discover the meaning of the name and how much it means to me'." She smiled at the recollection, a memory thought lost to the ages.

"Interesting. Your father used to own it. Where's your father now?" Barclay asked in a cautious voice.

Em glanced at Finch who stared at the floor. "He is no longer with us." Barclay would assume he was dead. To Em he was dead after abandoning his family, which resulted in the death of her mother.

"I am so sorry, my dear," Barclay muttered.

Finch said nothing of the truth, but his hand lightly patted her back.

She nodded in appreciation. Father's departure left Em with a permanent stab of pain in her heart. She held out her hand to indicate the seats for everyone to sit. "My concern, Doctor Barclay, is Denton may be up to something. The last I knew the mine fell into disrepair after father …"

Silence hung heavy in the living room.

"How did Denton get his hands on it?" Barclay picked up his cup.

Em shook her head. "I have no idea. This is the first I heard he owned it. I can't help but think he managed to buy the mine somehow." *Or steal it.*

Barclay waved his cup. "Well, there's the possibility Denton may have seized the mine if the taxes weren't paid. Either way, Denton must have legally acquired it."

"Did your father give you any history of the mine? We should hear your version." Finch leaned forward in interest.

She paused as she reflected. "The history — as I heard it — was the town's assayer Bill Newbury and Sam Quint discovered veins in nineteen twenty-four. Father said the history showed five lode claims." She ticked off her fingers. "One each for Bill, Sam and Margaret Quint, and Walt and Betty Denton.

"So they combined the claims." Finch grunted. "With each claimant entitled to twenty acres they end up with a single grouping of a hundred-acre claim," He turned to Barclay. "Sizeable."

Em nodded. "Walt, being the businessman of the bunch, established a company and filed for a group patented claim, which was granted in twenty-six, if memory serves. He is always in charge."

"The ownership history shows it changes frequently," Finch said.

She shrugged. "We get a lot of wannabe-prospectors come up here thinking they'll find millions. They lose interest when they find out how hard and dangerous hard rock gold mining can be." She paused then chuckled. "I suspect Walt waits in the wings then squeezes the desperate owner to sell cheap then sells high to the next interested party."

Em's thoughts spun furiously. A realization caused her stomach to cramp so hard she bent over. She clapped her hand over her mouth to stifle a scream and to stop her from vomiting in shock.

"Miss Olson?" Barclay's voice was full of concern.

She struggled to breathe. "If Father failed to pay the taxes and Denton seized the claim, or if Father sold it then failed to pay back the loan he took out to purchase the mine … the loan that I'm still paying on …"

Stating the fact out loud that her father may have left a huge debt for his daughter to pay back without an asset to her name made her stomach retch. "I—he—must not even have that property as an asset." She gasped in deep breaths and swallowed hard.

"What was the collateral on the loan?" Barclay asked.

"This hotel," she whispered.

Finch held up his hands to stop her. "Em, perhaps your father still owns the mine and Denton is his sales agent. Please don't worry until we know you know if there's something to worry about." He gently placed a hand on her shoulder.

Focus. Calm yourself. Think positive. She gripped her hands tightly. "I do recall Father talking about the likelihood of a rich vein. He and Magnus worked it hard. Beyond that I'm not aware of any more details."

Barclay and Finch both nodded.

Em snorted. She forced herself to straighten and fixed Barclay with a stern gaze. "Tread carefully." She looked at Finch. "Tread very carefully around this man."

CHAPTER 12

Em rubbed her eyes as she stirred the apples frying in the skillet. At three this morning when her windup alarm clock sounded, Em pushed off her bed covers to an exhaustion that hurt every muscle in her body. Getting the heavy steel of the woodstove hot enough to cook breakfast required an early rise. At least Barclay and Finch appreciated their large breakfast at five.

The men exclaimed loudly over her breakfast. "This will last me all day," Barclay said. "Good thing we'll walk all day, huh, Stone? It'll take me that long to work this off."

Just leave money, Em thought crossly.

Later, in a foggy haze of fatigue, she stared out the window as the edge of the sun's light touched the hills' peaks and slowly felt its way down. With a sigh, she turned back to stir the apples for Missus Doctor's breakfast, scheduled for nine. While preparing both breakfasts, she sneaked bits of the meal to eat. She felt too distressed about their news of the Ember Mine to eat with the geologists and she refused to eat with Missus Doctor and Sylvia.

She thought about her plan to have Sylvia prepare the room for more guests arriving in a few days, a honeymooning couple from California. *Will I ever be on my honeymoon?*

She thought back to Finch this morning. After breakfast as Barclay thumped up the stairs to grab his jacket, Finch caught her eyes and blew her a kiss. A large smile crossed his face. Em smiled back as a rosy warmth spread across her cheeks. His smile grew even wider. "See you this evening."

Em wished them luck. She considered giving them another warning but decided not to push the negativity. Barclay would have to decide which way he wanted to go.

I have to figure out what's going on with the mine and this hotel the first chance I get, she thought. *Hopefully Father – meaning me – owns something besides a huge debt.*

For the hundredth time that morning, Em glanced over her shoulder for Sylvia to open the kitchen door. *No hide nor hair of that girl.* Last night, Sylvia had been helpful, actions that softened Em's heart. Before heading to her room Sylvia said she'd be down early to help. Now, her heart hardened toward the spoiled child. Yes, Sylvia needed to go back home.

Em hurried to set the table for one and swept off the crumbs from the biscuits the men dropped on her linen tablecloth. At least they hadn't spilled coffee or syrup.

At nine, the food was hot and on the table. Missus Doctor had assured Em she would be on time this morning. With a sigh, Em returned to the kitchen and began to clean. No Sylvia. No Missus Doctor.

Em flung the dishtowel onto the wood sink. She stomped up the stairs, not worrying about disturbing anyone. She paused at Missus Doctor's door. No sound came from the room. She knocked loudly and paused. She rolled her eyes, then stomped toward Sylvia's room. She rapped on the door, listening for sound. Her room was as silent as Missus Doctor's. *The twit is probably still asleep,* Em thought. She rapped again, louder, until her knuckles began to hurt.

Tapping her foot, she grabbed the doorknob. Not wanting to barge in, she hesitated. No sound. She twisted the knob, pushed open the door, and gasped.

The room lay in shambles. The quilt, handmade by Em's sister Rose, lay twisted on the floor. The mattress was flipped. The pillow had been sliced. Feathers covered the floor. Shoe prints lined the walls where someone kicked the plaster.

Em's eyes widened as she took in the destruction. She felt nauseous. "Sylvia?" she whispered. *Had she been kidnapped?*

Em ran to the closet and pulled open the door. Other than a wooden dining chair thrown in upside down, it was empty of the few pieces of clothing her parents allowed her to take, forcing her to launder often. There were no clothes, no shoes, no personal effects. Her china doll was gone. Em dropped to her knees to peer under the bed. The suitcase was gone. Her mother's picture of Jesus had been kicked under the bed. Dizziness swept over her. Sylvia had run away and left a trail of destruction.

"How am I supposed to sleep in this dump?" The sharp voice stabbed at her back and Em whirled around to a rumpled Missus Doctor tying the sash of a silk bathrobe. "Christ, who does your cleaning?" Missus Doctor looked around the room.

"Would you please?" Em snapped. "I have enough troubles without you highlighting them." She turned back to face the disaster. How to get word to the sheriff about a runaway child and this damage? Without thinking she called over her shoulder, "Your breakfast is on the table—at nine—as you requested." She let her point hang in the air.

Missus Doctor snorted. "I was too tired to get up after all the racket." She headed back to her room.

"Wait!" Em called out. She hurried out. Missus Doctor halted in the hall. "Did you hear all this?"

"About five-thirty. Clary and Finch had gone to breakfast." Missus Doctor shrugged. "Of course, I can't get up that early, but the noise kept me awake."

"Did you hear anyone else besides Sylvia?"

"A masculine voice. They seemed to have a quite a good time destroying your room. All of a sudden it went quiet. Thank goodness. I thought about sending for the sheriff since it wouldn't have done any good to send for you to fix the problem."

The insult stabbed at Em's heart. She stared without thinking as Missus Doctor sashayed to her room and slammed her door.

Em leaned against the wall. Helplessness washed over her as her legs refused to work. She slid down the wall until she sat on the floor.

CHAPTER 13

Sheriff Benjamin Brodie stood silhouetted in the late afternoon sun streaming through the window. He hunched from rounded shoulders. His hands tucked into his gun belt as he listened intently to Em's statement. A brown horsehair braid interspersed with black beads rimmed his black cowboy hat. His lined face was wrinkled, yet kind.

Deputy Collins stood behind him jotting notes.

"I imagine your cousin grabbed one of those single miners to take her from here," Brodie said. "Where would she go?"

"I don't know," Em said. "Not back to Boston, I'm sure. Perhaps her parents sent her money to travel, otherwise I'm wondering where she got it," she wondered aloud. She froze with a horrifying thought.

Em raced down the stairs to her private office. Brodie's boot thumps followed her. Quickly, she spun the dial on the safe, then tugged opened the door. She seized the leather pouch where she stored her cash.

Heart pounding, she flipped the flap and squinted into the darkness of the empty pouch.

Sylvia had taken her few dollars. There wasn't much, but the money was hers and it was gone. With a groan, she slouched to the floor, staring at the pouch clutched in her fist as if willing her hard-earned money to materialize.

Sheriff Brodie kneeled beside her and cleared his throat. "Is your money all there?"

Clenching her teeth, Em shook her head. Her voice caught as the depth of Sylvia's betrayal sank in. "She took it."

"How much she take?"

"About fifty dollars." Stunned, Em tossed the pouch back into the safe. She nudged the door closed then spun the lock.

"She have the combination?"

Em nodded. "I thought I could trust my cousin." Numbness flowed through her body and her senses.

"Em, would this fifty dollars be all she had on her? I hate to ask if there's any chance Sylvia may have been involved in ... you know ..." He coughed.

"Certainly not!" Em stated. "Not here." Anger spiked at his suggestion that prostitution may have taken place in her hotel. After several seconds, Em glanced at the sheriff. "Not here, I am sure of it. But she seemed to disappear for hours at a time. She never divulged where she was when I questioned her."

The sheriff nodded. "I'll have my deputies search. We'll find her. She can't go far very fast." He patted her shoulder before he stood and left the room.

Brodie's and Collins' boot thumps echoed down the hallway. When the front door slammed shut, Em continued to stare at the safe. The tears refused to come.

How long Em sat there, she had no idea. She rubbed her face hard. "Augh!" she cried to the ceiling. Rising from the floor was a struggle and she collapsed on her office chair.

If this mysterious male Missus Doctor mentioned had a car, they would have had several hours head start. They'd be past Rock Springs by now.

She rubbed her eyes. Her shoulders slouched. Nothing I can do now, she thought. *No reason to mail a letter to her parents.* It's best to wait a few days in case Sylvia returned. Then Em would stick her on a train back to Boston—if the girl returned.

She pushed away from her desk and slowly headed for the kitchen to keep busy. She cleared the breakfast table and ate Missus Doctor's cold, congealed breakfast while standing at the counter. She couldn't afford to throw away food. She didn't taste it, but forced it down. She took her time washing the dishes.

Only preparing the pre-ordered cold-sandwich lunch loomed. If Missus Doctor threw a fit about cold sandwiches, then she should have been down for a hot breakfast. Dinner would be stew and biscuits, all easy things to make. But first, she would prepare the room for the honeymooning couple's arrival. "Do things early," her mother always warned her. "You never know when the best laid plans may upset your apple cart." Em smiled remembering her mother's confused sayings. How she wished her mother was here. She stared up at the kitchen ceiling, thinking of the comfort her mother brought to her daughter.

"I miss you, Mother," she whispered.

Somewhere, a knock sounded.

~ * ~

Em set the dinner table with large bowls gracing the center of her fanciest place mats. Her mother quilted the place mats. Their colors were vibrant even after years of untold washings. She stepped back to check the table. She loved this ritual of inspecting her table after all the work was done. The perfect table was the ice cream on top of her cake. She nudged a fork into position here then twisted her violet pot so the blooms looked best there. Em exhaled her first sigh of pleasure all day.

She trudged back to the kitchen to stir the moose stew on the wood stove. After a check of the oven's temperature, she tossed in another log in the firebox. Checking under the cheesecloth, the biscuits were rising nicely. In a few moments, she would brush them with the melting butter in the little pot on the stove's top, then in the oven they would go. Twenty minutes later, her mouth would water as she dumped the steaming biscuits into a towel-draped bowl.

The chugging of Finch's pickup stopped about an hour earlier. She was relieved the men returned with enough time to clean up before dinner. Occasionally, miners returned all dirty. Their soiled elbows on her clean tablecloth left spots that required a lot of beating on the washboard to remove. That the men, especially Finch, were back and hungry made her sad heart lighter.

She pumped the water handle to spew the forty-degree water and filled the water pitcher. The well water made for a refreshing drink.

As she bustled, she wondered where Sylvia was and if she was all right. She worried whether not notifying Sylvia's parents was the right thing. That morning, Em had begged Magnus to ride for the sheriff and report her disappearance and the room's destruction. He didn't want to go. Magnus vanished whenever the law showed up, but her distraught pleading made him agree to nudge old Rosybud to her fastest amble to the sheriff's office. Fortunately he ran into Margaret Newbury on her way out of town and she notified the sheriff.

Em set the big bowl of steaming biscuits on the table when boot thumps echoed. She turned with a smile, gratified Finch entered first. He blew her a small kiss, hidden since Barclay and his wife were behind him.

"Good evening," Em said. "Dinner is ready."

Missus Doctor wore a red silk sheath, resplendent with sequins along the low-cut bodice. Em wondered why she felt the need to dress so outlandishly in this country.

"The smell is heavenly," Barclay boomed.

"Thank you, Doctor," Em replied. "This is my mother's recipe of moose stew and her biscuits."

"Oh, that sounds wonderful. We're famished," Finch proclaimed as he pulled out a seat for Em.

"Only four plates? Your cousin isn't joining us tonight?" Barclay asked as he grabbed a biscuit, then juggled it to keep it from burning his hands.

"No, she won't." Em didn't feel the need to explain. She only hoped Missus Doctor wouldn't talk about it, but likely she already told her husband all about Sylvia's destruction and her disappearance. The bit about the sheriff being here was too juicy not to tell.

She handed the butter tray to Barclay, then she stood to ladle out the stew. She filled Missus Doctor's bowl, her husband's, then Finch's. While Barclay slathered on butter, Em fought a giggle when Finch juggled a biscuit.

Barclay groaned after he bit into the creamy bread. "Heaven," he muttered as he looked at Em as he chewed.

Em smiled. She thought about asking specifics with the Ember Mine, but she wasn't sure she wanted to know. She kept quiet, but listened to the satisfied groaning of the men. Missus Doctor sipped her stew with delicate slurps and gently nipped her biscuit.

"I would think your dinner would be more fancy than stew and bread," Missus Doctor sniffed.

Em tempered her anger. She felt no need to explain or apologize for this good meal.

"No, my sweetmeat, I quite disagree." Barclay stuffed another biscuit, this one unbuttered, into his mouth. With a loud sucking noise, he licked his fingers.

Missus Doctor stared with disgust at her husband's manners.

"Oh, this is wonderful," Finch said. "The flavors are spectacular together. Now with this, you could open a restaurant in the biggest city."

As the eating slowed, Barclay patted his stomach. "I didn't know I had waited all day for this meal, Miss Olson. My compliments to you."

Em brightened. "Thank you!"

"And I'll have you know this afternoon I signed and paid for a leasing contract on the Ember Mine."

CHAPTER 14

At Doctor Barclay's announcement Em sucked a gulp of water into the wrong pipe. She coughed until Finch patted her back. She wheezed. Finally, the water shifted and she could breathe again.

Em apologized and stared at Barclay, who beamed like a new father. Barclay looked to his wife then picked up her hand. "You will wear even finer clothing than you do right now, my cheesecake. I assure you the Ember Mine will take care of us as long as we live."

Missus Doctor removed her hand from his. "We'll see," she sniffed with a mild curiosity. "You don't expect me to stay in this godforsaken country while you dig in the dirt?"

"Certainly not, my chocolate bar. You may do whatever your heart desires." He patted her shoulder. She shrunk ever so slightly from his touch. He turned to Em. "Mister Denton was ever so helpful. He had all the paperwork prepared. Even had a notary to witness. He led me out to the mine via a trail, but he said it could be expanded to a two-track for vehicles, perhaps even into a road. Water is right there in Quartz Creek. There are even a few new shacks to work out of until the mill and offices are built."

Barclay ticked off his fingers then hesitated. "We'll need housing for the workers." He looked at Em. "What long-term rates do you have?"

Em's mouth worked in an effort to process the information he tossed her way. "Um, ..."

Barclay leaned forward. "Perhaps we could talk about my buying this hotel. It would make a fine place to house workers permanently." He sat back in his chair.

Em's face paled. Her breath came quickly, but the world blackened. "Um, ..."

"Well, think about it. Give me a price for long term or give me a price to buy the hotel." Barclay scooped the remnants of his stew.

Em stared at her bowl. Her mind raced too fast to think. There was an offer to either fill the hotel or buy it, but Denton was thick in this mess. She decided against thinking about selling right now. Barclay would get his rude awakening in the not-too-distant future. She didn't want to get her hopes up only to have them come crashing down when Barclay was forced to default on the agreement. Better to calm down and see how all this played out.

"I could work up a long-term rate for your workers, Doctor Barclay. How soon would you like that information?" Em asked, her heart pounding.

"Within a week," Barclay replied. "There's still much to do to forecast how many workers we'll have."

Finch slowly pulled apart another biscuit. Was he worried about this deal, Em wondered. Did he hope she would sell the hotel and join him on his travels? She banished that thought. Don't move so fast, she thought. A few kisses does not mean he was ready for marriage. A thought jolted her: *was she?*

She fought to blank her mind to calm the myriad thoughts screaming in her head.

~ * ~

After dinner, Em cleared the dishes and washed them in the wood sink. The Barclays and Finch were lounging in the living room after pushing away from the dining table.

A light knock sounded on the exterior pantry door. As she reached for the door knob, Em glanced out the window. Magnus waited, his arms crossed.

"Evenin', Magnus. Come on in. You know you don't have to knock." Em tossed a smile toward the little man as he stepped inside.

"Thanks, Em. I know. Rode out and got a hold of Margaret Quint like you asked. She'll come by tomorrow, late morn, to help," Magnus mumbled.

Em stared out the window, relief washed over her. "Oh, thank you. I'm glad. I could use the help." She rubbed her forehead while she thought. "I just have to figure out how to pay her."

"I'm a law-abiding man, Em. You know that. I can get some money. It'll be mostly legal but you can have it. You know you're welcome to all I got."

"You're such a dear, Uncle." Though Magnus didn't like to be touched, she leaned forward to give him a quick embrace. He squirmed as if he wanted to shake off the feeling of Em touching him.

Magnus shuffled his feet. He stepped back to the doorway. "Let me know what else I can do, Em. Night."

As Magnus pulled open the door to step out, Em said softly, "Good night, Magnus. And thank you." She watched as he trudged toward his little cabin on the corner of the property.

The coffee pot's glass top showed the bubbling black liquid. She arranged the serving tray and hefted it into the living room. Missus Doctor slumped in the wingback chair with one leg crossed over the other. One foot bounced in boredom. Barclay and Finch's debating grew heated. They became silent as she approached. In the oppressive silence she set the tray down and said brightly, "Your after-dinner coffee everyone."

How odd she stood to receive a stipend for giving information to Barclay and privy to information no one else had, yet they fell silent around her. Perhaps something else was up they didn't want her to know. Either way, she needed quiet time in the kitchen.

"Enjoy your evening coffee."

While the dishes dried in the rack, she puttered around the kitchen. Dinner and the coffee were done—she had only to wash the pot and the evening's cups. With a sigh, she thought about breakfast tomorrow. Thankfully, the men didn't ask for breakfast at an obscenely early hour. Breakfast time was the regular time at seven.

Leaning against the counter, she rubbed her throbbing temples. She didn't have time to make bread. They would have leftover bread. If she skipped eating, they'd have enough slices for toast. Breakfast would have to be oatmeal again; they would just have to accept that.

The thought of Denton flashed in her mind. *I should talk with him face to face.* She daydreamed that perhaps it would become heated. She would tell him what she thought of him. He would order her to leave the hotel as he owned it now and it was no longer her concern.

A small knocking sound interrupted her musing. Finch stood in the kitchen doorway looking unsure whether he should interrupt. Em stared for a few beats. "Can I get you something, Finch?"

He shook his head. "I'm worried about you." He hesitated. "Virginia told us what happened with Sylvia—that she's missing." His brow furrowed. "I feel responsible somehow. Is there anything I can do?"

Em gave a weak smile. "What happened isn't your fault. You just happened to be here when it did." Em picked at her fingertips. "There's some mysterious male voice in all this. Perhaps she had a boyfriend and they ran off together. I don't know. The sheriff said he and his deputies will look around the county."

Finch stepped into the kitchen. "Virginia said she overheard what you told the sheriff."

Em stared at Finch. Oh, please no, she thought.

"She said Sylvia took all your cash." He hesitated. "I can give you money, whatever you need."

Embarrassment flooded her that the man she cared for pitied her. She took a deep breath to push back the tears building up. Pressing her fingers into her eyes to stop the welling, she breathed deeply.

"No. Thank you. I'll manage." Swallowing hard, she forced her stomach contents back down. "If you want to help, please be patient while I work. I don't have any help now, though Margaret—you met her at the wedding reception—will be here tomorrow. The meals will be simple until I can get some permanent help."

"I understand. I will help in any way." He glanced over his shoulder through the dining room. "Even defend you to Missus Doctor Barclay should she complain." He smiled at her and approached Em.

Her arms raised on their own accord and encircled Finch's neck. He held her tightly and rubbed her back through her thin sweater.

"I wish I could wave a magic wand and makes things all better." Finch muttered into her hair.

Clicking heels sounded in the dining room. Em and Finch stepped back from each other as Missus Doctor swept into the room then out without acknowledging either. Finch rolled his eyes as she stomped up the steps.

Em turned to Finch. "I know this is none of my business, but I'm concerned for you and Doctor Barclay in dealing with Denton. How do you feel about this mine deal?"

He glanced over his shoulder to the dining room, then up the stairs to ensure Missus Doctor was out of earshot. He shook his head. "Denton was persuasive. I tried to recommend to Clarence to hold off, do a background check, verify it's available, but Denton said he had another investor wanting to meet with him to see the mine. The second investor promised top dollar."

Em closed her eyes. An educated man like Barclay had fallen for the oldest trick in the con artist's book. "Oh, dear."

Nodding, he said, "I can only hope, but I haven't finished my initial testing yet to confirm what I suspect is a rich vein. I'll find out tomorrow."

Finch and Em exchanged a deep gaze as Barclay's thumping footsteps approached the kitchen. Barclay walked through the kitchen and said, "I have to head to my room and plan for tomorrow. Breakfast at the regular time?"

"Yes," Em called out to his back. "Seven o'clock."

Barclay waved his understanding before he clomped up the stairs.

Finch watched as Barclay stepped onto the landing, then waited until he heard Barclay's door slam closed. He rushed to Em and swept her in his arms.

CHAPTER 15

"And she swung her handbag and smacked that cow moose right on the nose! The moose was so startled she ran into the willows." Margaret laughed until she bent over.

A snort escaped, sending Em into a laughing fit. Oh, how I missed a great belly laugh, she thought. "So, how was Pauline after that? She had a frightening escape!" Em gasped between laughter.

Margaret eased a wet pillow case from the washing machine's rollers then snapped the fabric to loosen the wrinkles. She draped the case over her arm as she recalled Pauline's story. "She just stood there not believing it. It happened so fast she didn't even think."

Em stuffed towels into the machine's tub and sprinkled some powder onto the towels. "Goes to show how careful you have to be when walking around the creek. Those thick willows hide a lot of critters."

Margaret nodded. "Pauline said she's taken that shortcut through those willows for decades and never surprised a moose, especially one only a few feet away." She paused. "She could have been hurt bad."

"I'm grateful she's okay," Em paused before turning the water handle to fill the tub. "And I'm grateful for your help, Margaret. I have to admit I'm not sure what I appreciate more, your physical help or your moral support and company. There are times when the hotel is full and I've never felt more alone."

"It's been a tough haul for you, Em. No one would fault you for selling out."

She slipped another pillow case into the rollers and turned the handle. As the rollers squeezed the water from the case, she eased the fabric away. "Have you made a decision on selling this place?"

Em paused. "No." She leaned on the edge of the tub and stared into the water. "I still hope Father will come through the door and tell me he's proud of me for taking care of his hotel … but I don't think that'll happen."

"Well, when you decide, Sam's been telling me he'll buy the place—although I'm not sure what I'll do with it!" She threw back her head and laughed out loud.

Em smiled at Margaret's point. As Sam's wife, she'd have the responsibility for running the hotel.

"If you want to keep the hotel, Sam said he'll buy the mine. Then you'd have some money to get you through until you decide what to do with the hotel." Margaret studied a stain on a sheet then stepped to a scrubbing board.

Em froze. She stayed still for so long Margaret turned to watch her. "You okay?"

Em shook her head and her hands lowered. The damp sheet pressed onto her dress. She barely felt the wetness seep through to her thighs.

Margaret stepped beside Em and placed an arm over her shoulders. She waited.

"A few nights ago I found out Walter Denton owned the mine somehow. I'm still paying on the second loan to him that got the money to buy it."

A hand flew to Margaret's face as she considered this news. "And your father didn't pay off the loan to Walt after selling it?" she whispered.

Em shook her head.

"Here's what you do, Em: go to Walter. He's almost a brother-in-law. Ask to refinance the loan. Perhaps he might give you some money since he's selling the mine."

Em stared into Margaret's eyes. Margaret shrugged, "It might happen. I've seen him do the right thing—not often—but I've seen it. Well, once."

Margaret patted Em's shoulder before stepping back to the washtub. "Have you seen the hotel and mine deeds here? Maybe you could just sign the things using your father's signature. Since he's not in any hurry to come back, you can get out from under it all by signing his name. Take the money and run."

"Forgery?" Em exclaimed, shocked at Margaret's suggestion.

"Look, Em, I know you're righteous, but you're his daughter. He left behind huge bills and you're working yourself to death to pay them off. When—if—your father returns and complains you sold off his property, well that's just too damn bad. He should have stuck it out like you have."

Slowly, Em shook out the pillowcase and tugged the damp skirt clinging to her thighs. "You do make a point." She pinned the case on the clothesline. "The only thing is I don't have the deeds."

Margaret straightened from rubbing the sheet on the washboard. "Check around. Sam told me the deeds have got to be here."

"Father must have hid them well then. Even still, because of the downturn of the property values around here, it's not worth much."

"Well, the mine should be worth a goodly amount, Em. Though Bill can't seem to make up his mind about the yield whenever he conducts his tests." Margaret owlishly studied the stain. Satisfied the blemish was gone, she dropped the sheet into the basin.

"Your brother's got how many years as an assayer?"

"Oh, 'bout ten. He's an expert on this area too, so it's surprising to hear him talk—in confidence mind you—how the assay results change."

The women worked in silence washing and hanging sheets and towels. When draped linen divided the basement Margaret turned to Em. "Go talk with Walt. He leaves in a few days, but he'll be home until then. He'll help."

CHAPTER 16

Em sat primly on the leather overstuffed chair, staring up at the exotic stuffed heads mounted on the dark oak walls. She studied the white horse with black stripes and a great gray beast's head with a horn sticking from its nose, a unicorn-like creature Em had seen depicted in an old book's engraving.

In each corner, huge leaves of tall plants brushed the oak-covered ceiling. The rugs were thick, Persian, she guessed. A massive chandelier holding twenty small oil lamps hung unlit. If it ever fell it would crush anyone sitting in the eight leather chairs and settees around the room's edge. Despite the magnificent furnishings, the energy the room exuded felt dark, unsettling.

Angry male voices argued, muffled through the thick oak door Em guessed to Walter Denton's office. She squirmed in the chair and smoothed the fabric of her best skirt. Flicking off a bit of road dirt, she inspected her outfit for any other soil kicked up by Magnus' speckled plug Rosybud on the miles out to the Denton mansion, near the neglected town of Hamilton City. The old mare was slow but gentle, which Em appreciated as she hadn't been on a horse for a while.

The voices grew louder and clearer, apparently they moved near the door. Em recognized Walter Denton's high voice. The madder he became the higher it rose. "I'll call your loan or I'll call the sheriff, Bill."

The door pulled open. Denton leaned on the handle. "I'll own your ass or your assay shop, either way."

"Rot in your hell, Denton." Bill Newbury screamed back. His face flushed dark red. He clapped on his hat then froze as he saw Em.

Both men stared at her but made no acknowledgement. Newbury moved stiffly toward the door in a suit she'd never seen before. Without a word to Em, he slammed the exterior door behind him.

Denton turned to her. His scowl made her heart feel like it would beat out of her chest. In the thick silence, Em forced herself not to cower. His musky cologne filled her nose. A fading bruise on his chin where Finch hit him at the wedding reception made his chin look dirty.

"You better have come to tell me you're selling the hotel," he growled. "I've had enough beggars for one day." The squinty eyes boring into Em's soul terrified her. A flash of saying *yes* entered her mind but the thought vanished just as quickly. She gulped hard and stood up.

"I don't beg, Mister Denton. I'm not looking for charity. I've come to talk with you about refinancing the loans on the hotel and the mine."

He grunted. "Surprised to see you here with your hand out since I sure as hell won't forget you barred me from the hotel." His eyes appeared to shrink as his face burned a deeper red. Finally, he waved his hand for her to enter his office.

Stepping into his office, wobbly legs staggered as her feet sank into the thick carpet. His office mirrored the living room.

As Denton stepped around the massive mahogany desk, he flicked a hand indicating for her to sit on a leather chair facing the desk. She sat before her trembling legs gave out. She took a deep breath.

"You have a magnificent home, Mister Denton. This is the first I've seen of it." Em meant the words in a conciliatory fashion as she sat stock-still while her eyes took in the sumptuous décor.

"Take a good look. This'll be the only time you see it." He reached for a cup of coffee and slurped a sip. He swirled the cup. He didn't offer her one.

Em forced herself not to react to his verbal slap. She affixed her eyes into his. "I want to talk about refinancing both my loans—father's loans. Sightseers are slowing because of the country's problems and property values' are dropping. I'm getting fewer guests. You were generous with my father when you sold him the Ember Mine. I am hoping you'd be so kind to lengthen the terms."

At the mention of Em's father, Denton's eyes grew cold. He leaned forward. "I wasn't 'generous' with your father. I sold him that mine he called the Ember for five hundred dollars lower than its already worthless value so I could clear some judge's order of restitution for shooting his drunk ass."

Em's eyes narrowed. "I suspected as much."

Denton snorted. "Sure you did. Now that we've got the preliminaries out of the way, let me be clear: I have no intention of lengthening the terms. If you can't make your ends meet then sell me the hotel. If you don't make your ends meet, the hotel's mine anyway. I just have to be patient."

Trembling throughout Em's body turned to quaking. She fought to calm herself. Denton smiled and leaned back into his chair. He was enjoying her fear.

"You assume I would sell you the hotel, Mister Denton. I have other interested parties." Em tried to exude a smugness she didn't feel. Dreams of Clarence Barclay's surprise offer and Samuel Quint's demand to buy her hotel swirled.

Denton tossed his head back on the chair's tall back and stared at the ceiling, "Ah, yes. Sam." He raised his head to focus on Em. "Where do you think the money for him to buy the place will come from? With Sam being my brother-in-law, it'll still be in the family. And you can bet his contract with you will have strict contingencies for you to comply with."

Em could barely breath. Her face grew cold. "I have another interested party," she whispered.

"I know about Doctor Barclay. He's so excited to buy your place to house his legion of workers," Denton's voice turned sarcastic. "A few words from me and he'll run away from your fouled well and collapsing foundation."

"I don't have either of those!" Em protested.

"Barclay'll believe what I tell him."

The weight of being trapped forced her to struggle to breathe. *Think. Father may still own the mine.* "I'm confused about Doctor Barclay's lease-to-own contract on the Ember. Perhaps you and I can make a deal on the mine. That should take care of most of my debt."

A satisfied smile crossed Denton's face. "You forget your own words from a few minutes ago how local property values are dropping. Even if I were to buy the mine from you, your debt would still exceed the value." He slapped his cup on the desk. "I would still own your loans."

Em clenched her fists until the blood left her knuckles. "Mister Denton, we've known each other a long time. Isn't there anything you can do? My father might return soon …" Em lost her train of thought at the realization she was reduced to begging.

Denton leaned forward and placed both elbows on the desk. He rested his chin on his hands and studied Em's face. Em dropped her eyes. His intense gaze made her want to run from the room for a bath to shed anything of him that remotely touched her. She feared what he would demand.

With a shiver, Denton blinked and dropped his arms. A scowl crossed his face as he slammed back into his chair. "You're apparently ignorant of the most important point, Miss Olson. I offer this lease or a purchase contract on the Ember because your father sold it to me and Sam Quint before he left. We own it. Your father snatched the money and ran away. He chose not to repay the loans."

He grabbed his coffee cup and drained the contents. For too long, he stared at Em then slammed the cup on the desk.

"So either you pay his loans or lose the hotel. And I don't give a tinker's dam what you choose."

~ * ~

The sun beat hot on the back of Em's neck. She tugged the wrinkled handkerchief from her sleeve and tucked it into her collar to block the strong rays. As Rosybud sauntered back to the hotel, Em forced her mind to stay blank and let the old horse's rocking motion soothe her jangled nerves.

As the horse crested the hill above the hotel, she stared at the structure with disinterested eyes. Magnus stood leaning against the hitching post mounted to the front porch. *Had he stood in the sun this whole time waiting for my return?* Her heavy heart swelled with love for him.

Magnus looked up to see Em and he pushed off from the post. He stood facing them as he watched his horse amble down the hill. In the slowly closing distance, Magnus and Em locked eyes.

Em slowly shook her head. Magnus hung his head and stuffed his hands in his pants pockets.

CHAPTER 17

The next afternoon, the purr of a black Hudson coupe pulled in the hotel's driveway. The soft vibration caressed Em, then ceased as the driver shut off the motor. This must be the honeymooners, Florence and Thomas Barton.

Through her private office window Em watched as the driver and his bride stared at the hotel to take in the chipped paint and the black logs. They exchanged glances and slowly disembarked.

Em liked to watch guests arrive and absorb the old hotel and their surroundings. She didn't like to watch when they seemed unsure about the condition of her hotel.

She hurried to the door to catch them before they walked in. The couple appeared to be in their late 20s. Freckles dotted Florence's face. Though dusty from the dirt roads, their tailored clothing highlighted fit figures. At the introductions, Em called the bride "Missus Barton." She enjoyed watching the new wife blush at the new name. Em led them to the register and Thomas completed the information.

Em preceded them upstairs to their room and gave them her spiel for new guests. "If you follow me, I'll show you the rest of the hotel so you can get your bearings."

They hesitated then looked into each other's eyes with desire. Thomas turned to Em. "Um, I think we'll remain here. We'll come down later to find our way around."

"As you wish. Call out if you need anything. Dinner is family-style at six in the dining room. Just walk through the kitchen." Em retreated from the room, hating honeymooners.

They always made her feel like an outsider in her own place. Their looks of longing made her uncomfortable — and jealous.

She closed the kitchen door behind her. In no way did she want to hear what they were doing. Her bedroom was below that of honeymooners or other frisky couples. The sounds embarrassed and mortified her.

Leaning against the kitchen counter, she thought of Finch, whose kisses were getting more intense and his embraces tighter. His hands wandered her body. *I wonder ...*

She busied herself by preparing dinner. A piece of meat the size of her head filled the cast iron pot. She grunted as she staggered with the pot to the woodstove.

She stacked the corn cobs, pulled off the green leaves then picked out the corn silk, and left the cobs to soak in a pot on the stove.

Perhaps she could set the table early — anything to keep her away from the hotel rooms.

Shouts of men outside the hotel poured through the open window. Em ran to the entry window and peered out. Finch, Clarence Barclay, and Walter Denton stood beside Finch's pickup. Barclay's face grew beet red. He shook his fist at Denton. Walt ignored the motion. They stared at each other, locked in their glare. After a moment, Barclay backed down and headed for the hotel's door.

Denton stared down at Finch before he drove off in a cloud of dirt.

Em stood aside, trying to make herself invisible. She didn't know what to say to them but "Good afternoon, how was your day?" was not it. She silently slipped down the basement steps.

Barclay shoved open the entry door and stamped upstairs, cursing under his breath. Finch slowly walked in and closed the door. Despite his heavy boots, he moved up the stairs as silent as a cat.

Em hurried from the basement and watched Finch's legs trudge up the steps. The legs stopped. Finch leaned down to catch a glimpse of Em. He held Em's gaze and shook his head.

Em steadied herself with a hand on the banister. *Oh, dear.*

Another door slammed open upstairs. Missus Doctor stepped down the first few stair steps and halted when she saw Em. Finch eyed Victoria as he stood a few steps lower.

"What type of whorehouse are you running here? Can you not hear those people down the hall? It sounds like a brothel!" Her face flushed with rage.

Finch's face remained impassive.

"Don't ever confuse this hotel with that. They are honeymooners. As soon as I get a chance, I'll ask them to be quieter. For right now ..." Em shrugged her shoulders. Her spite grew. "And as far as what a brothel sounds like, I wouldn't know."

Missus Doctor gasped. She turned back to her room and slammed the door.

Finch choked off a belly laugh and continued up the stairs.

A giggle erupted from Em's throat. The laughter released a welcome wave of joy. While she felt uncomfortable hearing people making love, often the circumstances dictated she plug her ears along with the other guests.

She stepped into the dining room to finish setting the table for dinner.

~ * ~

As Em felt satisfied the table looked right, Finch walked into the room, his hands stuffed in his pockets.

"I am so sorry, Finch."

He shrugged. In a low voice he said, "I tried to tell him to wait until the tests were completed, but he wouldn't listen." Finch looked over his shoulder to ensure privacy. "Now, Clarence's likely the owner of a worthless piece of dirt."

"Oh, no. I am so sorry."

Again, Finch shrugged. "I am very sorry it'll mean no long-term workers to stay here or the chance to sell the place if you wanted."

"I didn't think about it," she shrugged. "I knew Denton couldn't be trusted."

"You warned him. You were clear."

"Did you find any potential for a gold vein?" Em asked hopefully.

"The mine's been so salted, I can't tell what's what. It's possible it's a viable mine, but right now I can only recommend we start over with a clean slate."

Em grimaced. She knew several mines in the region had been "salted" by hucksters who added gold dust, nuggets, or ore from another mine to a worthless or played-out mine to make it appear rich. "Magnus told me once he came upon a mine and saw a man shooting a shotgun loaded with fine gold onto a shaft wall. He alerted other prospectors. The huckster barely escaped with his life and abandoned the country."

"Swindles like that ruin the reputation of every mine in a region," Finch added.

"Well, I take it that means there's a potential of value?"

Finch nodded. "A potential. I hope so for Clarence's sake. He's a good guy and got carried away. Never saw him get so swept away. Pure emotion. Don't tell him I said so."

Em shook her head.

"It's just this finding contradicts what other testing and results say." He paused. "You know Bill Newbury, the local assayer, I'm sure."

"Oh, yes."

"How's his reputation as assayer? How's his personal reputation?"

Em chewed her lower lip as she thought. "Good. I've never heard any prospector who stayed here complain about him. He's a good man. I like him." She hesitated. "I've heard he makes moonshine and runs it to Utah."

Staring at the wall, Finch seemed to consider this information. "That could leave him open to blackmail."

"I hadn't thought of that," Em said. "But you have to understand the culture up here. Rumors can be rampant and pure lies. I'm not sure if it's true. I've never heard anyone disparage his professional assayer results."

"Well, your recommendation is good enough for me," Finch said. "There's some confusion here I've never seen before. But for now, I have to clean out the mine of every rock laying around, maybe even scrape off parts of the shaft to clean it, a massive feat in itself, then start all over with collecting samples and testing." He tapped the back of a chair as he thought. "Do you know who has explosives up here?"

Em looked over in surprise. "Actually, it's all over. In fact, on the Ember Mine property there's a small rock structure where Father used to store his. The structure should still be there but I doubt the dynamite would be. Every prospector here likely has a stash somewhere, though you're required to have a license for it." A sudden thought made Em giggle.

Finch took a step toward Em and clasped her arm. "It's wonderful to see you laugh."

Em smiled. "It feels great to laugh." She waved her hand. "What made me laugh was once Samuel Quint took Bill Newbury's anvil up to the top of Drunk Swede Gulch and blew it up. Apparently Sam mistook his angle and knocked out Bill's porch." She giggled until she had to wipe her tearing eyes. "It's not funny, but at the same time ..."

A sobering thought crossed her mind and she stopped smiling. "Funny though, Bill refuses to talk about it. Sometimes I wondered if something else was going on. Anyway, perhaps there's dynamite still in the rock building."

I'll keep my fingers crossed." Finch said simply.

"I will too. If not, Bill Newbury, Samuel Quint, and Jamison Smith at the Assayer's Saloon have licenses to sell it."

"In the meantime, I'd avoid the Barclays' room if I were you. They're having a hell of a row."

"Oh, so Missus Barclay knows of your trouble?"

"By now, yes. But she was livid at the love birds down the hall," Finch's tanned face reddened to a pinker blush, apparently at the image in his mind's eye. "That's why I came down early."

Em watched his face. "I'll talk with them when they come down. They're on their honeymoon, but they must respect the other guests here."

He studied Em until he finally said, "You're a kind hostess, making sure your guests are comfortable, fed, and cared for."

Em hung her head at his compliments.

~ * ~

Hours later, flushed honeymooners Florence and Thomas Barton tentatively stepped down the stairs. Em couldn't look them in the eye. Leading them into her kitchen, she explained about breakfast time and dinner time. She led them through the dining room and into the empty living room.

She took a deep breath and faced them. "There's something I must discuss with you. I don't wish to embarrass you, but this hotel is old. The walls are thin—"

Thomas held up a hand. "Say no more. I understand. We're on our honeymoon as you recall." He reached out for his bride and pulled her to him.

Em averted her eyes. "I do recall; however, please refrain from too much noise ... honeymoon noise or otherwise. Sounds carry in this old place." Em stammered.

Thomas and Florence had eyes only for each other. She had made her point. "Dinner will be ready at six." She left the couple alone in the living room, wondering what the next guest would find.

CHAPTER 18

"Oh, Em, how do you manage with Sylvia's running away? It's like your father all over again. One minute here, the next minute gone!" Betty Denton stated pointblank after she'd dropped in unannounced the next morning. "Why you still hang onto this place I don't know. Walt and my brother Sam have told me they want it."

Em shrugged, unwilling to answer her nosy questions. "Betty, has Walter returned to you?" Em blurted. She felt like returning nosiness with nosiness and watching Betty squirm.

The older woman blushed. "Since the night of the wedding he only comes back for business in the daytime. Then he leaves in the evening." She stared at the counter a moment longer. Em noticed a slight darkening, fist-sized, on Betty's cheek. "I'll bet he goes off to his girlfriend's every night. Oh, that reminds me: when he did finally talk to me he said he's going to Salt Lake City on business and to visit family for a week. You can put the personal visit in 'Placer Claims' if you want. Well, I must go."

Good to see her go, Em thought, as Betty closed the front door behind her. Betty trapped Em in the kitchen and yammered while Em washed the breakfast dishes. Em appreciated someone to talk with besides guests, but she didn't appreciate being stuck in her own kitchen with the whining Betty. She stayed with a two-timing town cheat who beat her. She could have left long ago with her self-respect intact, yet she chose to stay with Denton because he had money. Betty was dependent upon him and refused to support herself. Em offered her room and board in the hotel if she would help with the cooking and cleaning, but Betty said she "could never do that". Others in town advised her to take the sizeable cash rumored to be in his safe and run, but she declined. Her choice, Em thought.

She relaxed for the first time that morning. Earlier, while the honeymooners, the geologists, and wife were at the table, Em informed them she could not provide lunch but only breakfast and dinner. If they wanted lunch, she'd order it for them through the Sage Restaurant. With Sylvia gone, she explained, she couldn't include lunches in addition to all her daily chores.

Breakfast had been tense between Finch and Barclay. Missus Doctor sat for coffee, but after a snap from her husband she grabbed a cup and returned to her room. No one spoke until the men stood and Finch gave Em a "Thank you." They left the hotel in silence.

No word came from the sheriff about Sylvia. She'd have to ask Magnus to put in a newspaper ad for a cook and a maid. Em sold some leftovers to a passing prospector yesterday, giving her a tiny stash of cash to pay for Magnus to ride Rosybud to Lander.

She checked her nearly blank reservation book. There'd be no other expected guests for another week. Relieved for the lessening work, the loss of any income would greatly impact her pocketbook. So many bills, so little income. How to raise money? If only she didn't have to worry about money — and help — she would live here the rest of her life. Until then, life drifted from one worry to another.

Distant sirens interrupted the silence and grew louder. Em hurried to the dining room window. The sheriff's car, followed by a deputy's, both in full lights and siren, raced down the hill from the east and whipped around the nearly blind corner in front of the hotel. The cars sprayed dirt and pebbles up the steep hill to the north then turned west, trying to gain traction.

Em mentally ran through a list of who lived to the west toward Atlantic City — no telling who or what they were heading for. Sylvia in danger flashed through her mind, but decided that was not the case. She returned to her kitchen to think about dinner.

~ * ~

Em set the platter of sliced pot roast on the table, then she fetched the big bowl of roast potatoes and carrots. Judging from the aroma the sweet rolls were about ready to come out.

At the footfalls on the kitchen's short stairway, Em caught sight of a grim-faced Finch. Behind him followed a red-faced Barclay. Missus Doctor wasn't with them. Not knowing how to address the men in this state, she settled for a nonchalant, "Good evening, gentlemen. Dinner will be ready in a moment." She unconsciously wiped her hands on her apron and stepped into the kitchen.

She helloed the newlyweds as they held hands through the kitchen and into the dining room. "Dinner will be ready in a moment." They barely acknowledged her, so enraptured with each other. Em rolled her eyes behind their backs.

She whipped off her apron and hung it on the nail. She dumped the steaming sweet rolls into a cloth-covered bowl.

"Dinner is served." No one spoke as they took their regular seats. Funny, Em thought, how once a person sat at a certain chair they sat at the same chair during their stay.

Thomas exclaimed over the pot roast. Florence commented how the vegetables were cooked to perfection. Both Finch and Barclay muttered how good it tasted. From the way they stuffed the meal into their mouths, Em wondered if they could even taste the food. Both men looked haggard, their thousand-yard stares betrayed a difficult day.

The honeymooners made polite chitchat as did Em. At some point, all three decided to give up and eat in silence. At the end of the dinner, Em collected the dirty dishes and fetched pieces of the yellow cake she felt up to making.

Everyone finished the dessert in silence.

As soon as Em stood to clear the dishes, Thomas and Florence excused themselves. "Good night," they called out to everyone. Only Em answered "Good night." Em said nothing to the men as she cleared the dishes. Finch and Barclay didn't seem interested in getting up from the table, but seemed satisfied to remain in her dining room. "I'll fetch the coffee if you'd like an after-dinner drink."

"Only if it includes whiskey," Barclay retorted.

Em shook her head. "Best I can do is cream and sugar."

"If that's the best you can do," Barclay muttered.

Em froze, anger spiked. "You know I don't allow liquor on the premises, Doctor."

Barclay stared at the table while his fingers spun a spoon.

Em carried in the tray laden with the coffee and the required items. She also balanced a small plate of cookies Pauline dropped off earlier. "Her gingersnaps are sure to rid any upset stomach problems," Em said half-jokingly.

Only Finch made an effort to appreciate the thoughtfulness. Em set the tray with the two cups on the table, not intending to join them. They were too immersed in their problems to want her around, she thought.

"Miss Olson, I am sorry for my poor attitude," Barclay said. "I would appreciate it if you would join us. We have something we need to talk with you about."

Em smiled her forgiveness, relieved at his apology.

Finch held Em's gaze. She felt good to be asked to be a part of something, though the looks in their eyes unsettled her. "Let me get a cup for myself."

She settled in at her usual place at the head of the table and waited for them to make the first comments.

After a moment's hesitation, Barclay looked her square in the eye. "Finch here made a most unfortunate discovery in the Ember Mine."

Em felt queasy. *Did he confirm the mine was indeed worthless?*

"I'm curious about your account of the mine's history."

Em nodded. "I haven't been there for a few years, but I told you all I knew."

Barclay nodded to Finch, who fixed his eyes on his cup, refusing to look at Em. "I descended the mine shaft today to begin cleaning ... I checked out a few of the drifts to check their condition." He glanced at Em. "A drift is a—"

"I know what it means, a horizontal passageway that follows along a gold vein, like a hallway."

Finch poked the cup handle. "In one drift ..." he coughed although Em suspected it was an excuse to pause.

Suddenly, Finch stared into Em's eyes. "I found remains." He swallowed hard. "Human remains."

Em's hand flew to her mouth to stifle a gasp. "Oh, my!"

"Doctor Barclay drove to the sheriff's as soon as I reported what was down there."

Barclay's face flushed back to beet red.

"That must have been why I saw the sheriff and the deputy fly past earlier! Do you have any idea who it may have been? I can't recall anyone missing. A prospector? There are a lot of abandoned shafts and open holes. I've heard of wanderers not watching where they're going and falling in."

"I helped the sheriff and the deputy to the drift. It was a tight fit with all us there. They weren't sure who it was. The body—a mummy essentially—was intact and the clothing was in good shape. They couldn't find anything on the body, like a wallet. When Clarence and I left they were still searching."

"Could they tell if the person died of natural causes?"

Finch took a deep breath. "When they were bringing down a board to load the body on and bring him up, they said a bullet hole was in his breastbone. And the poor man's head had been split open. Whoever wanted the man dead made sure of it."

Em closed her eyes. "A double-cross perhaps?"

"Don't know." Finch said. "Too early to tell."

Em sat in silence. "What was he wearing? Perhaps that could lend some clues."

Hesitating, Finch thought back to the monstrous memory. He reached for Em's hand and held it firmly. "A red checked shirt and a wood bolo tie."

CHAPTER 19

"Em, can you hear me?"

She groaned at the world whirling in her mind. Finch's voice sounded like he spoke through a water bucket. She gasped as a cold wet washcloth touched her face. "Miss Olson" sounded in her right ear. She flinched.

She opened her eyes. Finch's hand stroked her hair. Barclay knelt and touched her right shoulder. "My dear, are you alright? You fainted."

Em groaned, remembering. Shock caused her stomach to turn. She rolled onto her side, her back to Barclay, afraid she would throw up. Nausea roiled her stomach.

She pushed herself off the floor and leaned into Finch. His arms embraced her and he rocked her.

As the protective wall of shock lifted, she began to wail, lightly beating at Finch's chest. The tears would not flow, the numbness was too strong. The reality swam in her mind out of reach of her common sense and emotions. She needed time to face it: her father had not abandoned the family at all. He had been murdered and left in a deep grave.

A cry sounded far away. She shoved Finch and staggered toward the door. She threw it open and dashed toward the willows, toward the shortcut that would take her to the Ember Mine and her father.

"No, no …" she screamed as she ran. *Oh, please, no.*

A grip on her arms stopped her so suddenly she nearly fell. Strong hands pressed her to a chest she'd come to know.

"Oh, Em." Finch panted. He held her tightly when she tried to pull away to charge to her father. Each time he pressed her to him. "Honey, you can't. The police are working the scene."

He gripped her shoulders to turn her and half-dragged her toward the hotel. Her legs often collapsed and each time he caught her. As they neared the hotel, her legs finally gave out. Finch scooped her up in his arms. She gripped his shoulders and pressed her face into his warm neck. He carried her into the living room where Barclay stood behind a chair. Finch set her into the chair and kneeled in front of her.

She groaned. A vague awareness for Finch and Barclay's distress roused within her and she struggled to rise from the chair. Her legs refused to allow her to stand even though Finch held one arm while Barclay gripped the other. She gasped as she collapsed. "I am so sorry." She wiped her face with her hands. "I know this person."

"I know too," Finch whispered.

"Who is it?" Barclay cried, urgency in his voice.

She rocked, unable to speak the words.

"Em's father," Finch answered for her.

Silence fell thick behind Em and she couldn't see their faces. She didn't care anyway. "Perhaps we should tell the sheriff," Em said. Her voice felt so weak she wondered if they heard her. "I could send Magnus." Despite her shock her common sense started to function, but her emotional wall prevented her from fully comprehending the fact her father had not forsaken the family at all.

The exterior door opened. Magnus crept in. Tear tracks dried on his dirty face. He glanced at Finch and Barclay before he stared at Em. He reached for her hand as she reached for his. They locked eyes before Em pressed his left hand onto her forehead. He gently set his right hand on her head as a blessing. After a moment Magnus mumbled, "Sheriff's comin'. Deputy's outside to drive you … out there."

Em barely nodded as she stared at the floor. Finch kneeled beside Em and patted her back. "May I come with you?" He placed his hand on her shoulder.

Nodding, she seized his hand as if it were a lifeline. "I would appreciate that," she whispered.

She recalled Father's rucksack. She glanced at Finch. "Did you see a rucksack, by any chance? My father had it with him the last time I saw him. Did you see anything else?"

Finch's eyes sank, apparently unable to look into Em's haunted eyes. "Honestly, I didn't look for anything except for the opening of the shaft. Seeing it, recognizing it for what it was, I just wanted out of there. By the time the sheriff showed up, I had my wits about me." He shook his head, then looked at Em. "I'll go back and look. Perhaps I can find something."

Em smiled a sad smile as Sheriff Brodie walked through the dining room toward her. Deputy Collins stepped behind him. Em considered standing, but didn't have the strength.

"Em." The sheriff nodded his head, grimness threaded his voice. Deputy Collins nodded his greeting, but said nothing.

"We suspect the body in the Ember might be your father. I'm sorry. Mister Stone said you had described to him what your father wore the last day you saw him. The description matches what we found underground." Brodie nodded to Finch. Brodie never beat around the bush, and Em had come to appreciate his straight-forward approach.

Em nodded her head. "I remember clearly the last day I saw him. He was wearing a red check flannel shirt and my handmade bolo tie. The wood looked like a sunset." She pressed her handkerchief to her mouth and blinked back tears.

Barclay and Finch exchanged a brief look.

"And you never knew what became of him," Brodie prodded, softly.

"That's right. My family thought he had abandoned us." Em choked. Her shoulders shook from the strain of letting go of blaming her father these past two years. Finch gently massaged her shoulders.

"My father was having difficulty here. He turned to drink." Em turned to Barclay. "That's why I don't allow alcohol here."

She studied her dry hands. "It caused too many problems. My parents were fighting. Once I heard him holler at my mother he would leave for the California gold fields first chance he got. He was drunk." Em twisted the cloth. "He never knew I heard him. Then when he disappeared, we all thought ..."

"Did he leave with anyone that day? Did you see anyone hanging around him?" Brodie asked.

Em stared at the floor as if the answer might be intertwined in the floor's pine knots. She shook her head. "If there was anyone around, I just can't remember."

Brodie paused. "I hate to ask you, Em, would you be able to identify the shirt and the bolo tie?"

Em pressed her fingers into her eyes, trying to blot out an image of her father's mummified body from her mind's eye. She nodded. "If that's the only way." Em's head shot up. "He had a gold fountain pen in his pocket. Did you find it?"

Barclay shook his head.

"He had a gold tooth, right here." She pointed to her right incisor.

"There was a gold incisor with the remains." Brodie said.

Clasping her hand to her mouth to stop a wail, Em bent over, gasping. "I blamed him for so much."

"Do you remember if there was anyone interested in the Ember Mine? Perhaps this was a gold deal gone bad?"

At this, both Barclay and Finch jumped. Barclay said, "I signed a lease agreement with Walter Denton. He had all the proper paperwork. I paid him the lease money."

Brodie pursed his lips. "I've had complaints about Denton's business practices for years. Never had enough evidence to do anything about it. Em, do you know if your father owned that Ember outright or did he have a partner?" Brodie asked.

"Father was the sole owner," Em answered. "Once he hinted about considering a silent partner. He didn't mention who it was or the purpose of that partner. He was in a drunken stupor when he told me and Mother about signing the agreement with his pen, his gold fountain pen." Em craned her neck, seeking something. "Magnus might know. They were very close."

Magnus had already slipped away. Being around the law made him uncomfortable. Something about his bootlegging, Em suspected.

"Any of you seen anyone who has a gold fountain pen besides your father?" Brodie asked.

Em shook her head.

"Denton signed his portion of the agreement with a gold fountain pen," Barclay shot out. Already angry, his face grew beet red.

Brodie stared at Barclay, appearing to consider his comments. "Denton's wealthy. He'd likely have a gold fountain pen of his own."

"Father's pen had a row of baby teeth dented into it. My brother Michael chewed on it when he was two."

Brodie made a motion to the deputy who jotted a few things in his notebook. He stared at Em for several seconds.

A second deputy entered the living room. He strode quickly to Brodie and whispered in his ear.

Brodie nodded. "Em, you ready?"

CHAPTER 20

At the opening to the abyss known as Drunk Swede Gulch, Em stared into the shaft of the Ember Mine. She forced out of her mind the perceived image of her father lying in that deep grave. Finch gripped her arm with one hand and wrapped his other arm around her waist in support. Magnus stood close beside her. Barclay stood with arms crossed off to the side.

Sheriff Brodie and Deputy Collins stood behind a long, tarpaulin-covered box set on sawhorses. Brodie held his hand over the box. "These are just clothes and things, Em. The remains have been taken to Lander."

Em nodded. At least she wouldn't see her father in a state she would never rid from her mind.

"Ready, Em?" Brodie asked.

Em nodded, but as she stepped toward the box her legs gave out. Finch tightened his grip to hold her up. She closed her eyes and breathed in as if deep inhalations were the only thing that would keep her from joining her father in death.

Brodie whipped aside the corner of the tarp. Collins stepped back from the box. Em hyperventilated as she peeked. A red and white checked flannel shirt like the one her father wore lay crumpled.

"Does the left elbow have an 'X'-shaped tear?" Em whispered, her voice cracking. *Please, no, please let the cloth be intact.* "He'd joke how he'd wash his elbow for special occasions to make the outfit more formal." Em forced a laugh to lessen the stress and to cling to that fond memory.

Brodie reached into the box and gently shifted the material to find the sleeve. She moaned at the "X" tear at the left elbow.

"Tooth?" She felt as if her body was cracking apart.

Brodie stuck his hand under the fabric and scratched around. He held out the yellow bit. "An incisor."

Em had trouble breathing. Finch squeezed her arm in support. "His gold fountain pen?"

Brodie shook his head.

"Tie?"

Brodie reached back into the box. He cradled the bolo tie. The tie's shield portion was a sunset of different woods. He turned it to show the burnt "Father, 1930."

"The year he bought the Ember Mine," Em murmured. Her stomach retched. She pushed off Finch's supporting arms and staggered up the steep slope at the cliff's edge so she could vomit in private. Gasping for breath between wails, she forced her legs to propel her away from thoughts of his nightmare — and hers.

Behind her, Barclay screamed, "Don't go up there! Stop!"

In the evening's twilight she fell to her knees and heaved. The dinner she so carefully prepared lay on the ground. She leaned back to catch her breath, wipe her mouth, and moan to the sky. No longer able to hold her face to the heavens, her head lowered, and she stared into chasm.

Below her, partially hidden in the sages at the shadowy bottom lay a crumpled flatbed truck. Despite the twisted hood and broken spokes, it seemed familiar, almost comforting. Forgetting why she came to this ridge, she leaned on her hands to study the wreckage.

Her eyes flitted over the crushed top and ajar doors. Shifting her focus toward the flatbed, she comprehended a figure, a body that looked out of place.

Walter Denton's blank eyes stared into Em's. A large dot of dried-blood blackness punctuated his gray forehead.

Her screams sounded far away.

CHAPTER 21

The group of Em, Finch, Clarence Barclay, Sheriff Brodie, and Deputy Collins gathered in the semidarkness in the hotel's living room to discuss murder.

In a trance, Em wandered about the room lighting oil lamps. Mechanically, she waved the burning matches over the wicks and placed the stubs on the little metal shelf. Finch placed a gentle hand on her arm. "Can I do that for you?"

Uncomprehending, numb, she stared at him. "No." She sat on a chair. "Coffee," she mumbled. "Make coffee." She started to push off from the chair to head to the kitchen. Finch lay a hand on her shoulder and gently pressed her down.

She daydreamed about swatting away the gray fog of shock to concentrate on the questioning between Sheriff Brodie and Barclay about his contract with Denton.

Brodie studied Em then turned back to Barclay. "Would you say Denton treated you right on this deal?"

Barclay's lips tightened. "No. That bastard — sorry, Miss Olson — salted the mine." He indicated Finch. "My geologist here was cleaning the mine in order to collect samples to indicate if the mine is viable. But, I can't trust that scoundrel. If the mine's not viable, ..." He raised in hands. "I don't know what I would do with it."

Brodie turned to Finch. "How're your tests coming? Do you know whether Denton cheated your boss or not?"

Finch squirmed as he patted Em on the back. "I've been working on cleaning out the drifts, when I found ..." He rubbed her shoulders. "I found what may be a teaser vein that may bring us to a main ore body, but under the circumstances I haven't been able to return to check." He shrugged. "I can only keep my fingers crossed for a good outcome." He watched Brodie as he spoke.

"Fingers crossed, huh," Brodie grunted. "How scientific."

Finch shrugged again. "That's all I got right now."

"Either of you gentlemen seen Denton lately? Em, you?"

Em barely shook her head. "The night of the wedding reception here some time ago." She closed her eyes and silently groaned, remembering another time. "I went to his home a few days ago to ask about refinancing my—my father's—loans that he holds on this hotel and the mine. I haven't seen him since."

"Was he open to refinancing?"

Em shook her head.

"So it ended badly for you." Brodie's flat statement was not accusatory. "You do know you own this hotel and mine now," Brodie said. "And all the loans are yours."

Em stared at Brodie, eyes widening. She nodded. Although she'd treated the hotel and mine and the responsibility for paying on the loans as hers, now that they were in fact hers, she felt as if she'd bend in half under the weight.

"I haven't seen him today," Finch said too quickly as if to divert attention from Em. "But I've been hitting the mine and area pretty hard."

"Well, we saw him yesterday." Barclay's voice boomed in defiance. "The turd—excuse me, Miss Olson—had the nerve to come by and demand money to show us where good ore was or it would remain hidden. I was so angry I could have shot him on the spot." He flinched at his words.

The sheriff studied each person, in turn. Finally, he asked, "How well do either of you gentlemen know him?"

Barclay spoke up. "I only met him a week ago when he showed us the Ember Mine. I signed the lease and paid the first rent that day. He showed us around the area," he indicated Finch. He looked Brodie squarely in the eye. "Yes, Sheriff, a few days ago, after the initial assessment showed the mine had been salted, I was angry enough to shoot him; however, I did not."

"Had you seen Denton that day?" Brodie asked.

"I had seen him earlier in the day. He was snooping around, trying to find out what we knew. That's when he made his offer to show us the rich vein. After that he wouldn't speak to us, but when the work day was over he followed us here. We had words in the parking lot."

Em snorted. The men turned to look at her.

"Em?" Brodie prodded.

"You know Denton as well as I do, Sheriff. He's about as gutless a man as I've ever met." Em's voice was adamant. What she said was uncharitable, but she felt no sympathy at the moment. She indicated Finch. "The most bravado I have ever seen of him was during your fight with him last week." At Barclay and Finch's wincing, she realized she should have kept her mouth shut. She blushed.

"I heard of the fight. I intended to talk to you about it." Brodie said. Em felt relief she hadn't caused Finch any reason for the sheriff to suspect him. Finch's eyes reflected a slight irritation at Em before he turned to the sheriff.

To Em Brodie asked, "What was the condition of Denton's face when you talked with him at his home?"

Her mouth fell open, surprised. "His chin was bruised, but it was almost healed."

Brodie turned to Finch and affixed him a stare until Finch squirmed. "In the gulch, Denton's face was beat up, as if he ran into a boxer or someone who knows how to fight."

"I only saw the bullet hole," Em mumbled.

"Understandable, Em." Brodie didn't break his focus on Finch. "For such a short time here, you two already have a violent history." He let his statement hang in the air.

Finally, Finch waved his hands. "Everybody knows what happened at the reception. Not much to tell, Sheriff. The first time I met Denton was the evening of the Morenos' wedding reception. He was drunk and got abusive with his wife. I got him out of the building. He tried to assault me, but I got the upper hand. That's the only time I laid a hand on him. We had clashes about the mine, as you know. We haven't had anything to do with each other since."

"Sheriff, do you have any idea how Father's truck ended up in the gulch?"

Brodie waited until his deputy finished jotting his note. "I saw no tracks for the vehicle. I'd venture a guess it got there the day your father disappeared. It would have been rough going, but those trucks have low gears that'll make it climb a tree. The vegetation has recovered. The truck was already old so it looks like it's been there a decade. That's probably why nobody reported it."

"That's right, Sheriff." Finch sat and pointed an index finger. "Denton showed me around the property. He even pointed it out. He said it had been there since twenty-six when a miner pushed another miner's truck over the edge … something about a feud over a woman."

"True. He told me that too. I had no reason to doubt him." Barclay hesitated. "What a clever way to make that vehicle irrelevant."

"Genius." Brodie watched his deputy tap his pencil on his pad. He squared on Barclay. "Last question, Doctor: as Em ran up the hill this evening, you kept screaming 'Don't go up there! Stop!' Were you afraid of what she'd find?"

Barclay scowled. "Are you accusing me of murder?"

"He bilked you and made you look like a fool."

He jerked his thumb in Finch's direction. "Maybe you sent your fighter here to work him over like Denton worked you over financially," Brodie shouted. "There's a fresh bruise on his face." He jutted his chin at the faint swelling on Finch's forehead.

Finch held up a hand to his forehead. "Sheriff," fatigue threaded his voice. "This was from running into a jutting rock in the drift. As far as yelling to Em to stop, she was running to where we stored the dynamite."

CHAPTER 22

An exhausted Em walked Sheriff Brodie and Deputy Collins to the door, or more like they helped her to the door. *How much lower can I go?*

"I haven't heard anything about your cousin, Em," Brodie said, keeping his voice low. He nodded toward Collins. "Deputy Collins kept an eye out for her all over the county. No sign of her."

Em nodded to each man. "Thank you, Sheriff, Deputy."

She closed the door and leaned against it. Emotions tore through her body, scouring all her energy. The sounds of the lawmen driving away grew fainter.

A knock vibrated through the wooden door. Em started and managed to open it to see Doris Beers in the darkness. Her tiny frame wriggled in agitation. "A disgrace I tell you, an outrage! I demand you do something. It's an abomination!"

Em stared with uninterested eyes at her neighbor, a Californian who vacationed in Placer City. Doris Beers made it clear her husband's wealth allowed her to have much leisure time to spend the summers here. Em thought she was a lazy twit who had no business being around hardworking people.

"What're you talking about?" Her flat voice felt incapable of anger or interest.

"Nudity. Right here in your front yard. Just this afternoon!" Doris pointed at the deserted deck some distance from the hotel. "It was obscene. Flaunting herself for all to see! I demand you do something to stop this! I could see her from my yard! My children ogled her!"

Em stared at Doris' bottle-yellow hair sticking out on one side as if she woke up from a late nap.

"Then don't look." She shut the door on the sputtering Doris. She wobbled as she trudged back to the living room and sat with Barclay and Finch. No one said a word as they pondered the day's happenings.

Em gazed at Finch who studied her from across the room. "How did you find my father?"

He stood from the straight chair beside the small table and sat across from her in the tapestry-covered rocking chair. He filled Em's cup with coffee from the pot he made while Em finished with the sheriff, offered some to Barclay, who shook his head. He filled his own cup.

"I was down the shaft, poking around. Checking to see how many drifts there were. Cleaning up the bits of gold — pyrite, fool's gold actually — trying to see what I could see." Finch took a sip of coffee and winced at the steaming liquid. "There was something odd about a rock grouping. It looked too manmade, too tidy. There's no reason to have this rock pile stacked to make it look natural. I checked different portals — openings — getting my bearings. For some reason, I kept coming back to that rock pile. I decided to snoop since I learned not to trust Denton."

At this Barclay winced.

"I started picking up the rocks. They were rocks that had been blown up." He looked at Em. "Dynamite. I kept inspecting them and found a small grouping of white quartz. You know when you find white quartz, gold may be near. Anyway, the more rock I pulled out, the more of a hollowed-out space I uncovered. Pretty soon, I uncovered a drift. No reason to try to cover the opening unless you're hiding something." At that thought, Finch jumped and shook his head that his thinking was verified by a grisly discovery.

"I was getting rather excited. What's really down here, I wondered. About ten feet in, I stumbled — tangled up actually — on some fabric. I thought it was debris left over from another miner." He looked apologetically at Em. "It was a

141

segment of the red checked shirt. I set it aside and kept looking. Something was tangled in the cloth. I found a wood bolo tie." He stared into Em's eyes as she shivered from tension. The haunted look in his eyes made her want to stroke his face. "I could see it had been handmade. It had a sunset." Finch stopped talking while Em placed her face in her hands.

"Would you like me to stop?"

"No," she croaked. "I want to hear all of it."

"My headlamp started to run out of gas. The flame was sputtering, but I could still see. I took a few more steps. I tripped on something then accidently stepped on something else. I leaned in for a closer look. They were arms. Then I saw the head." Finch wiped his face with his hands. He sat silent for a moment. His breaths came faster. "The forehead was smashed in. The shirt was split open. I could see the breastbone. It had a hole in the bone."

Finch's hands trembled. "I think I screamed." An embarrassed smile flicked across his lips. "I stood up so fast I bashed my head against a jutting rock." He gingerly touched the soft swelling. "I got out of there. Clarence pulled me out. I told him what I found, and he took off for the sheriff's office."

"How awful." Em said.

"And I had no idea about Denton. I didn't know he was even around."

"Neither did I," Barclay interjected. "I'm not sure what I would have done if I saw him. I might have put the bullet in him myself." He looked guilty as he returned Finch and Em's shocked expressions. "I didn't off the guy. Though if he's such a scoundrel who preys on innocent, hard-working people he deserves it."

Em said nothing. She didn't condone violence, but the world was a better place without Denton. "Who would shoot him?" Barclay asked.

"Most anybody around here," Em whispered.

The sharp tacking of Missus Doctor's high heels grew louder. She swept into the room and headed for her husband, yet staring at Em. "Did you see that woman sunbathing nude on your deck? I can't believe you did nothing about it." Her red lips set in a tight line.

"A nude woman?" Barclay perked up. "Where? Here?" He hurriedly craned his neck to see out the window.

Missus Doctor shot her husband a cold look before turning to Em. "I would think you'd be concerned about the reputation of this hotel that you would stop such exposure. She displayed herself to the whole world, and her husband was nowhere around!"

"When was this?" Barclay asked. He was too curious and he'd pay for it later, Em thought.

"Oh, for heaven's sake, Clary. This woman," she pointed at Em. "Allows obscenity to be visible to anyone and does nothing about it."

"Now hold on there," Em interrupted. "I'm guessing you mean Florence. I'll talk to her. I didn't know about this until tonight when I was in the middle of an emergency. A nude woman is not an emergency. And, I would appreciate it if you wouldn't sneer at me or my hotel." She choked at the full weight of "my hotel". She turned her attention to Finch, seeking his support.

"Virginia." Finch proclaimed, "We've had a terrible situation happen—"

"I heard, I heard all about it." Missus Doctor waved her hand in dismissal.

"Well, there's a tragic incident along with it," Finch stated loudly.

Em didn't care about Missus Doctor, but she cared about Finch's defense of her. She gave him a look of warm appreciation.

"Miss Olson, we'll check out before the end of our reserved time here." Barclay said. "Unless Finch finds something with this accursed mine, I'm going to give it up. If it's a loss, it's a loss, and I'm a man not to waste my time or money. I'm aware you will charge us for the remainder of our projected stay, so I'll pay it. But we," he indicted himself and his wife, "are out of here soon."

Em paled. She glanced at Finch. She needed to know. "You will leave soon too?"

Finch appeared shell-shocked at Barclay's announcement. "I should stay to verify the mine. As soon as the sheriff will allow it, I'll go back down." He gulped at the memory, then he also looked to Em for support.

Her eyes pleaded with him to stay.

To Barclay he babbled, "It's worth it to keep looking. I think I may have found something, but finding the body interrupted me. I don't think this mine will be a total waste."

Barclay considered Finch's proposal. "You actually think it's viable?"

"There's a possibility. No promises, but there was enough there I might find something. And with the history of the mine," he indicated Em. "It's possible it's hot. Perhaps it's played out, but there's a hundred acres to work on for discovery shafts." He turned to Em. "Since Doctor Barclay will leave soon, can you recommend anyone to assist me up top and down below? A good man?"

Em's heart leaped. "Yes. Magnus. I think he'd be thrilled for the opportunity. You saw him. He's the one who came in earlier to tell me the sheriff was here."

"Magnus? That little gremlin who lives by the northwest corner?" Missus Doctor exclaimed. "He's hideous!"

Em affixed Missus Doctor with all the hatred she could muster. "Magnus is a sweet man. I expect respect for him. He's my adopted uncle." She turned to Finch and Barclay.

"He's a genius in a gold mine. He's reliable and hard working. He had a dynamite accident a few years ago that caused significant head injuries. The only lingering issues are he lost some memory and you have to give him time to develop his words. He's getting better every day. The doctor says he'll be back to normal soon. As I said, he's brilliant when it comes to finding gold. If you like, I can approach him and pose the question to him."

She paused, afraid her growing excitement would turn Finch off Magnus. "Folks for miles around turned out to help

144

with the hotel so Mother and I could care for him. That's how much folks think of him." The next question was between Magnus and Finch and Barclay, but she felt responsible for him. "You would pay him?" She quickly added, "You won't regret having him assist you."

"He has bad teeth!" Missus Doctor touched a lit match to a wick on an oil lamp Em missed earlier. She crammed the chimney on the lamp and tossed the match into the waste bin.

Em gasped and pushed off from her chair. She grabbed the match from the bin and, with an exaggerated motion, set the match on the little metal tray. Turning on Missus Doctor, she fought not to shout. "Never place a match in the waste bin but only on the tray." She turned to Barclay. "That's how the two-story burned down six years ago and I lost my brother."

Missus Doctor waved her hand in dismissal.

Em's exhaustion extinguished any rising rage. "Getting back to Magnus, his hygiene doesn't affect his mining brilliance."

Barclay snorted, trying not to laugh. He ignored his wife's icy glare. "Does he know anything about this mine?"

"Actually, he does. My guess is he knows far more than Denton does—did. He worked it with my father. Father said he 'had a nose for gold'."

The clock ticked on the wall while Barclay considered Em's proposal. Finally he nodded. He looked at Finch. "Would you stay here and work with this Magnus?"

Em's heart lightened.

"Absolutely. I want to see what this mine has to offer. Otherwise, it feels like it's beaten me." Finch looked at Em. "If you would get Magnus in contact with Doctor Barclay, they could work out the details." He looked to Barclay for approval.

Barclay shrugged. "Nothing left to lose."

"Wonderful." Em clapped her hands together. "Doctor Barclay, under the circumstances, are you required to stay or can you leave when you want? I mean, with Denton being found near your mine?"

Barclay stiffened. "The sheriff did not order me to remain here. Thus, I have another engagement I will head for. We'll leave soon."

"Good," Missus Doctor sighed. "Back to civilization and a real hotel."

The Barclays rose from their seats, preparing to head to their room when the honeymooners Thomas and Florence entered laughing, interrupting the serious mood.

"Em, we need you to settle an argument. We have a bet about why there's a saloon in Placer. Tom says the Eighteenth Amendment doesn't apply out here, so it's legal and can stay open. I say it does apply out here, and the saloon will be shut down. Who's right?"

"Neither." Their smiles faded. Incredulity spread across their faces. Em forced a smile. "Prohibition does apply to Wyoming, so actually, Florence, you are more right."

"It's open! The police don't enforce the law?" Tom asked.

Em shrugged. "This county is about the same size as Vermont, more than nine thousand square miles. Law is scarce. The state legislature just voted to repeal Prohibition. No one's going to trouble themselves to close the saloon now."

"But I saw the law running around in the past couple days!" Florence said.

"Nobody cares about a bar up here."

Missus Doctor immediately complained, "And the law should have stepped in when there was a nude woman on the deck. How revolting," she proclaimed. "Who would do such a thing?" she sneered.

Florence blushed. "That was me," she admitted. "I'm sorry for offending anyone." She muttered, "I thought the area was deserted." She looked to Em. "It won't happen again."

Em felt bad for her, but she did boldly commit an offense to many people. Still, Missus Doctor should not have chastised one of her guests. Talking with the offender was her job.

"I wanted to talk with you in private," Em said. "That's my responsibility." Her words were a rebuke to Missus Doctor.

The spiteful looks shared between Florence and Missus Doctor would freeze a teaspoon of water then boil it into steam. Discomfort and tension grew thick. Thomas and Florence bid their goodnights and fled the living room. Soon after, Barclay declared, "Good night." They headed to their room as each glared at the other.

In silence, Em turned down most of the oil lamps. Relaxing in the darkened room, she sat on her chair. The room shook. *Is that an earthquake or am I going mad?* She rubbed her temple to still the trembling.

Finch knelt in front of Em. He held her hands, then pressed his lips onto her reddened knuckles. "I am so sorry for your loss, Em. But as bad as it is, I hope knowing what really happened will bring you some peace." His eyes welled as they gazed into hers.

Em slipped a hand from his and stroked his face. She pressed her face into his hair. "Thank you," she whispered into his hair. Her tears overflowed and she couldn't stop them. Tears fell into his hair. A sob shook her shoulders. Finch held her as the sobs took hold. She cried herself out.

She gasped for breath and leaned back to stare at the ceiling. Wiping her face with her hands, she managed to stutter, "I am so happy you'll be here for a while. With everything that's happened, you are my bright spot." She paused, then looked him square in the eye. "I hope you can stay for a long time."

Finch lifted a work-worn hand to wipe off the tracks of her tears. "I hope so too."

Em reconsidered containing her desire and emotions around Finch, to keep that wall around her heart and make herself miserable. Another tack popped into her head: she could simply relax and enjoy the time with him.

With a boost to her worn spirit, she made a decision. "I will enjoy you while you're here." Her boldness pleased her.

He seemed surprised at her openness, then delighted. "I will cherish being with you." He placed a soft kiss on her lips.

"Thank you for your support with Magnus. He does have problems from his accident — but it's all coming back. I see him improving. He's brilliant. He can help you a great deal."

Finch nodded. "I trust your judgment and look forward to working with him. It'll be interesting. I could probably learn from him. I gather he could use the job and the income."

Em nodded. "Since his accident, he needs help."

He sat back on his heels. Em stroked his cheek then lightly touched the welt on his forehead.

"I hate to leave you alone, Em, but I must go to bed." He looked haggard. "I wish we could lay down together." At Em's widening eyes he quickly added, "Not like that. I just want the comfort of holding you."

Em's face softened. "I understand." She did too. The thought of curling up beside him, absorbing his warmth, was the greatest solace she could imagine.

Finch rubbed her knees, delaying the inevitable. Finally, he patted her knees and groaned as he stood. Em stood with him. With his fingertips, he tipped her face up. Their lips met. His kiss was soft then became more urgent. He leaned into Em, but she shifted back. Finch understood and stepped back. "I'm sorry. I just ... I don't want to leave you."

Then don't, Em thought. *Don't ever.*

CHAPTER 23

Lander Gazette Local News
"Placer Claims" reported by Em Olson
June 2 – June 9, 1933
- Next year, the county roads superintendent will add gravel where soft mud traps vehicles at the Roberts Gulches. Herman Newbury is disappointed at the news as he charges to pull out stuck travelers.
- Walter Denton visited family in Salt Lake City for a week. Betty Denton remained in Placer City. Editor note: he returned to Placer City earlier than expected.

Em stood above Drunk Swede Gulch, peering at the wreckage of her father's truck. With a deep breath, she reached for protruding rocks to step onto the cliff face. Even under her slight weight, rocks skittered under her feet, throwing her off balance. She seized the nearest jutting boulder to stop from tumbling. Jagged edges scraped her palms. Falling rocks hit other rocks and the gulch echoed from the clattering avalanche.

Climbing down the thirty-foot-high canyon wall was easier than fighting through the mass of gripping branches of tall sage and stiff bitterbrush bushes with limbs like wire that tore clothes, tripped legs, and hid the rockfall that twisted ankles.

She pressed her cheek against the boulder but only for a second. The sun's rays bored into the gulch, heating the boulder that burned her cheek.

The still air amplified the collected heat in the gulch. Sweat tickled down her chest. With a big gasp, she pushed off and stepped to a large rock.

Below her, Deputy Collins quickly stepped from rock to rock, gripping the sages for balance, then jumped to the ground. A dust cloud rose and he swatted it away.

Stepping quickly, she seized the thick stems of nearby sages as if they were a lifeline. More rocks skidded down. Stiff sage branches scratched her calves and tugged her dress. By the time she reached the gulch floor, she had slid down the cliff as much as she climbed down.

Sheriff Brodie held out a hand and she gripped it for balance as she carefully stepped around the boulder field to the crumpled mass that had been her father's truck. Staring at the wreckage in disbelief, she tried to feel her father's presence, but couldn't.

"I appreciate your willingness in taking a look, Em," Brodie said. "It took a lot of manpower to get Denton's body out of here. Since it's tough going and the truck'll stay here, I only want to go through this once. Now, take your time looking. Maybe you'll see something we don't."

Em nodded. Brodie stepped to the wreckage, touching, poking, and jiggling truck parts. Collins squirmed his way under the twisted bed. After a muffled shout, he tugged out a small toolbox and added the box to a stack of tools and a decaying coil of rope.

Plate glass bits from the shattered windshield sparkled on the ground. Two wheels had splintered wood spokes. One wheel jutted at a right angle from the frame. The twisted hood exposed the wiring's chewed fabric covering. A thick dirt layer covered the interior of the bed and the cab. Animals had chewed the leather seat. Through the large gaps rodents had stolen much of the padding.

From the driver's side, Brodie yanked open the half-door and stepped to the cab's edge. Em pushed open the already ajar passenger door. Mouse droppings littered the cab's floor. Larger droppings indicated pack rats had scoured the cab for shiny objects.

Brodie said, "My guess is if the fountain pen was here, that rat's got a nice writing stick."

"Probably right, Sheriff. I sure would love to find it though." She craned her head to search for Father's rucksack. What remained of the yellowed operator's manual lay open.

As if reading her mind Brodie said, "My deputies have searched down here and up top for anything that may have been flung out when the truck went over the edge."

She poked a dirt-covered mound that turned out to be decaying rags. "I don't see anything."

Brodie grunted.

The sun and heat bore down, making her feel as if she weighed a ton. Grasshoppers flew in slow motion; even their clacks sounded heavy. Like her, Brodie and Collins dripped with sweat. Their shirts were soaked.

Straightening, she stepped slowly from the truck and studied the ground for anything that might help, hoping for a glint of the gold pen.

Em threaded her way back to the truck.

"Well, it was worth a try." Brodie grunted.

Not yet ready to give up, she leaned into the cab and felt all over the bench seat. Her hand reached under the seat bottom and up the small space behind the back. Her fingertips brushed a piece of fabric.

"Sheriff" croaked through her dry throat. She didn't dare to believe she found the rucksack. Pushing her skinny arm up until her muscles cramped, she seized a strap and yanked. Dirt and mouse droppings fell in a cloud, but the rucksack was mostly intact. With a cry, she held up her treasure.

"Well done, Em!" Brodie cried as he scrambled over the rocks and reached for the rucksack. "It must have gotten jammed up there when the truck rolled. Our thick arms couldn't feel anything up there."

Reluctantly, she handed it over. He placed the bag on the dented fender, untied the leather strap, and flipped the flap. Em and Deputy Collins crowded beside Brodie.

He pulled out a worn leather wallet. After opening the slots, he handed it to Collins. "Empty." Brodie paused. "Robbery?" he mumbled. He pulled out some papers with chewed edges. He reached in and scratched around then peered in. "That's all." He handed the sack to Collins.

He held out the papers so Em could read along with him. The top paper displayed large text: "Quitclaim Deed."

Brodie mumbled as his eyes skipped over the page. "Quitclaim ... patented claim on the Ember Mine ... includes all rights to minerals ... before me appeared James Olson and parties of the second part Walter Denton and Samuel Quint."

Oppressive heat bore down on Em. *So Denton does — did — own it. Now Betty does. Perhaps she can lengthen my loans.* She leaned against the truck door, staring into the heat waves distorting the distant hills.

Brodie flipped the first page. In silence he held out the second page to get Em's attention. The spaces for the signatures and notary's seal were blank.

"Ha!" Em cried. "It's not signed!"

Brodie held up his hand, interrupting her celebration. "Not on this paper, Em. This doesn't mean anything. This could have been a draft. There could be a signed and notarized document somewhere. Plus, we don't even know who initiated this document."

Deflated, Em waved her hand to cool her burning face. She turned toward the truck for another look.

Brodie flipped the second page to expose the third and last paper. His body stiffened.

"You'll want this, Em." Brodie's voice was soft, quiet. He held out the paper.

She gripped the crispy, yellowed paper. As Brodie stepped away, Em immediately recognized her father's handwriting, a flowing copperplate.

> *My darling Bea,*
> *I won't tease you any longer. Your avid curiosity about how I named the Ember Mine has caused me much joy:*
> > *Em*
> > *Michael*
> > *Bea (the center of my universe)*

> *Edward*
> *Rose*
> *May my choice make you happy and feel loved.*
> *Your loving husband*

~ * ~

Deputy Collins drove Em back to the hotel and slowly walked her to the door. She felt so drained she wobbled as she walked. The deputy lightly held onto her arm to steady her.

"I'm so sorry, Miss Olson. But at least you found his rucksack, although the sheriff doesn't think there's a clue as to who may have done this. But sometimes those tidbits can develop into real clues and solve the crime."

Em nodded. "Thank you. I'll do anything I can to find out who did this to my father—and to my family. Thank you for the ride home. If you'll excuse me, I must write my sister."

Her legs hurt so badly she could barely climb the few steps to the porch. She pulled open the door to her private space, desperate to see no one, not even Finch. She needed peace. She needed to think and to absorb all that's happened.

A door slammed upstairs. Em had come to know that slam. Finch, Barclay, and Missus Doctor were the only ones in the hotel since honeymooners Thomas and Florence checked out that morning on their way to Yellowstone Park. Grateful for their income, she was just as happy to have them gone. An empty hotel, well, except for Finch, was just what she needed. Talking with Missus Doctor wasn't something she could handle right now.

"When is my husband ready to leave?"

The voice's sharpness scraped Em's last nerve. She turned her face toward the stairs. She wanted to stay angry but didn't have the strength. "I wouldn't know." She turned back to her private space.

"Well, you saw him earlier. What did he say?"

Em stopped but didn't turn, thinking about his words about her father. "He said, 'I'm very sorry for your loss'."

153

She trudged into her bathroom and closed the door. If Missus Doctor was stupid enough to follow, she'd find the energy to add to the growing body count.

~ * ~

Em sank into her bathtub. The tepid water and the hard bar of soap cooled and cleansed the dirt and sweat from her overheated body.

In the peace, she thought about her long-held belief her father chose to leave, that he rejected his family and their livelihood, a constant source of stress and heartache for both women. His heartlessness caused her mother's stroke and ultimate death. Em suffered and overworked herself being alone and running the hotel. All this time, she'd been wrong.

She would have to pen a letter to Rose about their father's murder, soon, but right now she couldn't do it. She struggled to get her legs under her to step out from the tub. After drying herself off, she climbed into her bed. Within seconds, she slept the deepest sleep she'd had in months.

CHAPTER 24

The next day, Em counted out two dollars into Margaret Quint's palm. "Thank you, Margaret. You've been such a big help with the laundry and cleaning. The ad for help is supposed to come out this week."

"You're welcome. I'll wash the sheets and towels tomorrow." Margaret threw a glance over her shoulder and whispered, "Jeez, were you ever right about the mess in the Barclays' room."

"She never leaves it unless Doctor Barclay takes her somewhere," Em lowered her voice. "Once she leaned over the railing—like she always seems to be doing—I told her she was welcome to take a walk around town. She said 'too dusty'. I told her she could sit on the deck. She shrieked that 'jungle animals' stalked her."

At that Margaret groaned and leaned her elbows on the kitchen counter. "Let me guess: the dreaded man-eating chipmunks, right?"

"Pretty much. I told her she could sit in the living room. She said 'too boring'."

Margaret straightened. "Oh, for heaven's sake, you have a beautiful living room!"

"Thanks," Em said. "I felt like she'd slapped me. The only good thing is she stays in her room and out of my hair."

"Well, that explains why stripping the room took longer than it should. I've never seen such a cluttered room, so many clothes and fashion magazines I could barely move around the bed. She even had a small suitcase of cosmetics!"

Em stared at Margaret. "You didn't open it, did you?"

Margaret waved a hand. "No! It was already open. After that, I cleaned Finch's room."

Em's interest piqued. She forced a nonchalant, "Oh?"

"He's awfully tidy. He even makes his bed! He'd make a good catch for a girl, Em." Margaret nudged Em's arm as she tucked the bills into her jeans pocket. She was one of the few women in Placer City who wore pants. "Call on me anytime. I know you need regular workers." As she stepped up the few stairs in the kitchen she turned. "Stop by the saloon. I'll buy you a drink." At Em's wrinkled nose, she laughed then trotted up the stairs.

Em cringed at the thought of drinking alcohol. Once, her father and Michael goaded her to try a sip of whiskey. The alcohol shock and strong flavors made her gasp. The drops went down her windpipe. She coughed until she was hoarse. Her throat burned for what felt like days. Afterward, witnessing the destruction the spirits caused her family, she vowed never to go near it.

~ * ~

Em pushed back from her desk in her private office and slumped. The handkerchief at her elbow was sodden. The flame's glare hurt her eyes and gave her a headache. Her office seemed so dark despite the oil lamp's light shining on the paper on her oak desk.

The letter to her sister was the hardest she'd ever written, even harder than the letter she wrote about considering to sell the hotel, the family's heritage, to a prospector after Mother's death last fall. This writing would inform Rose about their father's murder. They would never know who did it or why.

She lay her head on the desk. Their father was a drunk, but he wasn't a hothead and he wasn't a cheat to cause someone to kill him.

Off in the distance a truck chugged down the hill and pulled into the driveway.

Finally, she lifted her head then carefully folded the paper and slipped it into the envelope.

The front door squeaked open. "Mail call!" The door squeaked closed.

Right on time, she thought as she lurched for the door. Lewis Roberts stood on the bottom porch step, Em's mail held at his side.

"Afternoon, Lewis. How was your trip up the mountain?"

Lewis Roberts' face was more somber than she'd ever seen it. The twinkle in his eyes was gone. "Not so fine, Em." He hesitated. "I heard about your father."

Em nodded and fought against bursting into tears.

"I am so sorry, Em. Jimmy was a good man." He studied her face. "I wish I knew what to say to make you feel better."

Em gave a slight smile. "I appreciate that, Lewis. I just have to get used to the idea. And help the sheriff solve it if possible. I wish Father could have controlled his drinking. Maybe this wouldn't have happened."

Lewis Roberts had been Placer City's mailman for thirty years, longer than Jamison Smith owned the Assayer's Saloon, and acted as father confessor to drinkers about their personal problems. Lewis knew more of the gossip around the region than anyone. He was a trusted counselor and source, but he was judicious in what he divulged.

Lewis paused as he fingered the remaining mail in his pouch. "Jimmy wasn't just drinking, Em. He was grieving. He was grieving not just the loss of Michael, it was the loss of Bea's trust and respect too. Hard to know which was harder for him."

He stared at the distant hills before turning to Em. His Adam's apple bobbed from a big swallow. "I heard about Denton. Can't say that's unexpected. Figured one of these days he'd get what was due him."

Em snorted. "I'm a Christian woman, Lewis. You know that. But there's a time or two I wished I had the wherewithal to pull the trigger myself."

Lewis nodded.

"I can't help but remember how he over-charged us for what turned out to be inferior materials to rebuild the hotel after it burned down. He didn't care we lost Michael or it took all our money and a big loan to rebuild. I've never hated a human being so badly."

She stared at the far hills as a memory rose from the deepest part of her mind.

"Em, you here?"

She blinked. "I'm here. I had a thought I hadn't recalled in years. I remember Father telling Mother that Magnus threatened to kill Walt if he didn't readjust the payment schedule on the hotel loan — that I'm still paying on."

Lewis grunted while he rubbed his chin. "Would Denton use that as an excuse to kill Jimmy?"

"Father never said what Magnus did, but Walt did make changes to the loan. Walt's hated Magnus ever since."

He grunted. "Interesting." A smile flitted. "Magnus." His smile broadened. He held out a small stack of letters. "Here's a letter from your aunt in Boston, among others."

"I'll trade you." She handed him Rose's letter as she clasped the small stack of envelopes. After a quick glance for a stamp, he stuck Rose's letter into his small pack. "I best be going. I'll be thinking of you, young lady." He turned to head down the path to his battered Model T pickup.

How that thing ran was beyond Em, but she knew Lewis wouldn't hesitate to push it on his route.

She tucked the mail under her arm and headed back to her office. She tossed the mail bundle on her desk and fell into the wood rocker that served as her office chair. Moments passed as all Em could do was stare at the stack.

She flipped through the return addresses. A few letters were from all over the country, most were from Texas where most gold prospectors originated.

The one letter she feared reading came from an formidable force in Boston. Aunt Dee, Sylvia's mother, had written. Em's heart rate quickened at the rapid response to her letter requesting to send Sylvia back.

Em reached for her letter opener, a knife blade her father had refashioned, and slit the letter open. She shook out the single sheet of paper.

> *Dear Niece,*
> *How disappointed I am that you were unable to reach Sylvia and change her behavior. Perhaps you should try harder. Have you told her what you expect, threatened her with sending her back if she did not do what you wanted?*
> *We are unprepared to receive her. Do you want more money? I can wire money if that's what you want.*
> *I know you love your little town, however broken down it is, but would a large donation to your little log church entice you keep her?*
> *Let us know your terms.*
> *Aunt Dee*

She re-read it before tossing the paper toward the back of the desk. "Mother, can you believe a mother would reject her daughter so?" she asked the paneled ceiling.

Em listened for words of comfort. Somewhere in the room, a log wall popped, followed by a series of smaller clicks. "I don't believe so either."

She kicked back in the rocking chair and propped her feet on her desk. Obviously, Aunt Dee didn't want her daughter and was willing to bribe Em to keep her. She considered responding she required a lot of money to keep Sylvia, but the fact Sylvia ran away made that idea wrong.

For all Em knew, Sylvia might show up on Dee's doorstep. Wouldn't that be a surprise, Em smiled to herself. The smile faded imagining the lies she would tell her mother: how cruel Em was to force her to run away, or how Em allowed guests to force themselves on her.

Em tensed, afraid Sylvia would tell huge lies and get innocent people in trouble.

She stared at the letter. She had a responsibility to tell Aunt Dee that Sylvia had run away. No matter how nonchalant Aunt Dee took her responsibilities, Em took hers seriously.

She reached for her letterhead paper and lightly traced the logo. She had the papers preprinted with the Olson Hotel logo and address years ago when the hotel was flush. Soon, she'd run out of both—letterhead and money—and she'd have to use plain typewriter paper.

Dear Aunt Dee,

The front door slammed open. "Our room is upstairs," Sylvia said.

"I can make money off these guests," a male voice said.

Em bolted from her chair, dashed into the entry hall then stood, slack-jawed. She stared at Sylvia, who had lost weight and the gash of red lipstick appeared to slice her face in half.

Sylvia smiled smugly. "Surprised to see me, huh, cuz?" She held up her left hand to show the gold band on her third finger. "Well, we're here!"

Stunned, Em automatically stepped back. She stared as Sylvia sashayed toward her followed by a slouching young man with long, stringy hair. He grinned slyly. A tobacco plug peeked out from his lower lip.

Em felt her stomach flop.

"This is my husband, Mark Cutler." Without thinking, Em held out her hand. Cutler leaped forward and kissed Em's mouth. She gasped and stepped back, repulsed.

"Oh, Mark," Sylvia laughed. "My husband's a kidder. I'm tired and I want to go to my room. Mark, get our bags from the car."

Mark grinned again at Em and turned to head outside.

Em regained her senses. "Stop!"

"Go, Mark," Sylvia said, insistent. Mark turned to head out.

"Stop! How dare you just show up like this! You steal my money, destroy my room, and you run away. I was worried sick. Then you show up married and expect to stay here as if nothing happened!?"

Sylvia tossed her head. "Yes. We're in need. You're supposed to help family."

Em advanced on Sylvia. "I tried to help you, but you would have none of it. Now I'm supposed to just take you back?" She shook her head. "You were so desperate to make yourself emancipated." Em indicated Mark. "Now, you are." She pushed past Mark and opened the door to indicate they were to leave.

For the first time, Sylvia seemed unsure. Mark turned to Sylvia. "You said she'd take us, that we could stay here." His voice accused her.

"You have to let us stay. There's nowhere for us to go," Sylvia yelled.

Em's eyes narrowed. "What you did was unforgiveable. You squander every opportunity you're handed. You keep taking and expecting more and giving back nothing."

In the silence, Sylvia paused. Her face reflected Em would relent, a realization that made Em even angrier.

Suddenly, Mark moved forward and grabbed her around her shoulders. "Oh, come on, cuz. You want us to stay."

Em shook off his arm. The alarm bells ringing in her head were deafening. "Don't ever touch me again." She faced Sylvia, knowing her face grew hot and red. She growled, "You wanted to be an adult. Act like one."

She reopened the door, and jumped as Finch trudged up the porch steps, returning from his workday. Finch also recovered from the surprise and smiled, which faded as he noticed the angry expression on her face. He nodded to Em. "Miss Olson." When he looked past her shoulder and noticed Sylvia and the unfamiliar young man, his eyes turned hard.

"Doctor Stone," Em said tightlipped.

"Miss Wartzen," Finch said through tight lips. Hatred boiled from his eyes.

"Missus Cutler to you," Sylvia held out her left hand. "This is my husband. Surprised! Yes, I can get a husband." She said too proudly, a dig at Em.

"Finch Stone," Finch extended his hand to Cutler. Cutler shook the hand, but seemed unsure how polite he was supposed to be.

In the awkward silence, Finch seemed to understand the tense atmosphere. "Well, good evening." He skirted the group, then slowly headed for the stairs. He exchanged a furious gaze with Em as he reached for the banister, but made no indication he understood what was happening.

"I said you are to leave now." Em's voice was quiet yet threaded with anger.

Mark said, "Sylvia said we could stay here."

"She told you wrong."

Sylvia pushed the door closed and turned back to Em. "We'll work for you. We have to stay until we get on our feet."

"You won't work, Sylvia. You'll make excuses again. And frankly, I don't feel comfortable having him here." She flicked a glance at Mark.

"And why don't you feel comfortable, cuz?" Mark again reached for Em, but remembered his action would be rebuffed. He dropped his hand.

"You take too many liberties with someone you just met." She turned back to Sylvia. "And you can't be trusted. You're a thief." She pulled open the door again. When Sylvia reached for the door to close it, Em slapped her hand away.

"Don't you slap her," Mark growled, advancing on Em.

"If she's lucky, I won't call the sheriff and have you both arrested for trespassing. If you don't return my fifty dollars I will have the sheriff arrest you for theft." Em said. "This is your last chance to leave the property."

"You don't have enough money to steal. I only borrowed your measly fifty bucks." Sylvia screamed. "Come on, Mark. This bitch won't give us a break."

Em's hand rose on its own accord and caught Sylvia across the cheek.

Mark dashed forward and caught Em by the throat. Em's mind seized with anxiety. She couldn't breathe. She pushed Mark back but he wouldn't budge.

"Mark, stop it!" Sylvia screamed.

Below the roaring in her ears, Em heard a slapping sound before Mark was yanked away. Mark's tight grip on her neck threw her to the floor before his hand released. As Em breathed in welcome air, she barely heard a thud as Mark hit the wall. Another smacking noise and Mark screamed as his shoulder smashed into the door's edge.

"You heard the lady. Get out!"

Finch's voice was loud in Em's ears. She managed to see Finch propel Mark out the door and tossed to the ground in a cloud of dirt. Puffing, Finch turned to Sylvia. "Leave on your own or I'll throw you out too. Your choice."

Without a word, Sylvia ran past Finch. He slammed the door closed and threw the deadbolt. Panting, he knelt beside Em. "Are you all right?" He stroked her throat with the lightest of touches. "Can you breathe?"

Em nodded, too stunned to speak. She held out her arms to him. She squeezed him tightly, afraid if she loosened her grip he would vanish. Her breaths came in rasping gasps.

They knelt on the floor for what seemed like an eternity. A purring automobile pulled up outside. Earlier, the Barclays had taken a drive for his last look around the country before they would leave the next morning.

Carefully, Finch helped her up and held her until she felt able to walk. He steadied Em to her office, away from the Barclays' prying eyes and ears.

Em's body trembled. *How much more can I take?*

Finch leaned over Em while they listened to the Barclays bang the door open then wander up the stairs. "I cannot wait to leave this dump," Missus Doctor said. "And I want to go to a real restaurant, you hear?"

"Yes, my chocolate-covered peanut."

The door slammed upstairs and Em relaxed knowing she and Finch would be alone for a while.

Em studied Finch's face. He returned her gaze. Her fingers traced the lines on his face then down to his chin, speckled with a day's growth of beard. Her hand smoothed straying tendrils of hair behind his ear.

"What are you thinking, Em?" Finch's soft voice enticed her to keep going with her touch.

Without wanting to, she burst into tears and fell into his arms. She gripped him. "I don't want to lose you, and not because you save me from mean men." She blubbered, wiping her face. She stared into Finch's eyes with desperation, pleading with him to agree with her, that he wouldn't leave her — ever.

Finch kneeled and laid his head on Em's lap. He wrapped his arms around her waist and sighed.

Em placed her hands on his head and stroked his hair.

A pounding on the exterior door caused both Finch and Em to jump, startled.

"I should let them go away." She continued to stroke Finch's hair until he straightened, grasped her wrists and reluctantly pulled her hands from his head. He kissed her hands. "It could be the sheriff."

Em closed her eyes, knowing he was right. She let him help her off the chair, and she staggered to the front door. Finch stood behind her at a respectful distance.

She opened the door to an agitated Sylvia and a smug-looking Mark. Sylvia threw up her hands in resignation. "Okay, okay. You're right. As always. I'll do better. Now, can we come in?"

Em stared at Sylvia, then at Mark. His smirking face, bruised from Finch's knuckles, froze as he looked behind Em and saw Finch staring back.

Saying nothing, Em closed the door and threw the lock. She turned around to see a small smile flit across Finch's mouth. "That's brave."

Em considered his words. "Not brave. I just can't tolerate her or her lies. And I don't trust him."

He held out his arms and she pressed into his chest. "You might have some trouble with them. They may try to wriggle their way into your forgiveness and your hotel."

Em nodded. "Perhaps. I'm concerned what responsibilities I have to her. She's family."

"Yes, and you are family." His voice grew angrier as he spoke. "How much is one family member supposed to take at the hands of another family member? It's about time you thought about yourself, Em. You help others, but no one seems to help you."

Em smiled a sad smile. "Except you. You help me. You help me a great deal."

Finch's face turned grim. "I'm not family."

I wish you were, Em thought as she pressed into Finch's chest. He kissed her cheek. *Oh, how I wish you were.*

CHAPTER 25

During the early breakfast, Em, Finch and the Barclays ate in silence. Missus Doctor seemed especially happy. Before breakfast, the Barclays spent much time packing Missus Doctor's extensive wardrobe. The wood floors creaked under their constant movements. Suitcases piled high on the Packard, but they weren't done yet.

"We'll settle up after breakfast," Barclay said.

Em nodded. His bill had been ready for a couple days now. The money would help pay expenses in the coming weeks. He hadn't mentioned her stipend for giving them information, but she wrote it on his rate sheet. If he were angry about the status of the Ember Mine, he had only himself to blame.

"Finch, I've been reconsidering. If you can't find anything in the next couple days, I need you to head to the Jewel Box Mine in Colorado."

Em froze. She felt cold.

Finch stammered, "I thought I was to remain here until all testing's finished. I suspect there's something there in that drift. I just have to find it." His face seemed pinched with stress. "Plus there's a lot of unexplored surface to look at."

Barclay shrugged. "I'm prepared to let go of the Ember. I've had enough trouble here. No offense to you or your fine hotel, Miss Olson." He tipped his head at Em. "Enough is enough, and I've had enough."

Finch chewed his biscuit then sipped a bit of coffee. "Magnus has been most helpful." He glanced at Em in acknowledgment of her advice. "I think he does have that 'nose for gold.' If you allow me to stay and pursue it, it might be worth your while, Clarence."

A snort escaped from Missus Doctor. "Well, aren't you getting along so well with the little cretin."

Em's face grew hot with rage. Finch studied Missus Doctor. "Virginia, he's brilliant. Have some compassion for his mining accident that hurt his brain. He's a good man, worthy of respect. If anyone can keep you in gold jewelry, it'll be him."

As Em's face turned back to its real color of cool, Missus Doctor's face reddened with embarrassment at Finch's chastisement.

Barclay grunted. "He's that good, huh?"

Finch nodded as he smeared his biscuit in the gravy. "He's that good. It's worth a look if you'll let me remain."

Barclay stabbed a piece of ham and stuffed it into his mouth as he considered. "What's the minimum time you need to make it a go or no-go?"

Finch sipped his coffee. "Two weeks. In that time, Magnus can fully refamiliarize himself with the mine. The accident caused a loss of his knowledge, but it's coming back fast. Plus, I can have samples collected and sent off. All we have to do is receive the assayer's report. One way or another, two weeks is the minimum of what I need."

Em held her breath. Two weeks was better than nothing. *Please say yes.*

Barclay covered up a small burp. His tongue bulged his lips and he sucked out food bits from between his teeth. He leaned his elbows on the table and affixed a stern look at Finch. "You have two weeks. Find the gold."

Finch nodded in decision. "Two weeks. Either way you'll know for sure."

Barclay pushed himself away from the table. "Let's settle up," he commanded.

Em said nothing as she stood. She followed Barclay to the hallway stand where she checked out guests.

She showed Barclay his rate sheet. For their almost-two-week stay, he owed her forty dollars for room and board and for her consulting fee—a fortune to Em. Barclay stared at the amount, and pulled out five ten-dollar bills. He tossed them on the stand then turned away. Em stared at the bills. "There's too much here, Doctor." She held out the spare ten.

"With your hospitality, and at great personal sacrifice, I fear it's not enough, my dear." He retreated up the stairs.

Em's breath came faster as she stared at the bill in her outstretched hand. Gathering her senses, she grabbed the rate sheet. *Could he think he was paying for Finch too?* She checked the sheet. The bill only stated the Barclays' stay, their meals, and for her information. He had checked it carefully.

Dipping the pen into the inkwell, she wrote "Paid" on the sheets, one for him and one for her records. She stepped into her office and carefully placed the cash into the leather envelope and her copy of the bill in her safe. She locked the door, spinning the dial several times and feeling a bit faint.

A heavy suitcase thumped on the stairs. She hurried to the hallway as Barclay stepped to the floor. "Doctor Barclay—"

Barclay held up a hand to stop her. "My dear Miss Olson, you have been a most gracious hostess—regardless of what my darling says. Be strong. Good luck to you."

He turned to leave then looked back. His eyes twinkled. "You can have Finch to yourself."

CHAPTER 26

Lander Gazette Local News
"Placer Claims" reported by Em Olson
June 10 – June 16, 1933
- A group of men stopped in at the Assayer's Saloon. From their discussion, the bartender said they were Ku Kluxers heading west. They caused no trouble except to several pints of beer.
- Herman Newbury reported a bunch of drunks got stuck in Big Roberts Gulch. He made them sober up before his horse team pulled their automobile from the mud and charged them double.

A week later, Em sat across from Finch at the dining table as they ate their first breakfast alone.

The morning Clarence Barclay drove his vehicle and that irritating Missus Doctor out her driveway, Em never felt so relieved. She felt excited to have Finch to herself.

That afternoon a knock on the door ruined that dream. A transient showed up at her doorstep. Sam Brady, a man as wide as he was tall, came to try his hand at panning for gold. He strutted like a gold baron who already owned all the riches in the country. His ignorance was clear. Em heard her mother's voice: "He has more dollars than sense." He'd heard in this area anyone could kneel and pan the nuggets that flowed down the creeks.

Finch spent most evenings in the living room explaining how placer mining worked, explanations that always met with quarrels from Brady. "I tried my hand at hard rock prospecting in California and it's not that way," he would argue. Finch, always patient though at times it was with great effort, would say, "This isn't California and we're talking about placer mining here."

After the second time at being chased off a claim by the business end of a shotgun, Brady decided Wyoming was not the place for him and headed to Utah where "the gold's so thick you trip over it on the way to the outhouse."

Em accepted his money then showed him the door, fully resenting this irritating greenhorn who had stolen her most precious time.

Finch poked at his bacon. He said little that morning. Em hoped he would talk as openly as he usually did regardless of the company. Perhaps he felt uncomfortable being alone with her now their time grew short.

"How's the bacon?" Em prodded.

"Good. As always," Finch's quick smile faded as he hung his head. His movements told Em he was either lying or something else was bothering him.

"Are you feeling alright?"

Finch nodded. He stared at his scrambled eggs. He looked Em square in the eyes. "I ... I'm almost finished with the Ember Mine." He left the statement flat.

Em knew what that meant. A cold hand gripped her stomach. She forced herself to breath normally.

"You'll be leaving soon, and not having found good ore." Em's voice was soft, afraid to speak too loudly for fear her voice would crack along with her heart.

"Yes, Em." He cleared his throat, trying to make his voice louder. "I haven't given up hope yet. There's still samples that have to be mailed. Magnus' memory is clearing all the time. His mind has started to work again. It's rather fascinating to watch him."

Em brightened. "That's great. For him. I hope he remembers something that will make the mine successful." And keep you here longer, she thought.

She swirled the scrambled eggs on her plate. "I've decided to change the kitchen. I've been thinking about what you said when we sat on the old bench on the other side of the creek.

It's time I made things easier on myself. That old water pump needs to go. Having modern plumbing would be a great help to the ol' arm." Em forced a laugh and gripped her right arm with her left hand and moved it into a pumping motion. "Modern kitchen plumbing! Who would have thought it?"

Finch smiled a sad smile. "Well, I can help you if you need a hand. I don't know much about plumbing, but I can try." His head dropped. "If I'm still here, to be honest."

The dash of verbal cold water washed over Em. She poked again at her eggs. She stole a glance at him.

Through the large window in the dining room, she could see Magnus trudging toward the front door. He always stopped by in the morning to fetch Finch. He always turned down Em's invitation to breakfast when she had guests. While Em enjoyed having Finch alone she worried what Magnus ate. "Magnus is here," Em said softly.

Finch pushed back from the table. "I'm sorry, Em. I can't eat this morning."

"I understand," Em whispered.

"The food was wonderful. The company even better." He planted a quick kiss on her cheek. "I'll head up to my room and get my stuff for today." He left without another word.

Em watched him step through the door. She sat for several moments at the table, feeling if she moved the warmth and touch of his lips would fade.

With a sigh, she stood to clear the dishes.

As she forced the pump handle down, she thought how much she would enjoy being able to turn on a faucet. At the Sage Restaurant she turned the handle on its kitchen faucet. To get that gush of water with a simple twist of a knob made her feel like she was inserted in a magic trick.

She stuffed the soiled dishes in the wood sink, then decided to let them soak. She had no energy for menial labor.

While seated at her desk, Finch's boot thumps upstairs announced his movements. She took an odd comfort in knowing he was in the hallway or back in his room. Reaching for her letterhead, she habitually tapped the pen on her front tooth as she decided who she would write first, her sister Rose in California about the release of their father's remains or her aunt in Boston of the latest developments concerning Sylvia.

Her sister needed to know of the findings of their father. Sylvia was now a married adult and no longer Em's responsibility. As she wrote the day's date on the letterhead, a pounding on the front door caused her to squiggle the date. Irritated at the error, she hurried to the door.

Sylvia stood alone at the foot of the steps. Em froze, not saying anything. Both seemed oddly content to stare at the other until Em felt irritated at the interruption. She slammed the door closed.

"Wait!" Sylvia cried out.

Finally, Em thought crossly. She opened the door and stood in the opening but said nothing.

"Aren't you going to invite me in?" An irritating whine threaded her voice.

"No."

Sylvia squirmed, unsure what to do next. "I'm your cousin."

"Yes." *Sadly.*

"You're not going to help me?"

"Excuse me? You're sullen and lazy. You lie. You accused a valued guest of improprieties. I had to trick you to admit you lied. You ran away like a thief in the night, which you are since you stole my money. Lie in the bed you made." Em panted as she ran out of breath.

"Oh, cousin, you forsake me?" Sylvia's voice was petulant.

Em's eyes widened. "You're married now. Go to your husband. Find a job. He can take care of you with my fifty dollars." Em stepped back, adding, "I'm writing your parents today. I will let them know what has transpired." She paused. "Do not return to my hotel."

She closed the door then stepped to the window where she could watch the front yard through the sheer curtains without being seen. Sylvia stared at the door, her face getting redder. She spun on her heels and strode to an old truck—actually a coupe that had been cut down to make it into a truck—parked almost out of sight from the front door. Mark Cutler sat in the driver's seat. From their gestures, they were arguing.

A moment later, Sylvia stepped from the vehicle, slammed the door, and hurried to the porch, clutching a wad in her hand. Jumping on the porch, she pounded on the door as Finch stepped down the stairs to head for work. As he turned for the door, Em held up a hand for him to stop.

Sylvia opened the door and screamed, "Here's your damn money!" She threw the bills at Em who involuntarily ducked. The bills fluttered like large confetti.

Em trembled in her rage. From the corner of her eye, Finch stooped to gather the bills. He smoothed the stack in his hands. Slowly counting the bills with grand hand gestures, he stepped toward her. "Fifty dollars, Em."

Forcing her voice flat she said, "You have repaid your debt. Hear me, Sylvia: if either of you return to this property I will have you both arrested for trespassing."

Em slowly closed the door as Sylvia's eyes widened in shock and threw the bolt. Trembling overtook her as she turned for Finch. He drew her to him. As they loosened their embrace, Finch held up the bills. "Your hard-earned money, my lady."

Her chuckle vibrated then cracked as she clasped the bills. Relief flooded her and her eyes welled. She had her money back and with any luck her cousin and low husband would never pound on her door again.

She and Finch slipped to the window to watch Sylvia's actions. She plopped on the truck's seat, waving wildly. Mark made an obscene gesture toward the hotel, started the old truck, then jammed the gas pedal to shoot out the driveway. The vehicle chugged up the steep hill toward Atlantic City. Before the vehicle crested the hill, Mark drew back his hand and backhanded Sylvia.

Em gasped. Finch grunted.

Should she should have relented? She was family no matter what, but Mark would be abusive whenever he didn't get his way, and Em would always be wary after he'd attacked her. The thought of him in her hotel was unacceptable. No, she had little sympathy for Sylvia and zero for Mark. Both were the type of people who burned their bridges before them then complained they had nowhere to turn.

Finch placed a gentle hand on her shoulder. "I'm sorry, Em, for so many things."

She nodded. Finch kissed her temple. He whispered, "I have to go." He patted her waist, unbolted the door, and he was gone.

Back at her desk, she contemplated the paper with the date. She decided to write to Aunt Dee while she still felt upset. With quick strokes of her pen, Em wrote about her difficulties with Sylvia and that she ran away to marry a boy. She was gone from the hotel. Em elected not to divulge about Mark's abuse or that Em refused to let them stay with her. That was Em's business about protecting herself, her hotel, and her guests. She pondered about including the news of Father, but right now she couldn't write the words. For years, most letters from her aunt contained a dig at Placer City, its residents, or Wyoming.

She decided upon: "I'm sorry the outcome is not more happy for us all. I tried my best." Em signed the letter then stuffed it into the envelope.

In the quiet, Em thought about Rose and their father. She penned the letter to her sister about their father's remains. She added their father would be buried in Placer City's cemetery just outside town to the north. Would Rose help with the costs of burial? The mounting costs were jolting.

Money from Barclay lay in her safe, but she'd hoped to use it to fix the kitchen. Money was tight though. Letters requesting reservations had dropped. A sign of the Great Depression, Em thought. She had money now, but later ...

Em wrote that she hoped Rose could come for a memorial service. She wrote all she knew. With a flourish, she signed her name. As she stuffed the envelope, she heard the mailman's truck chug into the driveway. *Perfect timing.* As she stood, her legs ached. The familiar pain returned.

"Mail call!"

"Afternoon, Lewis. How was your trip up the mountain?"

"Mighty fine, Em. Here's that Sears catalog you've been expecting. Got a letter from Rose." He held out a small bundle of letters and took the ones she offered. He flipped through them to ensure there was a stamp on each envelope. He jerked a thumb over his shoulder in the direction of Atlantic City.

"Thought I saw Sylvia in a truck heading toward Atlantic. Don't know if you knew that ... if you were still looking for her." Lewis was always respectful in his search for answers, yet had ways to get people to talk freely.

Em nodded. "I can't believe it, Lewis. She ran away to marry a boy, Mark Cutler. Do you know him?"

Lewis blinked in surprise. He ran his hand over his cap. "Nothin' good, I'm afraid. The Cutlers are rough. I can't imagine that girl got hooked up with someone from that crowd." He added quickly, "But maybe he's one of the good ones. There are a few who seem to be alright."

Em recalled the backhanded slap. She swallowed hard. "I can only hope. That reminds me, I need to let the sheriff know Sylvia's turned up so they can quit looking."

"Well, they know. Deputy Collins mentioned to me he found them in their truck sleeping at South Pass. They were using an abandoned cabin's outhouse and washing in the creek. I suppose you won't want that in 'Placer Claims'."

A snort escaped from Em's mouth. "Um, no."

CHAPTER 27

"Finch, your lunch is ready." Em placed the pail on the kitchen counter as he stepped through on his way to the mine. A wave of excitement to escape the drudgery crashed over her. "I see Margaret Newbury coming down the hill and I don't want to keep her waiting. Is there anything you need from Lander?"

"Just your sweet face coming back through the door," Finch smiled. "Have a safe trip and, Em, have fun."

Em smiled back as she whipped off her apron and hung it on the nail. "I should be back before it's time to start dinner, but if I'm not there's some sliced beef in the icebox and bread in the pantry. I hope you don't mind that."

"I'll just head for the Sage and eat there. A beer sounds good. Have a good trip. I'll see you this evening." He headed for the door.

Em dashed to her office and unlocked the safe. She reached for the leather pouch and flipped the flap. She breathed a sigh of relief that the cash was there. The shock of her cousin stealing her money hadn't yet faded. She reached for her jacket and her hat and purse. Grateful to be able to pay her property taxes and pick up some fresh food at the grocery, she stuffed the pouch into her purse.

At the Chevrolet's horn, Em trotted to the door.

~ * ~

Em waited patiently while a clerk with a nametag of "Jane" accepted Margaret's tax payment and wrote a receipt.

Margaret stepped aside while Em stepped forward. "Can't believe how much property taxes have dropped. We aren't worth what we used to."

"A mixed blessing," Em added as Denton's voice echoed in her mind about her debt exceeding the property's value. She placed the tax bill and the cash on the counter.

As Jane counted the money and wrote out a receipt, a thought entered Em's head. "I would like to verify the owner of record on another piece. It's five patented lode claims in one continuous group on a hundred acres, but specifically, the Ember Mine. It's to the west, about a half mile from this property." Her fingertip tapped her receipt. "I expected the tax bill for the Ember, but I haven't received it. I don't want to take a chance of not paying the tax."

Jane raised a finger. "Let me check the books." She stepped aside and hefted a large leather-bound book, beautiful with gilt lettering, and tried not to slam the heavy book on the counter. She gently flipped the large pages.

As Jane searched, Margaret leaned over. She whispered, "Are you going to transfer ownership of the hotel from your father to you?"

Em shook her head. "I'm not ready to proceed with probate." *It's just too soon.*

Jane's finger moved down the page then stopped. "I show James Olson owning that property. I show no change of title, such as a warranty deed or even a quitclaim. I show this address as the same as yours. You should have received the tax bill."

Surprised, Em said, "I've heard Walter Denton owns it."

The clerk's fingers tapped the page as she considered. "Perhaps he hasn't submitted the contract or quitclaim yet." She shrugged. "I've seen it many times, especially for the rural properties, the deeds don't come through for some time."

"But the tax payments on the property ..." Margaret said. "Have the taxes been paid?" She turned to Em. "If not, that could mean trouble. Walter could have snatched it at an auction on the courthouse steps."

Uneasiness washed over Em.

Jane stepped to a wood file cabinet and pulled open a drawer. Flipping through the card stack, she pulled out a card. "This is the list of tax payments on that property. The card also states James Olson as the owner. The taxes were delinquent last year, but the taxes are paid and caught up now."

"Well, if Em didn't pay the tax, who did?" Margaret leaned on the counter beside Em.

Staring at the card, Jane nodded. "Well, if Denton owns the land he's paying the taxes." She snapped her fingers. "Your man Magnus came in before the notices went out and paid the taxes. I gave him the receipt a few weeks ago."

~ * ~

Em thrust her arm out the Chevrolet coupe's open window and let her fingers flutter from the breeze. She closed her eyes and wished the wind would blow her to California, to sister Rose. *Was Magnus — my adopted uncle — not as loyal as he appeared?* Thinking the question made her heart hurt.

"You okay?" Margaret shouted over the wind noise.

Em shook her head.

"Don't read into it, Em. Magnus loves you. There has to be an explanation."

Em braced herself as Margaret pulled on the steering wheel, first in one direction then in the other as the coupe leaned through the tight corners of the Red Canyon road.

"It just doesn't make any sense," Em shouted back. "If Denton somehow owns the mine then why is my Magnus paying the tax bill?"

"Is Magnus working for Walt by any chance — hold on!" Margaret stamped on the brake, flinging Em against the dashboard. The car skidded to a stop. A red Angus cow stood in the road, chewing, staring at the vehicle. Margaret beeped the horn. The cow ambled away.

Margaret stamped on the gas pedal and Em's head snapped back as she was flung into the seat. She gripped the door's edge to hang on.

"I mean, it's possible, isn't it? Magnus worked the mine with your father. Maybe he's working it with Denton despite his brain injury."

Em stared out at the blood-red cliffs as they flashed past. "I don't think so, Margaret. I thought work stopped after my father was killed. Magnus was hurt about that time so I don't think he could have done much. From the tidbits Finch says there's been little sign of excavation. This makes no sense."

"But Magnus has been doing well. He works hard. There's no reason why he couldn't be working for Walt. And Walt had to have given him the money to pay the tax. Magnus just wouldn't pay it on his own. Plus don't forget, that's a big property, a hundred acres. There's plenty of land to explore besides the Ember."

As the coupe headed up the steep hill out of Red Canyon, Margaret downshifted. The coupe lurched. The grinding gears sounded above the wind noise. "But I'll agree with you there's a lot of things that don't make sense going on around here. My brother Bill's been doing a lot of assaying work for Walt. He can't seem to make up his mind if there's gold in that mine or not. Seems every time he's brought a sample it's either good ore or useless."

"Is he feeling okay?" As the vehicle turned sideways to the never-ending wind, the gusts blowing straight through the coupe loosened her hairpins. Tendrils of hair whipped at her face. A dirt cloud from the skidding tires blew in the window.

"He hasn't been himself lately."

Em braced herself against the dashboard as Margaret stamped on the brakes in front of the hotel.

"His business is in trouble."

~ * ~

Em and Magnus lifted a table and carefully hefted it down the narrow basement stairs. The table's legs caught the stair's doorways, and they struggled to maneuver it without losing their balance. They placed the table in its usual corner where it was stored. Em leaned on the table to catch her breath. Magnus, not even breathing hard, trotted up the stairs.

After a moment Em pulled herself up the stairs as pain gripped her thighs. She plodded into the kitchen, desperate for a break. "Magnus, want a cup?" She lifted the coffee pot.

He shuffled his feet. "I will … if you tell me what's wrong," he mumbled softly. He didn't meet her eyes.

Tension gripped her stomach. *Am I that transparent?* She reached for two cups and filled them. She set the pot back on the wood stove and stuck in a small piece of wood in the firebox. Magnus picked up his cup and held it under his nose, expectantly.

"I went to town today with Margaret Quint. I paid the taxes on the hotel. I checked the county records for the mine deed and it still shows Father's name even though Walter Denton told me he owns it." She gulped. "The clerk said you came in and paid all the taxes, including the back taxes."

Magnus swayed back and forth and hung his head. He sniffed as his thick mustache narrowed as he pursed his lips. "I'm caught then."

He set his cup on the counter and took a tentative step toward the pantry door. "I'll never lie to you, Em. I been working for Denton doing assessment work on his unpatented claims over by South Pass. You know about those: the owner of an unpatented claim must do a hundred dollars' worth of improvements every year to keep it." He paused. "And I been working for him around the Ember, the patented claim." He held out his hands in surrender. "I just did it to save up a few dollars, but I stopped when Barclay signed the contract."

Through the large window, Em watched a cow moose and her calf amble on the distant hillside. "I guess there's no crime or disloyalty for working for someone who owns a property, however much I think he is — was — a scoundrel. A man has to make money, especially in these tough times."

He hung his head even further. "Thanks, Em," he whispered. "I should have told you, but you already have heavy burdens."

She gave a grimace before giving him a small smile. Suddenly her brow furrowed in concentration. "He didn't get you to pay for the improvements on his unpatented claims, did he?"

"Ah, he tried. He's good at turning a man into a sucker." His mustache broadened as he smiled. "I'm a law-abiding man, Em. You know that. I figured since Denton owns most of the mines up here I figure he owns most of the equipment. I just relocated some of it."

CHAPTER 28

Lander Gazette Local News
"Placer Claims" reported by Em Olson
June 17 – June 25, 1933
- *Lewis Roberts, mailman to South Pass City, Atlantic City, Placer City, and Hamilton City will bring his Post Office district supervisor with him on his rounds.*
- *The annual Cowboys versus Miners football game will be played behind the Assayer's Saloon on August 5. Reminder: Since the Cowboys lost the game and the bet last year, they have to wear women's skirts, though they are allowed to wear the leather helmets.*

Wiping her hands on the dishcloth, Em sighed with satisfaction then tossed the rag on the counter. The breakfast dishes dried on the rack. The kitchen was clean.

From a distance, a sudden conversation of male voices floated into the kitchen. The voices seemed to come from within the hotel. Curious, she stepped into the dining room. The voices grew louder. Two men sat around her large desk in her living room.

"Here's the sample I pulled out of that drift." Finch held up a rock. He caught sight of Em and stopped talking. Bill Newbury, the assayer, sat upright into his chair.

"Oh, I heard voices. I wasn't sure who was here. I'm sorry to interrupt." Pleased Finch would be around her today, she said, "Hello, Bill. Can I get either of you some coffee?"

The men looked at each other. Bill nodded. Finch turned to her. "That sounds great, Em. Thanks."

She hurried back to the kitchen and loaded a tray with the fresh pot and cups. She skipped the cream and sugar since she guessed Bill took his black, as did Finch.

After setting the tray on the table next to the desk, she filled a cup and offered it to Bill. "You take it black, right, Bill?"

Bill nodded. "How're you doing, Em? I'm sure sorry about Jimmy. I respected him. He was a good man."

She froze, startled at the sudden mention of her father. A surprising warmth washed over her that Father wasn't the cruel man she had come to believe out of habit. "Thank you, Bill. He was." She brightened. "Yes, he was."

She poured a cup for Finch. His fingers brushed hers as he accepted the cup. "Thank you, Em."

As she straightened to take her leave she glanced at the desk littered with maps, geological and assayer reports, an old gold pan held black sand, and two geology books.

Back in the kitchen, Em strained to hear the men's conversation. Their voice tones were often even-keeled. Occasionally, Finch's voice rose. "The calculations are off for this drift ...," before his voice lowered and their discussion continued.

Moments later, Bill's voice grew louder. "That's not the right conclusion. Further up in the gulch it's so steep you have to climb like a mountain climber. There you'll find the proof dispelling ..."

Uneasy with eavesdropping and learning the man she cared for deeply erred in his work forced Em to head to her office. She stared at the increasingly smaller stack of reservation letters. With a glance at her calendar she realized the summer was half over. Winter arrived early in this country and reservations dried up even earlier. She reached for Father's letter opener and the top envelope.

~ * ~

Boot thumps approached through the kitchen, Finch's footsteps. Em knew their sound and cadence. The sunlight shining through the office doorway darkened as he leaned in. "Can I interrupt you?"

"Anytime." Her smile faded as she recognized the serious look on his face. "Is Bill still here?"

"He left some time ago. Could I buy a stamp from you and would you give this to your mailman?"

"Certainly." She reached for the loose stamps as he extended the envelope. "Good timing. Lewis should be here soon." She licked the stamp and as she pressed it to the envelope she noted the words "Mining Company" with a Salt Lake City address.

~ * ~

The hotel's front door pushed open. "Mail call!" The door closed. Em pushed back from her desk and headed for the front door. Lewis stood in his regular spot on the step. Behind him was a tall stranger, the regional postmaster she guessed.

"Afternoon, Lewis. How was your trip up the mountain?"

"Mighty fine, Em. Here's your coal bill."

She reached for the envelope he extended. "I'll trade you." He accepted her letters then flipped through the envelopes quickly. He always ensured stamps were affixed. In the stress of the past year she'd forgotten a few times.

He turned to indicate the man. "This here's Ed Wilson, my district supervisor." The slender man in trousers nodded.

"Oh, yes, I put that you'd be here in 'Placer Claims'. It's a pleasure to have you see what Lewis does for us. Welcome to our mountain."

Wilson sniffed. "I saw that piece. I wished you hadn't done that. People will act differently with the supervisor around."

Em noted his pale skin. "Oh, I wouldn't worry about it, Mister Wilson. Folks up here don't care about bureaucrats. But we do care about Lewis here."

At his widening eyes and with Lewis' hand hiding a smirk, she felt satisfied. As the soft summer breeze ruffled Em's dress, she felt a soothing sense of laziness, a feeling she hadn't felt for what seemed a decade. She stepped back. "Do you two have time for a cup of coffee?"

Lewis hesitated. As Wilson turned back toward the vehicle Lewis piped up, "You know, we do have time." He stepped in. Wilson stared at Lewis' back then followed. They headed to the kitchen.

Finch had returned the coffee tray, and set the cups in the wood sink and the coffee pot on the wood stove. *How thoughtful.*

Hefting the half-full pot, "Black, if I remember right."

"You remember right."

"Mister Wilson, black or cream and sugar?"

"Cream and sugar. Call me Ed."

Em stifled a small smile as she took the cream pitcher from the icebox and set the sugar bowl and a spoon before Ed.

Both men settled into the chairs at Em's peninsula counter. Em leaned against the wood sink. "How're you enjoying traveling with Lewis? Have you been up here before?"

Ed grimaced at the strong coffee. He took his time answering as he studied Em's kitchen. Oddly, the tension in his body seemed to release. He smirked. "You know I grew up in my grandmother's kitchen, which was very similar to this. I'd forgotten how relaxing it felt. And it always smelled good."

His face went slack as he stared at the stove. To Em he appeared to be far back in time.

With a blink, he waved a hand. "To answer your questions, this is my first time traveling with Lewis. I had no idea this region was such a tough route." He glanced at Lewis. Respect seemed to grow in his face. "A tough man taking care of a tough route." He slapped Lewis on the shoulder.

Lewis blinked in apparent surprise. He nodded in acknowledgement.

Ed drained his cup and set it on the counter. He placed his hands on the counter as if preparing to push back. "Do you mind if I take a look at your place?"

"Not at all." She held up her hand toward the dining room. "The dining room's there and through it is the living room."

Without a word, he pushed back and strode through door.

Em and Lewis exchanged a surprised look at the quickness of his warming up. Lewis leaned close to Em. "What the heck was in that cream? Until now he's been a solid stuffed shirt."

Em waved her hand to indicate the humble kitchen. "I see it all the time."

Lewis sipped his coffee. "How you doing, Em? I hope it's getting easier for you."

"Actually it is, Lewis. Thanks to you telling me about Father's grieving, I had an epiphany this morning how he really was a good man. I've thought only bad things about him for so long it had become a habit. It feels good to let all the bad things go."

"I'm relieved. Any word who might have done it?"

Em shook her head. "I doubt I'll ever know. The sheriff asked some questions, but I haven't heard anything. When I think about it for too long, the anger builds up, and I feel I'm going to scream."

"Folks are worried about you, Em. A lot of 'em say they'd be happy to see you sell out, now the hotel's yours. No one would think less of you."

"Seems like that subject keeps coming up. Sometimes I want to scream 'sold' on the spur of the moment."

He stepped to the woodstove to top up his cup from the coffee pot. "If you ever feel that breeze and do it, just scream to me. I keep my notary kit in my truck."

"Notary kit?" Em set her cup on the counter.

"In addition to the mailman, I'm a notary. I keep my seal embosser, blank quitclaim and deed forms, annual assessment affidavits, and mining claims on hand. You'd be surprised how many times I've been stopped by a prospector or someone needing a document notarized." He hesitated. "You know, maybe a trip to the Assayer's Saloon is what you need."

She stared at Lewis. "Never! I won't do that, no matter how angry I am." Ambling footsteps sounded from the dining room as the footfalls slowly headed toward the kitchen.

Lewis said, "Don't let absolutism rob you of the simple joys of life, Em." He glanced over his shoulder to make sure Ed was still in the dining room. "I'm a follower of profound quotes. My father said: 'Sometimes a stiff drink will do you more good than stiff knees while in prayer.' Here's another paraphrasing Mark Twain: 'Profanity provides a relief denied even to prayer'."

Ed stood in the doorway but faced into the dining room, studying it.

Lewis leaned on his elbows toward her. "The main thing for you to understand, Em, is what that dandy Oscar Wilde said: 'Everything in moderation, including moderation'. My view is anyone on either end of the swinging pendulum of life is where people make their biggest mistakes … and find their greatest sadness."

CHAPTER 29

Finch loitered over his breakfast. He often leaned back into his chair and studied the dining room. His eyes studied the oil lamps mounted on the walls, the sloping floor, and the hanging tapestry only she knew covered a damaged portion of the wall where the roof had leaked last year. "It's nice to see you so relaxed," Em said softly.

He smoothed the linen tablecloth. "Feels good to relax." He met her eyes. At a sudden thought he lowered his eyes. Em suspected the thought was he'd leave this ol' place soon. "Do you have plans for today?"

"Yeah, uh, since I'm done collecting samples and snooping around, me and Magnus are going to take the time to poke around. I find sometimes I need to step back and relax. Not focus on specific things. That's when I usually discover something or have a thought that changes the situation. You?"

"Actually, I do have plans for early this afternoon." She slapped her napkin on the table and fought back the giddiness. "I'm going to the saloon."

~ * ~

Pushing open the saloon doors, Em tentatively stepped into the Assayer's Saloon. Coming out of the bright sun into the dark interior, she couldn't see. The remnants of cigar smoke tickled her nose. The sour smell of beer made her sneeze. She felt, more than she could see, people staring.

Blinking, she could just make out Margaret walking toward her from behind the bar. "Well, as I live and breathe, Em! This has to be your first time here."

Em nodded as she tried to discretely wipe her runny nose.

"Hey, everybody, we got a virgin here!" Margaret yelled to the few men who sat around the back table playing cards. The men turned to study Em then turned back to their game.

"Margaret!" Em spun to escape out the door as Margaret grabbed her shoulders and pulled her to the bar.

"They know it means the first time someone's come in here, Em. Don't worry." She pushed Em to a stool and stepped behind the bar. Slapping her hands on the bar, she declared, "I've been wanting to say this to you for the longest time." She grinned. "What'll ya have?"

Em hesitated. She didn't know how to answer.

Margaret leaned on the counter. "How 'bout a root beer? On the house. It's a soda pop, but it has 'beer' in the name. It'll get you started down the road to hell." She slapped the counter before turning for the icebox. She expertly popped the cap off and set the dark bottle before Em.

Em took a sip. The chilly drink, its surprising flavor, and the bubbles felt wonderful in her mouth. "That's great!"

As she sipped, she focused on the room, dark despite the sun streaming in the small windows.

The paneled wainscoting was the same dark oak as the huge bar running the length of the room. Above the wainscoting, deep burgundy wallpaper ended in a yellowed pressed-metal ceiling. Thick dirt covered a hundred crystals hanging on the chandelier.

Margaret leaned forward and whispered, "So really, Em, why're you here? I'm glad you came in, but you've never been here before. What's changed?" Her face knowingly smiled. "It's that geologist, isn't it?"

At that last question, Em felt her face turn to fire. Margaret seized Em's hands. "That's it, isn't it? He comes in for lunch and a few other times. Only has one beer. He said he didn't want to overindulge before going to your hotel." Margaret slowly nodded her head as she spoke. "He is handsome."

Em couldn't meet Margaret's eyes so she concentrated on picking at the bottle's label. "He drinks, but he's a great man." She stared at the liquor bottles littering the back bar. "Yesterday, Lewis Roberts made a comment that got me thinking, how everything we do should be in moderation. That makes sense." She leaned her elbows on the bar as she thought. "I only saw the extreme, the damage that too much liquor did to Father, to Michael—gosh, my whole family. So I went to the other extreme, refusing to be around it, even sneering at anyone who might have a drink. I guess it never occurred to me good people—like Finch—can have a drink and it's okay."

Margaret straighten and lightly slapped Em's arm. "Well, good for you."

"Honestly I'd begun to think how low someone must be to even enter this place ..." She gazed into Margaret's eyes. "Even to work here. I was wrong. You're my friend. And if such a place is good enough for you, it's good enough for me," she said stoutly. "If I ever made you feel bad because I was so sanctimonious," she blinked back tears. "I apologize."

"Ooh!" Margaret stepped around the bar and embraced Em. She laughed. "Well, I'll start you on the road to hell, but you won't have to walk the whole way by yourself." She stepped back behind the bar.

"Lately, so many things have happened and been said to me that made me rethink a lot of things. And there's another reason why I wanted to come here. I've been thinking a lot of Father. He spent a lot of time in here." She paused. "Can I ask you some questions about Father when he was here, about the Ember Mine?"

"Sure."

"I remember Father saying he came in here when he 'struck it rich' at the Ember."

"Yeah. He did. I was bartending when he said it."

"Who overheard it and did you tell anyone?"

"Heck, everybody heard it. That's big news. Vaguely—that was a long time ago—it was busy, so a lot of people heard it. Besides, if he wanted to keep it quiet he wouldn't've announced it in a bar. We don't have confidentially here." Margaret threw her head back and laughed. "I know I told Sam. Of course, I tell him everything."

Em pondered. "And Sam works closely with Walter Denton." The local business connections and back room dealings started to line up in her mind.

Margaret shrugged. "Well, Sam may have told his sister, Betty, and Betty may have told her husband Walt."

Em sipped her root beer. The bubbles built up in her stomach. She pulled out a handkerchief and silently exhaled bubbles into the cloth.

"Were you here when Walt and Father had that fight back in April 'thirty?"

Margaret pffted. "Seems like I'm always here. Yeah. The place was jumping. Your father was drunk—as usual. He was sitting over there." She pointed at a stool along the bar. "Your father was talking garbage—and loud."

She indicated the stool Em sat on. "Walt sat where you are. He had about eight cases of beer in him. He yelled about how much better off Bea would've been with him 'than with a drunken worthless bum'."

Em closed her eyes.

"Yeah, bad, huh? Your father hollered, 'She saw I was better than you.' Well, Walt yelled, 'Yeah, *was* being the key word.' Boy howdy, the cussin' started, the stools went flying, and the fists came up. Then Walt's gun came out."

Margaret arched a thumb behind her shoulder to indicate the cracked mirror on the backbar. "That's how that got broken. The bullet passed through your father's arm, then hit the mirror."

"I can't believe they'd fight over Mother." Em sipped her root beer.

"Are you kidding? You didn't know how bad Walt had the hots for your mother when they were young? He was crazy

191

about her—I mean *crazy*. Walt really wanted Bea. He'd beat up men who tried to get close to her. I even saw him grab his gun and chase one guy!"

Staring into the depths of the bar she muttered, "When she married your father, he settled for Betty. Walt's hated your father ever since."

CHAPTER 30

The willows swayed in the soft breeze. Talcum-like clouds poofed with every step on the dirt road. Em paused at the footbridge across Quartz Creek. She smiled at the story of Pauline Highsmith surprising a moose in these willows and smacking her with her handbag.

She let the peace the rugged country exuded wash over her. Leaning against the rail, she stared into the creek's clear, slow water. Tiny brown trout darted for the eddies shaded by the willows. She didn't know how long she stood there when a large automobile drove past then pulled into her drive. With a sigh, she pushed off from the rail and stepped onto her yard.

Samuel Quint stepped out of the late Walter Denton's Chevrolet Deluxe Coupe. Slamming the door, he sauntered toward Em. "Well, Miss Prude, whatya say?"

His taunt infuriated Em. She stepped onto her porch and opened the door.

"Now, now," he tried to soothe her. "This is business. You're a businesswoman. I'm a businessman. We can discuss this rationally." He reached for Em's arm, but she moved her arm back, giving distinct notice of "don't touch me."

"If you're a businessman, then act like one. I don't appreciate your rudeness, and I could slam this door in your face right now." Em's tight voice allowed the hatred of this man to come through. She trembled with anger.

He held up his hands in submission. "Okay, okay. Miss Olson, I wish to discuss my desire to purchase this hotel." He extended his left arm up and swept his right arm in front of his stomach as he bowed.

By attempting to be businesslike, his sarcasm made matters worse. "Mister Quint, if that's the best you can do, you give me no choice but to tell you no. I will not conduct business with a man who has no respect for me or my establishment. Good day." Em stepped back to close the door.

"I will offer you a sum this place is worth," Samuel called out to the closing door. "Eight thousand."

Em pulled the door open slightly. "I have real plumbing and forty acres here!" She hesitated. "Respect given is priceless, Mister Quint." She started to close the door, but slower this time.

"Fine. Ten thousand dollars. Final offer." Samuel's voice faded as Em closed the door. "Cash on the barrelhead."

She pressed against the door as if to prevent it from opening on its own. Her soul screamed "sold." She covered her face with her hands, and a loud groan escaped her open mouth. Against her back, someone pounded on the door. She gasped and spun to open it.

Samuel held up two fingers. "This offer's good for two weeks, Miss Olson. After that, it's gone." He bowed an exaggerated bow and turned away.

Em closed the door, gasping for air. She stepped aside to the window and watched Samuel pull open the coupe's door. He fell into the driver's seat. Em squinted, curious as to who was with him.

As Samuel spun the coupe around in her driveway the sun reflected off the hood's chrome air inlet covers. She winced and blinked.

Adjusting her hat was his sister, the widow Betty Denton.

~ * ~

Em felt distracted for the rest of the day. She remade her bread dough because she put in the wrong ingredients. Ten thousand dollars! Well, she still owed over five thousand dollars on the loans for the patented claim and the hotel, but she would be free from the hard work and stress of the hotel. If Betty and Samuel—and his wife Margaret—worked together, three people running this hotel would handle the load so much easier.

She'd have the money to do what she wanted. *Maybe even follow Finch.* The thought caused her to pause. *Would I actually follow a man? Would he even want me to?* Finch was a single man, used to traveling and meeting young women such as herself in the many hotels he stayed in. *Would he want an entanglement?*

Focus Em, she told herself, as she turned to the dough.

A pounding on the door startled Em. *Now who?* She wiped her hands on her apron as she hurried down the hallway to the door. An unknown man in a uniform stood on the porch.

"Telegram for Doctor Stone," the man called out in a no-nonsense, official tone.

"Doctor Stone's staying here at the hotel, but he's out in the field right now. Do you need to talk with him or shall I sign for it and give it to him when he returns?" Em asked. She had never signed for a telegram, but recalled her mother's spiel to the deliveryman years before.

"You may sign for it. Just give it to him as soon as he arrives." His official tone never wavered as he held out a clipboard for Em to sign. He handed her the envelope. With his index finger, he touched the bill of his cap in salute before he climbed into his Model A pickup. The vehicle chugged out her driveway.

Em studied the envelope. "Western Union" was boldly printed at the top. On the front, "Doctor Fincelius Stone, Olson Hotel, Placer City, Wyoming," was scrawled in pencil. She turned the telegram over and read the sender: "Doctor Clarence Barclay."

Curious, Em lay the envelope on the flat-topped post at the foot of the stairs where he would see it. Her stomach churned at what that telegram might contain.

CHAPTER 31

The front door slammed closed as Em removed the browned biscuits from the wood stove's oven.

"Finch, there's a tele—" She froze at his grave face as he stood at the bottom of the stairs, staring at the telegram in his hand. He flipped over the telegram to read the sender.

Em swallowed hard, not wanting to pry. A tremble spread throughout her body. "Dinner will be ready in a few moments," she called out, not knowing if he cared or even if she did.

Finch barely nodded as he went up the stairs. His steps were slow, exhausted. To Em he looked like he lost everything he had in the world. He hasn't lost me, she thought.

She busied herself placing the meal on the table. Perhaps the telegram stated Missus Doctor left for a junket to Timbuktu and Doctor Barclay would return to the hotel immediately. Perhaps it was as simple as that.

With the table set and the food steaming on the table, Em had nothing to do but wait. She watched the steam rise and twist in the slight draft from the open windows. She forced herself to become mesmerized by the vapor.

Footsteps tromped down the stairs, slowly. Em's heart turned over, afraid of what Finch might say.

He trudged into the dining room and pulled out his chair. He hesitated then sat as Em stood to dish out his meal. She didn't want to act as if he owed her an explanation of what was in the telegram.

"Thank you, Em," Finch muttered.

"You're welcome, Finch," Em muttered back.

They ate in silence while Em stole glances at Finch. Through her eyelashes, she could see he stole glances at her.

Finally, she couldn't take the tension any longer. "How was your day?"

Finch chewed and kept his eyes fixed on the stew. He took a deep breath and set down his spoon. "Not good. Magnus seemed to go crazy, like he had a horrible memory and lost control. He ran screaming into the hills."

The spoon fell from her fingers and clattered against the bowl. "I've never heard of such a thing."

"I spent all day trying to find him. Your mailman, ..."

"Lewis Roberts."

"Roberts happened by. He pointed out where Magnus may have run to, Magnus' 'safe house' he called it. I found it—after about an hour walking. He was curled up in the corner, whimpering. Kept mumbling … I think he said, 'Shot … Denton … Denton'."

Finch reached for another biscuit, but studied it like a rock. "Don't know what 'shot' was. I finally got him out of this … delusion, but he was in poor shape and so was I. We managed to get back to the Ember. That's why I'm so late. I've never seen such a thing." He stared at the biscuit.

"Did you bring him home?"

Finch nodded as he split apart the biscuit and slathered on butter. "I walked him straight to his cabin and he yanked out a whiskey bottle by the front door. Said he needed to think. That bottle's empty 'bout now I'm sure."

"How are you?"

Finch sighed. "My bottle's going to have a dent in it tonight." He flinched with a sudden thought. "I'll take it down the road."

Em waved her hand in dismissal. "You're welcome to drink in your room."

He blinked in surprise at her permission. "Thanks. I appreciate that. It was horrifying. I pity the man. I can't imagine what he's been through to have a reaction like that."

"What do you think set it off?"

Finch chewed while he recalled. "We were above ground near the shaft to the Ember." He leaned back as he thought. "I heard a distant explosion at a mine a couple hills over, either a small explosion above ground or a large one deep in a shaft. I turned to Magnus to make a comment. He had this oddest look on his face. He started screaming and ran off. It happened so fast."

He stared at the wall as he thought. "Do you think there's any potential Denton killed your father, Magnus saw it, then Denton set off the explosion that caused Magnus' problems? And being in that spot and hearing that explosion at the right time triggered his mind to remember?"

Em gasped. "I hadn't thought of such a thing. We had always thought the explosion was an accident!"

"Well, maybe it was. I'm just conjecturing." Finch stuffed the biscuit into his mouth. "It would explain a lot. You said Magnus always helped your father."

"Yes!" Em cried. She pushed back from the table in her excitement. "If Magnus was there when it all happened that does explain so much!" She turned to Finch. "Do you think I ought to notify the sheriff?"

He shrugged. "Wouldn't hurt. Perhaps with a doctor's questioning, Magnus might recollect something."

"I'll do that as soon as we're done eating." Em stopped. "Well, I have to figure out how to notify the law. Magnus has always been my runner for the hotel. I can't send him on Rosybud to the sheriff so he could be questioned."

Faces ran through her mind of who might deliver a message. "Jamison Smith ... no. Lewis Roberts. He'll come by tomorrow and I'll ask him to notify the sheriff. That'll work." Em pulled up her chair and began to eat with relish, excited over what may become of this latest revelation.

At the end of the entrée, Em stood to clear the dinner dishes and fetch the mincemeat pie she baked that afternoon.

She cut two large slices and returned to the table. She set one plate in front of Finch then walked around to the other side and sat. He stared into the distance as she waited. With slouching shoulders, he dug into his slice. In an unsettling silence, she stabbed her own slice.

They ate with a few appreciative groans from Finch. As he chewed his last bite of pie he placed his elbows on the table. His head hung low as he stared at the empty plate. He took a sip of coffee Em poured for him. "Thank you," he muttered.

"You're welcome."

"You, uh, you didn't ask what was in the telegram." Finch looked her in the eyes.

"I wouldn't ask. It's none of my business."

Finch cleared his throat. "Excuse me." He patted his chest and took a deep breath. Her breathing came faster and she feared what he might say.

"The telegram was from Clarence Barclay."

Em nodded.

"He has changed his mind about giving me more time on the Ember Mine. I'm to go to Salt Lake City to collect all the assayer's reports then go to him in Colorado.

"I'm to leave tomorrow."

CHAPTER 32

As the sun set and the light faded, Em made no move to light the living room's oil lamps. They seemed content to enjoy their final evening in deepening darkness. On the couch, they sat tightly pressed together. Either they held hands or Finch draped an arm over Em's shoulders. She didn't want his last looks of her to be a weepy mess, and she fought hard not to cry. She couldn't talk for the tightness in her throat. A lone tear would course down her cheek. Finch constantly apologized when she wiped away a tear. As they murmured about nothings, at times his voice broke.

She considered asking him if she would ever see him again, but she didn't want to hear the inevitable "no." With a deep breath, she decided to simply take what time he could give her. That was all she had. "I cherish this time with you, Finch." She pushed away from his chest and studied his face in the dim light. A smile suddenly crossed her mouth. "You've been the best guest I've ever known."

~ * ~

Breakfast had been sumptuous. She wanted him to remember the delicious breakfast and the full lunch pail she packed for him. Neither said much during their meal. There was nothing to say.

As Finch lifted his bags into the truck's bed she'd never seen him move so slowly. Finally, "I have to settle up."

In the hallway, he studied the rate sheet. Em couldn't speak or she'd burst into tears. He set the cash on the stand and grinned a small smile. "I feel really odd paying you when I feel the way I do."

With a quick smile she whispered, "I understand." She quickly counted the bills—a habit—and wrote "paid" on the copies. She held out the extra bills to him. He shook his head.

Em tried to protest. "That's a lot," she whispered of his huge tip. Finch's eyes held hers. "Miss Olson of the Olson Hotel, you are worth far more than that." He kissed her lightly, softly. His soft lips caressed hers.

He held his hand on her shoulder as they walked out the door and down the porch. At the driver's door, he turned to her, his eyes welling. At his emotion, Em's throat tightened and tears blurred his face.

He cupped her face and pressed his cheek into hers. "You're the finest woman I've ever met," he whispered. A soft groan escaped. He kissed her cheek then turned away. Without another glance, he climbed into the cab, started the Ford, then drove out the gate.

The control on her emotions released and sobs shook her shoulders as she watched him drive the steep hill toward Atlantic City.

As he crested the hill, his left arm extended out the window and up in salute.

~ * ~

Em stared at the hill, trying not to comprehend he had gone. Slowly she turned back to her hotel. In the silence of the morning the weight of being the only person in the world nearly staggered her.

She lurched into the kitchen. Leaning against the counter, she wept as if her broken heart would never mend. There was nothing she could do for it. She fell to her knees. Her shoulders shook with the agonies of a lifetime. How long she knelt there, she didn't know or care.

201

Finally, her knees began to hurt. She shifted to sit on the floor. She hugged her legs while she stared at the wood stove that stood there, solid and dependable, for decades.

She closed her eyes and touched her lips as she remembered their last evening together. Recalling the warmth of his lips caused her to weep. The handkerchief she stuffed in her sleeve grew sodden. Struggling to rise from the floor, she tottered to her bedroom. She pulled out a fresh handkerchief and sank into her bed. Soon that cloth was in the same condition as the first.

With a loud cry, Em threw the handkerchiefs as hard as she could. She panted as the cloths fluttered to the floor. She shoved herself off the bed.

"Keep busy," she yelled to the empty hotel. Em purposefully stomped her feet as she headed for the porch, forcing herself to enjoy the morning's fresh air. She allowed herself to stare up the road, hoping against hope to see his Ford pickup crest the hill.

A vehicle—a Ford pickup—crested the hill. She held her breath before she recognized Lewis Roberts' older, boxier pickup as he descended the hill and turned in her drive.

She wiped off the dried salt streaking her cheeks. Her face was puffy, red, she knew; her eyes were swollen and she didn't care. She dully watched him as he gathered her mail and stepped toward her. He gave a wave. "Mail call!"

"Lewis. How was your trip up the mountain?" Her stuffy nose betrayed her forced happy voice as she breathed through her mouth.

"Mighty fine, Em." He approached her as he scratched in his mailbag. "Got a couple 'Placer Claims' for you. Pauline's putting together a recital of music and patriotic essays on the Fourth of July.

"Now for the really big news: Jamison Smith sold the Assayer's Saloon ... to Margaret Quint!" He finally found the envelope he sought and extended it. He froze at the sight of her blotchy face. "Em!"

She reached for the envelope. "Rough day. Coffee?"

They walked into the kitchen and Lewis sat at the counter. Em reached for the coffee pot and poured them both a cup. She cut two large slices of pie and slid a plate in front of him. They sat silent while Lewis stabbed his slice. Em poked hers with the fork.

Halfway through his pie Lewis said, "Ran into Doctor Stone on his way out of town. He asked me to make sure I stop and talk with you before heading out of Placer." He stabbed the slice and paused. With a glance at Em's face he seemed to understand.

Em swallowed hard to prevent herself from weeping at the sound of his name. She nodded. *How kind of him.*

Talk or explode. "Big news about Margaret owning the Assayer's, huh?" She stabbed the slice and swept a piece in her mouth. The bite tasted like cardboard and she swallowed hard. "She'll do well at it."

In silence they ate.

She finally felt strong enough to tell Lewis what Finch and Magnus endured yesterday. "I can't help but wonder if Denton may have been the one to kill Father and set off the blast to kill Magnus too, but that failed. And Father's gold fountain pen is missing. It wasn't on his body and it wasn't in his truck or left behind here in the hotel."

Lewis stared at Em, the pie unchewed in his open mouth. Em wondered if he thought she were crazy. Mechanically, he chewed the pie.

"Lewis?"

"I'm dashed, Em, but not just because of what you suspect." He turned to Em. "I remember that day clearly because I saw Denton. Now, normally I wouldn't remember a certain person on any certain day but I remember this because Denton clearly didn't want to be around me. He was angry, jittery. He tried to hide a gold pen. I asked to see it. He refused. 'Get along with you, mailman.' I kept needling him. He was very nervous and twice he dropped it. All of a sudden he was too polite, almost bootlicking, something I've never seen out of him before. But what really makes it stick in my mind was right before I ran into him I saw the explosion cloud at the Ember—"

Both stared at each other. Em shoved herself off the stool and paced the floor, unable to control herself. "Oh, my God. Oh, my God."

"Now, Em, there's no telling what all this means. Likely nothing," Lewis held up his hands in warning.

"I know you're right. And even if we were right, I don't know how it can be proven. Would you notify the sheriff for me? Finch—Doctor Stone—said Magnus was in too bad a shape to ask him to go."

Lewis turned. "I'll go fetch him right now." Without another word, he grabbed the remaining section of the slice before he dashed out the door.

~ * ~

Em paced the floor while she waited for the sheriff and tried not to think of Finch. *I have to do something or I'll go mad. Think.*

She had no guests to prepare for, and the rate money and tips Barclay and Finch left ensured she had enough money to last for weeks.

Finch appeared in her mind. She closed her eyes and moaned as his lips touched hers. His hands on her back pressed her into his chest. She breathed in his scent. The warmth of his mouth felt so real that when she opened her eyes she was shocked he wasn't standing before her. Her fingers brushed her lips. Finch was gone.

Suddenly, smoke choked her throat as the memory of Michael's body being removed from the smoldering ruins of the two-story hotel seared into her brain. Sweet, funny Michael was gone.

Then Rose's screams as she raced out the door, chased by their drunk and cursing father, echoed in her mind. "Rose!" The name burst from Em's mouth in her great need for her sister. Rose was gone.

Gasping for air, Em followed the horse-drawn wagon bearing Mother's coffin on the rocky two-track to the cemetery at the top of the hill. Mother was gone.

Em had sworn her father's abandonment killed her mother when the whole time he lay dead, cruelly murdered, hidden and buried in a mine. Father was gone.

Her fists clamped to her head to block out the streaming images. She screamed with all the force she could muster to give the pain a chance to escape. Her fists struck her head as the images refused to stop. Her screams faded to wailing.

Raising her head and gasping for breath, she stared at the sink and the pump. The handle jutted out at a right angle from where she lost the energy to press it. *That damnable water pump.*

Rage gave her strength. She snatched the empty coffee pot. Lifting the pot over her head, she swung the pot and smashed the cast iron pump, again and again until the pot crumpled. With a grunt, she threw the ruined mass into the pantry.

Groaning loudly, she reached underneath the cabinet to wrench the rusty inlet handle closed. Before her power gave out, the handle turned. She shook out her strained hand.

Screaming at the ceiling as if all her cares hovered above her, she ran to the storage closet and grabbed her father's hammer and chisel from the tool box.

Stabbing the chisel as hard as she could behind the counter and the backsplash, she hammered the chisel deeper. As the backsplash came loose, with a cry Em yanked the splintered wood to expose the counter carcass. The pump's cast iron and galvanized drain refused to yield to her frenzied pulling.

"I'll get rid of you if that's the last thing I ever do!" She ignored the loose hair sticking to her sweating face and hammered the drain and the supply line until they shattered.

Wheezing for air and with her strength fading, the counter loosened and she gave a huge yank. Fueled by her anguish, the momentum and weight of the pump, the broken drain, and the countertop flung her across the room, sending her crashing to the floor in front of the stove.

She gasped at the dirt cloud and waved her hand to keep it away from her face. For minutes she lay on the filthy floor sneezing and coughing as the grime settled.

She sat up to survey the damage. Splintered wood, drain pieces, and the pump lay about her. She kicked them away.

Leaning against the wall, chuckling, an oddly self-satisfied feeling swept over her.

Despite the hammering and pulling, a white envelope stuck to the wall where the backsplash had been attached.

Curious, she struggled to her feet then stepped over the debris. She tugged on the envelope. A dot of paint had dribbled behind the backsplash where Em painted the wall the past winter. Trying not to tear the paper, she peeled it off.

Staring at the envelope, she recalled her mother reaching for this very envelope. That was the day they returned from Lander and were unloading the new sink and faucet and groceries. Mother called out to Father they had returned from town. The envelope had been tucked into the top edge of the backsplash. As she reached for the envelope a sudden pounding on the front door jolted Mother's touch and the envelope slid behind the wood.

Breathlessly, an anguished Herman Newbury told them of Magnus' accident and his dire condition. Through the following traumatizing days filled with caring for Magnus and realizing Father actually carried out his threat to abandon them, she and Em promptly forgot about the envelope.

Em unfolded the flap, expecting a reservation request or a guest's note. She tugged out three papers. Two were official-looking documents, complete with raised seals. The other was a hand-written note Em instantly recognized as her father's copperplate, though she also recognized the scribbles of his drunken haze.

She swallowed hard as she stepped back in time.

My Darling Bea,
You had been so adamant about getting a new pump and sink I knew you would find this.

First, drink has seized me and makes me say things I don't mean. I would never leave you despite what I say in my grief. Forgive me. I don't know how to release its hold on me.

Walt and Sam are after me to sell them the mine — as you wish it gone. They're pressuring me to turn the mine over to them for less than what I know is its real value.

Here are the deeds to the hotel and the patented claim. With you, they're both safe now. Walt and Sam can't get to the mine without going through you. The decision to keep or sell your portion of the mine is yours alone.

I believe in my heart with the Ember Mine you can have the splendor you deserve. Em can hire workers to do her bidding whilst you become pampered.

Your loving husband,
Jimmy

Her legs refused to hold her and she sank to the floor. She stared at the papers clenched in her trembling hands. She looked closely at the quitclaim deeds to the hotel and the Ember Mine's patented claim. Her hands shook so badly she could barely make out any words. She fingered the raised notary seals. Her eyes welled as she stared at her father's signature.

The light of reality blinded her: that's why Sam Quint and Walt Denton wanted the hotel so much. They were looking for these papers!

She stared into the ruined kitchen as the sun set and thought until darkness hid the damage. Em pushed herself off the floor and leaned against the damaged counter. A thought to run after Lewis Roberts to tell him the latest news entered her mind, but prudence kicked in. Lewis was long gone.

She struck a match. At the oil lamp mounted on the wall, she touched the tiny flame to the wick. The flame cast a soft glow on her kitchen. As she replaced the glass chimney, she squared her shoulders.

They'll pay a huge price for it.

CHAPTER 33

Lander Gazette Local News
"Placer Claims" reported by Em Olson
June 26 – July 3, 1933

- Businesses are set to change hands this week with the new owners intending to reopen in the coming weeks.
- Pauline Highsmith has recruited several local children to put on a program of music and patriotic essays at the Sage Restaurant on the glorious Fourth. A carry-in will follow with the Sage Restaurant providing the baked ham and beef.

Three days later, Lewis Roberts stared at Em with an intent gaze before she pushed open the screen door to let him in. Behind him, Samuel Quint shifted from foot to foot. His sister, the widow Betty Denton, clenched her hands. To Em's surprise, behind Betty stood the assayer Bill Newbury, who stuffed his hands in his pants pockets.

Em stepped aside. "Good morning, everyone. Let's go into the dining room. It's the best place to read papers and we can spread out." Her tongue stuck to the roof of her dry mouth as she spoke.

Her legs wobbled as she walked, so anxious she might faint at the thought she would actually hold papers to sell off her hotel. She led them into the dining room and held out a shaking hand for them to sit. She glanced at Lewis Roberts as he set a canvas satchel beside his chair.

He saw her studying the case. "My notary kit." Lewis stood tall. To the others at the table he announced, "Besides the mailman, I'm the game warden, fire chief, and you know I'm a notary to verify signatures."

Em smiled a sad smile and swayed to the kitchen. She loaded a tray with cups and the full coffee pot. She balanced the cream pitcher and sugar bowl on the cups.

"I don't need coffee." A sneer rang through Samuel's voice. "I want to get on with this."

"Well, I want Em's coffee." Lewis' nose rose as if to exude an air of importance. "The papers will be signed in good time." He took the offered cup of coffee and bowed his head in gratitude. Em smiled tightly.

"Betty?" Em held out a cup to her. Betty's lips pressed together so tightly a white streak slashed her face, making her already pale face appear tan. She took the cup. With trembling hands, she poured almost half the cream into the remaining space of the cup, almost overflowing the precious liquid.

"Bill?"

He shook his head.

"So, you'll move out immediately," Samuel ordered, and indicated Lewis. "Once this notary does his business, you're out of here."

Em's stomach flopped, then flipped back into place. She felt she would fly to pieces.

"Have a heart, Samuel," Lewis chastised.

"Shaddup." Samuel's hands turned into fists. The more animated he grew the more relaxed Lewis became.

"If you kill me, you'll not have anyone to notarize the document." Lewis sipped his coffee, a satisfied smiled crossed his lips.

Samuel slammed back into the chair, sighing loudly. He reached into an interior pocket of his jacket, yanked out a roll of documents then slapped them onto the table. "Enough jaw-jackin'. Let's get to it. Here's the contract." With a heavy hand, he swiped flat the papers.

He held up a hand to indicate Betty. "My attorney and Betty's have looked at it. It's all in order. For ten thousand dollars, all properties, furnishings, structures, and mineral rights transfer to us. Nothing's left behind. You take only your personal things."

As he spoke Em nodded, her face turning cold.

Betty reached into her purse and extracted a thick envelope. Samuel snatched the envelope from her hand and slapped it on the table. "Ten thousand. It's all there. Count it if you don't trust me." His voice grew louder as he spoke.

"I will because I don't," Em stated with a bravado she didn't feel, forcing herself to look him square in the eye. Samuel dropped his eyes to stare at the envelope.

Em picked up the papers and unrolled them. The papers stuck to her sweating hands. She glanced at each of the five pages. Her brow furrowed.

"Your properties are made up of several parcels so the contract shows the legal description for all of them," Betty said. "The descriptions are correct. The county assessor verified them." She held out a gold pen.

Her heart racing, Em reached for the offered pen. She held the gold fountain pen and stared at the neat row of tiny tooth indentations. Feeling the floor fall away, she forced a calming breathe and set it on the table. "Nice pen."

"Pretty enough for you to sign the papers?" Samuel growled.

Em forced herself to slow down and read the papers. "It does list all the properties just as you say."

"It's all straightforward I tell you," Samuel almost yelled. He grabbed the pen, popped the cap off and stuck it on the barrel. He held out the pen.

She forced herself not to be intimidated. "Why, Samuel, you wouldn't want all these witnesses to think you pressured me into signing, would you?" she said with a voice as sweet as honey. "Even though they'd swear not to tell anyone."

Samuel's face turned red. He tossed the precious pen on the table. A drop of ink squirted onto the tablecloth.

"Please, don't drag this out," Betty pleaded. She picked up the pen and held it out. "Sign the papers and be done with it. Think of all the stress that'll go away the instant you sign."

Em studied Betty, forcing her face to remain expressionless. "Why do you want this old place, Betty? You have the most magnificent home in the whole county."

Betty's mouth worked. Her lips twisted. Her body trembled so hard the coffee cup rattled on the saucer. She set it on the table. In a deadly voice she growled, "I'm going to burn it down."

Silence weighed so heavily Em could scarcely breathe. The papers dropped from her hands. Horrified, all she could do was whisper, "Why would you do that?"

"Every time I see this place I hear Walt complaining how Bea belonged to your father. When he was drunk he'd say he was stuck with me. He'd say even with all his money he was stuck with a poor man's Bea!" She slammed her hand on the table. "I put up with this for years—years!" Her body jerked so much Em thought she was having an apoplectic attack.

Speechless, Em turned away from Betty's crazed eyes and retrieved the papers that fell on the floor. Betty sank to her chair and spun to face away from everyone.

Em cleared her throat to loosen the choking tightness. "There's no provision for paying off the two loans my father made to Walter. Ten is not enough."

A gurgling noise from Sam was the only sound. "You think you're entitled to *more*?"

"I've been paying faithfully on the Ember Mine loan although you both own it. And I've been paying on the loan when Walt overcharged my family for using inferior material for the hotel's two-story. That's more than my fair share to Betty, which means I'm left with very little."

"Oh, for hell's sake, Em!" Sam roared.

Betty spun back and slammed her hands on the table. "I'll forgive the damn loans," she screamed. A tear dripped off an eyelash. "Sign the papers!"

Lewis sat tall in his seat. "If you're sincere, Betty, I have a form in my kit." He snatched his satchel, flipped the flap then whipped out a form.

"I am sincere."

While he wrote furiously, Betty glared at Em.

"How much are the loan balances, Em?"

"The balance on the hotel is one thousand, four hundred." The room darkened and she was afraid she'd faint. She gripped the table. "The balance on the mine is four thousand, one hundred."

He shoved the paper toward Betty. He declared, "Read it carefully, Missus Denton. Make sure it's correct. Indicate you choose to forgive Miss Olson's two loans by signing it. I'll notarize it. Em, Bill, and Sam will observe."

Betty snatched the paper, grabbed the gold fountain pen, and signed the form. She threw the pen on the table and the paper at Lewis, who carefully signed and squeezed the embosser to press the seal into the paper.

He turned in his chair toward Em and held out the completed form to her. Her hands shook as she reached for the form. She stared at Lewis, who winked. When he faced the table, "Now, may we proceed?"

"Finally," Sam growled.

Em licked her dry lips. "Thank you, Betty."

Betty sat staring out the window with her back to Em. She waved a hand in dismissal.

Her fingers refused to work as she tried to separate the papers. Forcing herself to breathe normally she muttered, "Where were we?" She reread the document and focused on one segment.

"Now what?" Quint groaned.

"Only my father's name is shown on the contract as the owner of all the properties," Em said loudly—too loudly for the heavy silence in the room.

"You're his heir. All you have to do is take his death certificate to the courthouse. The properties are all in his name." Samuel voice grew louder with every word. "What other name would be on it?"

"Mine."

A soft gasping sound rose from around the table as Magnus, ashen-faced, creeped through the living room door.

Sheriff Brodie, Deputy Collins, and two other deputies followed. The lawmen circled the room, each with a hand resting on their revolvers' butts, stone-faced and silent.

Lewis stood from his chair and stepped backward to the wall. He flipped aside his jacket to show his filled holster. He too placed his hand on the butt of his revolver. "I've also been deputized," he said dryly.

Finch walked in and stood beside Magnus. Staring at him, Em's face grew cold and she swayed. *I'm hallucinating.* Finch glanced at Em then focused on Quint.

"Say, what is this?" Quint snarled.

Bill stared, wide-eyed, at each lawman. Betty gasped, stood up, and stepped backward.

"Don't move anymore, Missus Denton," Brodie ordered.

Em stood and stumbled away from the table. Her heart raced until she thought it would pound from her chest at the stress of facing her father's killer.

"What's all this about?" Quint's voice wasn't so full of bravado. His face took on a bit of nervousness.

"Samuel Quint, Betty Denton, Bill Newbury: you're all under arrest."

"For what?" Betty gasped.

"For the murders of James Olson and Walter Denton, the attempted murder of Magnus Ollsen, and for the attempted thefts and fraud of the Ember Mine and this hotel." Brodie declared, his voice loud, authoritative.

"No!" Betty screamed.

"Where did you get the fountain pen, Betty?" Em demanded. She snatched the pen off the table. She pointed the pen at Betty as if it were a sword. "This was my father's. He always had it with him. The dents are from my brother Michael's teeth. I'll stake my life it was in his shirt pocket the day he was murdered!"

All eyes stared at the pen. Betty's eyes widened in horror.

"Walter gave that to me. He said the pen was used by a captain in the Spanish-American War." She stared at Sam until she pressed her hand over her mouth.

"You twit," Quint yelled.

Tears poured down Betty's face. Her face sagged, weighed by years of ridicule. "I didn't know the pen was Jimmy's. I thought the beauty of the pen would sway Em and with her desperate enough to sign the contract, she'd just go away!"

She bent over, clutching her stomach. She retched.

Deputy Collins leaned to check Betty's condition. She made a grab for his gun in the holster, but he shoved her to the floor and pulled his weapon. Brodie and the other deputies, Lewis included, raised their weapons and trained them on Sam and Bill. Bill raised his hands.

Betty wept as she curled in a ball. "I hate him, I hate him."

"Shaddup, sister," Samuel growled.

Betty pushed herself from the floor, ignoring the tears pouring down her face, and raised a beseeching hand to the sheriff. "Walter was a maniac for Bea. He beat me because I wasn't her. He chased loose women because he had me. To relieve the aggravation at not getting her he did against me. May he rot in hell." She fell back to her knees weeping.

"I didn't have anything to do with that." Samuel said.

Sheriff Brodie took a step forward. "Quint, if you tell us what happened in the Ember Mine, I'll tell the prosecutor you cooperated."

Samuel's mouth twisted into grimaces. He glared at each person in the room. His mouth worked as he considered Brodie's offer. He spat onto the floor. "You can't prove a damned thing."

"I can." Magnus trembled. He took an unsteady step toward Em. "I remember. Walt and Sam both were at the Ember Mine with Jimmy."

With a trembling hand, he pointed at Sam. "They told Jimmy the mine was worthless. Jimmy'd been under a lot of pressure from Bea to sell. Walt told Jimmy to go home and get a paper to sign over the deed and Sam would be back to collect the paper. They all left."

Magnus shoved his hands in his pockets. Slouching, absorbed in his memory, he swallowed hard. "I went to work on a discovery shaft about a hundred yards west. When I went back to the Ember, it was about one o'clock. I could hear Sam and Jimmy arguing in the shaft. Sam told Jimmy the 'only thing down here are drunks, dirt, and salt'. That got Jimmy cussin'. He said he believed me, that there was gold down there, that he had signed a quitclaim and hid it in the hotel, and only Bea knew where it was and she had all the power."

The old man trembled so hard Em feared he would collapse. "I heard a clang, then a gunshot." Staring at the floor he whispered, "I don't remember what happened after that."

Lewis spoke up. "That's about the time I saw the explosion's dirt cloud. It was later that people found Magnus in real bad shape."

"And you have a license for dynamite," Brodie stated.

Quint hung his head. "Yeah, you can tell the prosecutor we fought," He turned to Brodie. "I struck the drunkard. When I dragged him into a drift I took the pen. I set off the dynamite to cave it in. I didn't know 'short stuff' was around until I saw him crawling away as good as dead. I gave the pen to Walt when I told him everything Olson said. I went back later to make sure the drift opening was blocked."

Em covered her face and tried to block out an image of her father's assault and death.

"Don't worry, he was so drunk he didn't feel a thing," Sam sneered as if that would make it all better.

"That's why you and Denton wanted the hotel. You expected to find the deed proving you were the owner. That was a valuable piece of paper," Brodie said.

Samuel nodded.

No one moved. The silence grew thick.

When Brodie finally spoke he turned to Betty then Sam. "And then there's the fraud of Sam and your husband presenting the mine for lease and accepting the lease money when it wasn't legally theirs."

Em found her voice. "According to Walt, Father sold the mine to him and you, Sam. That was a lie."

"I had nothing to do with it!" Betty screamed. "Walt and Sam came up with that scheme." She pointed at Sam, then enraged, she weakly punched him on the arm.

Suddenly, Samuel lunged. The lawmen braced themselves and pointed their pistols at him. Samuel froze then moved slowly to grab the envelope of cash forgotten on the table. He stepped toward Em.

Finch nudged past Magnus and stepped in front of Em. Samuel glared at Finch and slapped the envelope on the table in front of her. He pointed at the envelope. "There's Barclay's damn rent payment, plus more, so there's no fraud."

Em stared at the bundle. She glanced over to Magnus, whose eyes widened. Her hand shook as it reached for the envelope.

Brodie held up a hand. "Em, if you accept Quint's offer, I won't pursue fraud and conspiracy-to-commit fraud charges. If you reject his offer he'll go to prison for them too."

She pulled her hand back while she considered his words. The silence grew heavy as everyone watched. She stared at Magnus who stared back. He blinked a message of support.

Slowly, she picked up the envelope and pressed it to her chest. With a glare at Quint she said, "On behalf of Magnus and myself, I accept, since you're going to prison for something far more important."

Brodie nodded. The lawmen collectively exhaled in relief.

Betty screamed at Sam. "That's my ten thousand dollars!" She turned to Em. "Give most of that back. You know it's way too much for your 'rent'." She stabbed an index finger at Finch and shrieked, "You know how much your boss paid in rent money for that lease!"

Finch shrugged. "I don't recall."

She turned to Brodie, arms waving. "I demand you make her return most of that money."

With an impassive face Brodie stated, "Both parties agreed to this business transaction, witnessed by five deputized lawmen. If you have a problem with an element of the transaction, you'll have to take up the matter with a judge. It's a civil matter."

Betty sank into a chair, her mouth hung open.

Em turned to look at Magnus, Finch, and the sheriff. Their faces were expressionless as they stared back. To the envelope clenched in her hands she forcefully stated, "This doesn't begin to cover what your family has done to mine."

With shaking hands Betty pointed at the contract. "This is a legitimate contract! I demand you let me go!"

"It is not legitimate," Magnus said. His soft voice was small in the stale heat of the room, yet all movement and sound stopped at his words.

Em whisked the contract off the table and handed it to Brodie. From under the table she pulled out a folder she had taped there earlier. She opened the folder and handed the documents to Magnus.

Magnus held out two documents. "Here are Jimmy's real signatures quitclaiming the Ember Mine to me and Bea and the hotel to Em."

He pointed at the signatures and the notary's embossed seals. "These are the real documents. When Em read your contract she gave a signal: 'listing *all* the properties'."

"Even you two said so yourselves, Quint, Missus Denton," Brodie said.

Em pointed at the contract the sheriff held. "Betty, you mentioned my properties are made up of several parcels. True. Well, tucked in among all the legal descriptions is the legal description for the mine," Em stated.

"Sam and Betty, you both tried to pressure and intimidate me to sign the contract without a careful reading. If I signed it then you would have legally owned *all* the properties—the hotel and part of the mine—and getting them for only ten thousand."

"But the mine's worthless!" Sam yelled.

"The mine is not worthless," Finch said. "My samples show and my company's assayer attests it has a high grade ore with a high grade deposit."

"Which means attempted fraud and conspiracy charges," Brodie stated as he scooped up the folder and the documents from Magnus. To Sam and Betty he stated, "Em partially owned the mine though you told her she didn't. Denton produced a fake deed to prove to Barclay that Denton owned it and so could offer it for sale or lease. Since Em had no idea where the deed was and with the circumstances of her father's 'abandonment', she had little choice but to believe it." He stuffed the folder into his waistband.

Brodie lifted his chin in Finch's direction. "Why don't you tell us what you know?"

"My boss sent me to Salt Lake City to talk with our company assayer. He had gathered copies of all the reports going back to nineteen twenty-five by various assayers testing the mine. We spent hours going through them. Nothing made sense. First, the report was glowing. Then the next showed the mine was played out. The next was glowing again."

Bill wavered and his hand reached for the table.

"The results differed depending on who was selling. If the owners were Denton and Quint, the report basically stated it was the proverbial gold mine and could sell it for a high price. If someone else owned the mine, it was played out and worthless so they could buy it cheap. When I pieced together who owned it and when, I noticed all the conflicting reports in the past several years were signed by the same assayer: Bill Newbury." Finch paused as he watched Bill sit. "As soon as I figured it out, I headed back here to report it to the sheriff."

"Great work, Doc. So the only question left is the killer of Walter Denton." Brodie stated. He turned to face Betty. "Anything you want to say … Widow Denton?"

Betty stood from her chair. She pressed the palms of her hands to her stomach. Her eyes grew so wide Em thought they'd fall out. Her face turned from beet red to dead white. Her head shook "no" so hard she looked like she was having a fit. "I hated him. He abused me. But I didn't kill him." She paused and sank into the chair. Barely audible she whispered, "I only got him to the gulch."

"It's all connected, Sheriff." All eyes turned to Finch as he stared at Newbury.

Bill shot off his seat. His fists clenched so hard his knuckles whitened. Finch braced his body but never took his eyes off Bill.

"And you know Newbury killed Denton, how?" Brodie prompted.

"Driving back I recalled a meeting with Bill in Em's living room." He glanced at Em and indicated the room behind him. "At one point he mentioned Drunk Swede Gulch. It's a crevice so deep it's more like two cliffs. No one prospects the cliffs as they're almost inaccessible. He described some exposed quartz there. I haven't heard of anyone who knows anything about that gulch except for him.

"It's where Em's father's vehicle was crashed. Since the Newburys have lived here for decades and knew the Olsons, Bill had to have known about the vehicle and who it belonged to." Finch turned to Bill. "Since you couldn't have carried Denton, he had to have climbed down there. You made Denton walk to the truck before you beat him up and then shot him."

Bill Newbury leaned forward and buried his face with his hands. "He ruined me as an assayer. At the gulch, I gave him one last chance to renegotiate my loans. He refused. He demanded I keep issuing reports that went as he directed. We argued. He was mad, crazy. He ignored I had a gun on me. He came at me with his fists raised. I couldn't take his threats anymore." A sob burst out. "I hit him again and again. … I pulled my gun. … He came at me. … I pulled the trigger."

He faced the sheriff. "He blackmailed me to sign those false reports. He said he owned me since he owned my loans, that he'd take my land and my business."

"I heard that blackmail, Sheriff," Em spoke up. All eyes turned to her. "I went to Walt—as you know—to ask about refinancing my loans. I heard him threaten Bill."

"Thank you, Em," Bill whispered. He hung his head.

Quint turned on Bill Newbury, who cowered below the huge man. "You found the lease agreement to the Ember Mine with Walt's and my name on it. You acted like a little boy when you tried to turn the tables on us — blackmail us — to join this little group and be rid of your loans."

Grimacing, Sam turned his body and fixed his murderous eyes on Em. Her blood ran cold then hot. The suffering inflicted on her family blazed through her body. A red curtain of rage passed over her eyes. She screamed, "You killed my father! He was a good man! I'll see you hang!"

With a roar, Quint dove over the table for Em. She retreated to the wall to escape, but his thick hand seized her shoulder. She screamed at the pain as his strong fingers dug in her flesh and she could only swat at him.

In a furious blur, Finch and Magnus wrestled Quint away from Em before a *crack* rent the air.

Samuel's head snapped forward and he fell onto the table. His limp body knocked Magnus to the floor, then slid on top of him, pinning him. The only sound and movement were everyone's panting.

Bending over Sam, Sheriff Brodie gripped his pistol high after he knocked out Sam with the butt of his gun.

Beside Brodie, standing over Samuel, Finch's fists clenched. He breathed hard as he stared at the unmoving form.

Magnus squirmed, pinned under Samuel's thick leg. He bit Sam's knee before kicking off the dead-weight leg. He scrambled away then stood panting beside Em.

At the silence, Betty wailed and fell to her knees.

"Get them out of here," Brodie ordered.

~ * ~

The sheriff and deputies dragged out a struggling and screaming Betty. With eyes and nose streaming, she cursed her dead husband, her brother Samuel, and Em's father and mother for ruining her life.

Little powerhouse Magnus hauled out a groggy Samuel limping from his damaged knee. Sam pressed his cuffed hands to the back of his head as a gash dripped blood down his back. In a flash of selfishness, Em felt relief he hadn't bled on her clean floor.

A deputy handcuffed Bill, who walked out without resistance.

Em stepped into her kitchen and watched as Betty, Sam, and Bill were pressed into separate deputies' cars. Against the dazzling sunlight, beside the sheriff's car, Brodie spoke briefly with Finch then shook his hand. A moment later the lawmen drove out of her yard, their vehicles' sirens blaring.

After discovering the quitclaim deeds, Em sent for Brodie who had responded immediately. She showed him her father's note and quitclaim deeds and told him everything she'd learned. They planned the whole thing.

She gave him the idea for her to announce to Sam Quint and Betty Denton that Em—as Father's heir—would sell the hotel to them, expecting them to produce a falsified contract and perhaps get Quint to confess for killing her father. The sheriff and deputies had hidden the vehicles behind Em's barn while they listened from the living room to the conversation in the dining room.

She hoped the gold fountain pen would show itself. Em breathed a huge sigh of relief she had been right.

Unbeknownst to her, Finch had returned and notified the sheriff of his findings. Thanks to Finch, they also solved who killed Walt Denton.

Brodie had won himself a reelection, she thought.

As the sirens faded, Em collapsed on the kitchen stool and slumped forward. She was too exhausted to sort through the maelstrom of what had happened to think about any one of them. Wrapping her arms around her shoulders in a hug, she winced as her hand struck the injury Sam had inflicted.

Finch's boot steps and Magnus' tentative footfalls approached the kitchen doorway. Magnus' soft footsteps stopped beside Em and he lightly patted her back. She pushed back to sit upright and studied his old face. His mustache drooped lower than she'd ever seen it.

Tears flowed unchecked down her cheeks. "I am so proud of you, Uncle."

His eyes welled. "And you're the bravest person I ever met, Em." He bowed his head and paused. "I have to go for a bit."

He needed a drink, Em knew. For once, she didn't "tsk" as he turned for the steps. A fleeting thought passed that perhaps a sip sounded appealing. As Magnus skirted Finch, he clapped a hand on Finch's shoulder then staggered toward his tiny cabin near the corner of the property.

"I must be dreaming." Em listened to the world's silence as she watched Finch standing in the doorway.

He shook his head as he descended the steps. He leaned on the counter beside Em and glanced over at the new sink, kitchen faucet, and counter. The twinkle in his brown eyes returned and his smile broadened.

She looked away. The thought of him leaving again hurt so badly. "It is so much easier." She tried to joke as she focused on her clenched hands.

Finch chuckled at Em's reference to his earlier suggestion to remove the old pump and wood sink.

"You saved me from a mean man."

"I have a habit of doing that."

"Thank you for coming back," she said softly. "You solved a murder and uncovered Sam and Walt's scheme that ruined a lot of people. The whole town is obliged to you."

She rubbed the calluses on her fingers to stop from snatching him up in her arms. "Can you stay?" she whispered.

"I can't." His voice was barely audible. For a moment, they listened to the robin singing in the aspen tree outside the kitchen.

"I must go," he whispered. "It's too painful to be here knowing I just have to leave you again." He pushed off from the counter and straightened.

"Goodbye, Miss Olson of the Olson Hotel."

And he was gone.

CHAPTER 34

That afternoon, Em and Magnus sat on the hotel's east porch steps, now shaded from the intense sun. Magnus puffed slowly on his father's churchwarden. After a century of regular use the carved bowl had smoothed. They watched silently as the shade's edge crept eastward.

Magnus was squirmy. Em knew he had something on his mind. Finally, he cleared his throat. His voice went to a high pitch. "Em, I'm a law-abiding man, you know that … Well, except for the whiskey thing. … And that woman turned out to be already married. … And somebody else stole Rosybud before I took her. … And—"

Em lightly bumped his shoulder with her own.

He cleared his throat. "And I filched Denton's gold—but that don't count none since it was my gold anyways." He rooted around in his jacket's deep pocket, pulled out a leather pouch, and held it out to her. "Well, our gold."

Stunned, she hefted the pouch.

"I sold some to pay the taxes. The rest I squirreled away." He gestured with the pipe toward the pouch. "There's only about three ounces there, about a hundred dollars' worth. Since we're officially partners I kept three ounces for myself."

"Why did you …?" Em was so stunned she couldn't even think of a good question.

"Filch the gold and pay the taxes on the patented claim when Denton 'owned' it? I didn't trust Denton." He shook his head almost violently. "No, sirree—he kept giving me different stories about how he got it. So I pretended Jimmy owned it and made sure everything was right by him." He nodded his head like Rosybud did.

She leaned and kissed Magnus on the cheek. "You're wonderful." Her smile felt it was the broadest of her life as Magnus fought to not wipe off his cheek. "And I'm one-quarter owner of the Ember Mine," she declared.

Magnus glanced over to her.

"Father signed the quitclaim to you and Mother. Rose and I are her heirs so we each get half of her half." Em stared at the leather pouch. "She suffered too."

"You're a good girl, Em."

"Not yet, Magnus," she cried and dashed into the hotel.

A moment later she hurried out and plopped next to him. She held out a white envelope. "Partner, here's your half of the mine's 'rent' money."

His mustache narrowed from pursing his lips as he peered inside the envelope. His mustache widened as he grinned. "Holy moly, but me and Rosybud are headin' for the Assayer's Saloon tonight!" He giggled until he wiped his eyes.

Magnus chuckled as his fingers riffled the bills. "I figured for sure you wouldn't take that money out of principle, Em." He pulled out the bills and stared at the stack. "Then you could have knocked me over with a feather how you got Betty to forgive your loans."

She nudged his arm. "I'm a law-abiding woman. Magnus, you know that."

~ * ~

The coffee pot percolated on the wood stove. *Gosh, fresh coffee sounds good right now.* She filled her cup, topped it with cream and sat at her counter.

Justice had finally come to the Olson Hotel and her family.

Father hadn't abandoned the family and proved his love to them. His killers were identified. They had even confessed, and they would be severely punished.

A fortune in cash was locked securely in her safe, enough to last for years.

Her two loans were erased and she was debt-free.

With a jolt, she sat straighter. She was the full owner of the free-and-clear Olson Hotel! She was a quarter-owner of the free-and-clear Ember Mine!

Majority owner Magnus would be taken care of.

Em closed her eyes to give a prayer of gratitude.

Out the window to the hills beyond, the sagebrush in the sunlight glistened with their pale green summer glow. The only sound were the clacking wings of the flying grasshoppers.

Where the lengthening shadows darkened the gulches, doe antelope grazed on the hillside as they watched over their galloping fawns.

Em leaned back in her chair to view her domain. She giggled as her stresses and cares fell away. She flung her head back and allowed herself an open-mouthed laugh. She took a big gulp of her coffee.

Feeling invincible, she stepped into her dining room — her dining room. The room remained a shambles where Quint dived over the table after her. Chairs had been shoved aside where Betty fought against being handcuffed.

With a swipe of her hand, she straightened her mother's pure white linen tablecloth. With a whoop she spun, her arms wide, and laughed. The rest could wait until tomorrow.

She had no guests to concern her today. For now, she'd head to the other side of the creek and swing the remaining daylight away.

Stepping onto the porch and blinded by the setting sun, she could make out the silhouette of a truck pulling into her drive. Not wanting to see anyone for the rest of the day but in too good of a mood to be irritated at a drop-in guest, she waited. When they approached for a room she would turn them away.

She held up her hand to shade her eyes from the sun's harshness.

The driver's door opened. A head's silhouette rose above the cab's top then moved around the back of the truck and approached Em.

"I'm sorry to drop in like this," a man called out. "I don't have a reservation. I hope you have a room for the night."

Welling tears burned her dry eyes and blurred Finch's face. Her chin trembled from daring to believe in his return.

He stepped close. His fingers brushed her cheek to sweep away the escaping tears.

"I got as far as the county line. I had to come back." He swallowed hard.

"Do you have a room in the hotel for an out-of-work geologist and homeless prospector?"

CHAPTER 35

Lander Gazette's Local News
"Placer Claims" reported by Em Olson
July 24 – August 1, 1933
- *The Assayer's Saloon and new owner Margaret Newbury hosted a grand opening. The Cow Chips provided the music until dawn when the saloon ran out of beer.*
- *Newcomer Dr. Fincelius Stone was announced as head geologist for the incoming dredge operation, which is expected to bring several workers and their families to Placer City.*

"Mail call!"

Lewis stepped around the corner of the hotel. Em smiled as she pinned a pillowcase on the clothesline. She strolled across the little bridge over the creek to meet him. "Afternoon, Lewis. How was your trip up the mountain?"

"Mighty fine, Em. Got a letter from your aunt in Boston."

"Thank you, Lewis." *She's responding to the news about Father, perhaps word about Sylvia?* Em tensed.

He tapped his cap's bill and turned to head to his truck.

"Lewis."

He turned back.

"I never did tell you how much I appreciate what you did for me last month with the Dentons and Sam Quint, and my loans. Thank you."

"You deserve for good things to happen to you, Em. I'm just happy to help." He paused and smiled broadly. "Besides, it was Betty's idea to forgive the loans."

She laughed. "Can I ask you something else?"

Lewis waited.

"Why didn't you tell me Father signed and you notarized the quitclaim deeds?"

He took a step toward Em. "Couple reasons. I don't read the documents I notarize. What's stated in the document is none of my business. I only verify the person is who they say they are and witness that the person signs of their own free will. Besides, Jimmy asked me not to say a word. 'It was a surprise for Bea'." He shrugged. "I didn't say anything because I didn't know what the contents of the documents stated, and if I did know I would not violate my promise to Jimmy." He smiled and turned for the corner of the hotel.

Em tucked the letter into her apron pocket and pinned the last damp sheet onto the clothesline. She stood back to watch the breeze sway the laundry.

She pulled the letter from her pocket, sank into the swinging bench and pushed off. She tore it open.

> *Dear Niece,*
>
> *I'm gratified to hear James' disappearance was solved and the blackguards caught. I always warned Bea that the people in Placer were no good, but she never listened.*
>
> *Sylvia and husband showed up at our door last week. She told me dreadful stories how you worked her so hard she was forced to marry this boy and run away.*
>
> *The boy doesn't belong here and Sylvia has grown belligerent during her time in Wyoming. I gave them money and ordered them to return, but she announced she was with child and demanded to remain in my home.*
>
> *Can you explain how things went so wrong?*
> *Aunt Dee*

Em rocked the bench to watch the undulating linen on the clothesline. She folded the letter then slipped it into her apron pocket. Whether Sylvia was indeed pregnant or throwing a tantrum, Em was comforted Sylvia was home and safe — and not coming back to Placer City.

Movement by the hotel caught her eye. Finch hurried around the corner striding toward her. His pants were dirty and the knees sagged. Drying sweat stains encircled his arms. Pushed up on his forehead were goggles, which had protected his eyes and made the clean skin appear to pop out of his head. The rest of his face was covered with dirt.

"What a pleasant surprise to see you so early this evening."

He took a deep shuddering breath. "We found something."

Fear flashed through her, a remembrance of him finding her father's body. She whispered, "What is it?"

"Magnus and I finally cleared out all the rubble on that collapsed drift we found last week." He held out a small vial filled with water.

Em studied what appeared to be a half-ounce of tiny nuggets. He nudged the vial closer. She grasped the vial and gently shook it. She smiled as the bits immediately settled to the bottom.

"The vein Magnus was expecting." Finch smiled.

She threw back her head and laughed out loud. Leaning forward, she kissed his dirty cheek then quickly wiped the grit from her lips.

"I'm so happy! Congratulations on your success—and Magnus'." She gripped the vial in both hands and tucked them under her chin as she grinned at him. "Father always knew Magnus was right." She ignored the tightness in her throat and held out the vial for Finch to take back.

"It's *your* gold." He held up his hands, refusing to take it back. "This is your quarter of the gold we recovered just today from your mine. Magnus has his half and Rose's quarter," Finch stuttered gently.

Em gasped. She gazed at the contents then held the vial out to him. "We agreed you'd keep my portion of the gold as wages for working the mine between your time preparing for the incoming dredge. This is for all your hard work."

Finch hesitated then took back the vial. "Okay, it's mine."

He held her gaze as he bent slightly. A slight groan escaped as he kneeled onto one knee.

Em's heart pounded as she stared down at him. She studied the dirt in his hair, the lines around his warm brown eyes, his full lips.

"I said once you're the finest woman I've ever met. I meant it. I'm in love with you, Em Olson of the Olson Hotel. You have made this world where I want to stay forever."

His eyes welled as he held up the vial. "This is your wedding ring—in raw form. I ask you to accept it and me."

Her legs grew weak. She sank to her knees in front of Finch so close her breasts pressed against his chest.

With the lightest touch her fingers stroked the stubble of his beard and the grit on his cheeks. She gently kissed him.

The End

~ * ~   ~ * ~

Afterword

The South Pass region attracts an abundance of unique personalities that shine through the decades. These fascinating individuals spark stories that are told and retold—most are even true—and influenced this novel.

With great respect, several characters in this novel were inspired by some of those individuals.

Ellen Carpenter and mother Nellie Carpenter, both hard-working pioneers, were held in the highest regard along with their renowned Carpenter Hotel in Atlantic City and were the models for Em Olson and the Olson Hotel.

The motivation for Magnus Ollsen was newly lost Roger Fullerton and long-gone Scottish gold miner James Cassie. Sporting huge drooping mustaches, both men were small in stature yet large in their gentle impact on this community.

The inspiration for Pauline Highsmith was Philippina Halstead, a distinctive free soul I miss even today.

Inspiring Lewis Roberts was the intrepid and tough mailman Clarence Roe. Clarence made the trek thrice weekly to deliver mail, often on snowshoes. Newspaper articles expound on his ordeals and his commitment to delivering the mail. Thankfully, the incident of Lewis fighting for his life in a blizzard for two days is fiction.

Margaret Quint's zest for life is inspired by two remarkable women: Zoie Green Fuller and Laurel Nelson.

The Old Church is modeled after St. Andrew's Episcopal Church in Atlantic City, consecrated in 1913. It's a very spiritual place and the quintessential mountain church.

Whenever I typed the Cow Chips, I was thinking of the renowned Buffalo Chips, a musical group responsible for some of the most memorable events in the region. The esteemed members are Bob Lewis, John "Johnny Mac" McIntyre, John Mionczynski, and Quentin Roberts.

The name Fincelius came from the fascinating subject of the riveting book *Finn Burnett, Frontiersman*, a pioneer to the area.

Lastly, the bad guys and the town of Placer City, Wyoming, were invented to suit the story.

About The Author

Barbara Townsend's writing journey began at the University of Wyoming. During her first fiction writing class she felt compelled to write a mystery. The thought of twists, turns, red herrings, clues and making them all fit into one story fascinated her. That first short story, *Murder at Wainwright,* she later wrote into *Clear and Convincing Evidence*.

An internship in the Toppan Rare Books Library led her in another direction. With books dating from the 1800s, she wrote a thesis that examined women in nineteenth-century Mormon polygyny. That paper won a student competition at the university's American Heritage Center. Her accumulated research led to historical mystery *Blood Atonement*.

Her writing credits include the university's newspaper and Air Force newspapers. She was first a student then a faculty member of the Wyoming Writing Project. She graduated *summa cum laude* with a Bachelor of Arts degree.

She lives in Wyoming's Wind River Mountains.

Books by Barbara Townsend

Blood Atonement
Clear and Convincing Evidence
Tarnished Gold